Start

with the

Backbeat

Start
with the
Backbeat

A NOVEL

By

Garinè B. Isassi

SHE WRITES PRESS

Published 2016
Printed in the United States of America
ISBN: 978-1-63152-041-9
Library of Congress Control Number: 2015953826

Cover Art Credit: Zabel Isassi
Book design by Stacey Aaronson

For information, address:
She Writes Press
1563 Solano Ave #546
Berkeley, CA 94707

She Writes Press is a division of SparkPoint Studio, LLC.

This book is dedicated to every person with a heart and head filled with music, especially Adrian, Sofia, and Zabel, whose hearts and heads I had a hand in developing.

I PEERED INTO WHAT WAS ABOUT TO BECOME MY VERY OWN office. The painter, a stocky guy in oversized coveralls, threw a puzzled glance at me before shoving the roller up the wall. Maybe he didn't expect a short girl with red-streaked hair to be hovering in the doorway. I eagerly surveyed the buckets and splattered drop cloths. I had picked out my personal shade of corporate white from the Benjamin Moore color wheel. I chose "AF-35—Vapor," mainly because I liked the name. It was on the yellowish side. It was so exciting!

I quickly twisted my grin into a smirk, making sure that nobody walking along the hallway might have seen my puppy-like reaction.

The nameplate on the door seemed way too formal for the music business, though. I tapped it with my black-polished fingernail. "Jillian Dodge," it announced stiffly in etched, fake wood. Nobody called me Jillian. Not even my mother.

I liked my name as "Jill." It was short and sharp.

"Jill" was kinetic.

"Jill" was strong.

"Jill came tumbling after."

Working at a record label had been my dream since forever. Of course, I didn't realize that breaking in would mean years of wage slavery. Technically, I didn't even work here. I was a perpetual temp. I self-titled my position as a "glamour job," where you get to be seen with the rich and famous, but are too poor and ordinary to be counted among them. The crazy low pay I got from Mega Big Records did not translate into food, clothing, and the New York City version of shelter.

My parents agreed to help me with rent for a while, but "a while" was well defined.

"Two years," my dad said the weekend he came to cosign the lease to my apartment, where I moved in with Luann. "If you don't have a living wage by 1989, you're coming home."

My father's veterinary practice did well enough, but in Conroe, Texas, the outskirts of the suburbs of Houston, people didn't carry spoiled pets in their purses and pay premium for doggy surgery. Throughout my school years, I spent way too much time holding down angry felines. It's a miracle that my forearms still have skin.

Dad had gazed out the restaurant window at the people rushing by on the busy sidewalk.

"Personally, I'd rather die in hell than live in this goddamn parade," he told me, doling out his version of encouragement. "But if it's what you want, you'd better ride fast or you'll have to jump ship."

He had a way of talking like some kind of cowboy sailor all the time.

I barely made his deadline. I had spent almost two

years in abject poverty when finally, last fall, the product manager job opened up. I jumped on it like a cat on a ball of string. So now, I had health insurance and a real salary, and would have an office soon. But it was technically "probationary" for the next six months. That was the word on the contract, anyway.

I still lived in that seven-story walk-up building, with the cosigned lease and Luann. She had her own glamour job at *Soap Opera This Week* magazine and we lived on the fifth floor. We had mice in our building, an odd smell in the entranceway, dubious neighbors, and no elevator. It was a dump, but affordable. Plus, we both developed very shapely legs.

I MADE MY WAY BACK TO MY CURRENT DESK, WHICH WAITED IN an alcove off the hallway, jammed in with four other desks and a variety of file cabinets. I slogged through the half-full boxes of vinyl LPs and cassette tapes that littered the floor. We called this area the Admin Pit and for the past two years, I was one of the admins, short for administrative assistant, the new wave term for secretary. It was like calling the garbage man a sanitation engineer.

These desks were hand-me-downs from a real 1950s-style secretarial pool in some posh advertising agency and had the water rings and deep gouges in the wood to prove it. God only knows what debauchery they had seen over the years. But we, the admins, carved our own initials into the sides and claimed them for a year at a time, until we either moved up or moved out of the company.

The real nitty-gritty work of Mega Big Records happened in here. All the mailings went out from these desks. All the letters were typed from these old typewriters and faxed out through the beeping fax machine in the corner. The phones rang almost constantly with calls from the public, industry executives, musicians, delivery guys—everyone from nuts to crazies. We were paid to either block them, help them, or transfer them to their rightful owners.

Nobody stayed here for long, so nobody made anything look nice. The executives and artists never even walked down this hallway, and the place was a center of frantic activity and noise. It was like a bizarre cross between a frat house and the engine room of the *Titanic*.

I sat down, picked up my three-hour-old coffee, and sipped the now-cold liquid. Glancing around the mess of my desk, I looked past the to-do list that Jenny, my boss, left for me to the various photos on the corner. There was a photo of my mother and father. There was another one of me, my roommate Luann, and our poker buddies at Coney Island. There was a photo-booth picture strip of Jonathan, my sometimes boyfriend, a sound guy on tour with a band called Flying Flock. His chiseled features cut an almost colonial look against his long, disheveled hair. Right now, he was lost somewhere in the middle of the country, making stops at nightclubs with names like Club Foot and The Depot.

And then I had a framed 5x7 headshot of Gordon Sumner, a.k.a. Sting, my muse and first musical love.

Even though I attended every Police concert that came through Austin while I was in college there and went to all the solo concerts that Sting did in New York, the one and only time that I was in the same room with him traumatized me. It happened when I had been working here at Mega Big Records for almost a year.

Jenny, with her massive curly hair, big teeth, and tight pants—a female version of Jon Bon Jovi—greeted me that morning with her usual schedule of who and what was on that day's agenda. I had figured out that being excited all the time was somewhat tiring and leaned more toward slightly jaded at that point. After the gloss of meeting famous musicians wore off, you learned very fast that the business world, even among rock stars, was exactly like high school. There was the Popular Crowd (Top 40 stars in overpriced fashion), the Stoners (mostly garage bands and Brits), the Nerds (managers, legal reps), and the Jocks (session musicians, backup singers, heavy metal bands in broken-down buses). The difference was that the gossip and backstabbing was national entertainment, broadcast nationwide on the radio, TV, and in print. And there was no school principal to step in and call your parents to come take you home.

Jenny always liked the fact that I didn't get all googly-eyed and freaked out around the artists. So I was able to stand in line for the bathroom with Cyndi Lauper or ride the elevator with Ozzy Osbourne and say, "Hey, how's it going?" to them. It always helped, though, if I wasn't exactly their number one fan. It must be said that most of the artists we worked with never got that famous or rich. We pushed them on MTV and tried to get radio airplay and press coverage. But most of them didn't sell enough albums to get a gold record or even make a living.

Off the cuff during her list, Jenny said, "Oh, and Branford Marsalis showed up this morning with Sting. A surprise visit. What a pain. They want us to talk up the

Bring on the Night live album." She sighed. "It's not even our release! They will be in the conference room in fifteen minutes and we all have to go."

My normal response would have been a shared groan with her. We hated it when the bigger stars showed up during our workday without warning. Everyone had to drop everything.

Remember all that stuff I just said about how cool I was around all these rock stars? Well, with Sting, it was different.

I loved him.

I didn't only mean, "I loved his music," which I did. I didn't only mean, "I loved his look," which I did. I meant I loved him! Years before, he was the poster on my fifteen-year-old self's bedroom ceiling. I knew every word to every Police song. I thought it was the epicenter of cool to make a jazz album after being a punk rocker. His songs expressed my hormone-filled teenage solitude and angst. The British accent, the hair, the hips—oh my God! He was my first crush, even before my first date with David Peterson in the tenth grade, and now, years later, he proved to be an intellectual, Shakespeare-quoting dreamboat. I was ready to groupie myself out, which I never did as a rule.

At the time, his photo was on the bulletin board next to my desk. It was not obvious among the dozens of other band pictures, but I talked to that photo when I was stressed. I'd look at his calm face and call him by his real name, Gordon. Of course, nobody else in the office suspected this. That would have appeared completely pitiful, that I still felt lingering teenybopper adoration. I was an adult now. A music industry pro. A composed businesswoman.

So while Jenny was standing in front of me expecting the eye-roll, she got me nearly spitting out my coffee instead. My eyes widened and I squeaked, "Whaaat?"

She did a double take and her eyebrows lifted to the curls on her forehead. I worked my face into some semblance of nonchalance and rechecked my cool, saying, "Oh . . . yeah, right. I'm coming."

I slipped into the conference room, hiding behind her left shoulder, thinking this was the only time I might benefit from being the shortest person in the office. I fumbled into the corner, plastering myself against the wall, and gawked at Sting, who sat at the end of the table, a mere five feet away from me. I was unable to speak, move, or breathe.

Jenny scrutinized me with glances back over her shoulder. Noting my shallow breathing and dilating eyes, she followed my gaze as it landed squarely on Sting/ Gordon's beautiful face. She nudged me with her elbow, maybe just to make sure I wasn't about to faint or anything. I jumped at her touch. The senior vice president was doing his banging-of-the-fist-on-the-table thing and saying something about how we had to promote our artists even when they put something out on a different label. The two famous musicians appeared to be uncomfortable, shifting in their seats and eyeing each other.

When the speech was over, they mingled for a few minutes and all of my coworkers, Jenny included, rushed them to shake hands and get face time.

I tried to shimmy around Michael, one of our radio promotion guys and also one of my best workmate buddies, to get out the door so I could breathe. Michael could have passed himself off as another Marsalis brother, super jazz guy, with his dark mocha-colored skin, clean-cut button-down shirt, and cropped hair. He turned and frowned at me, so I ended up peering around his elbow to ogle Sting/Gordon and avoid being seen.

It was ridiculous and I knew it. I didn't want to meet Sting/Gordon and possibly shatter my dream confidant. I knew I'd gush if I had to say something to him and if I did that in front of Jenny and everybody, I was done for. If I did it in front of Michael, I'd be the butt of his jokes on an hourly basis, and I would have to move back to Texas to escape from the humiliation.

I practically ran back to my desk. As I rummaged through the drawers for a paper bag to hyperventilate into, Jenny appeared in front of me.

"Sting's your teen idol, huh?" she asked bluntly.

"Huh?" I stuttered. "I don't know what you're talking about."

"We all have one." She flipped a frizzy curl from her forehead with the back of her hand, a move I often imitated at the monthly poker parties when describing her to my buddies. "That one star that got us interested in this business in the first place. The one we knew would marry us one day."

I stared at her.

"Don't worry," she said as she turned on her heel and headed into her office, "I won't tell anyone."

Of course, that was a lie.

Now everybody knew about my Sting fixation. It only got worse later that year, when the *Nothing Like the Sun* LP came out and I found out that he was even doing yoga.

Eventually, Jenny started coming to the poker nights, where I could imitate her moves in her presence and openly mock her for her breach of confidence. Meanwhile, the comments from Michael were still unrelenting, but I brushed them off.

Some people needed to exercise. Some people needed to drink or do drugs. I needed My Gordon.

JENNY WAS ON MY LEFT AND TONY, ANOTHER PRODUCT manager, was on my right in my very first managers' meeting. We sat against the back wall of the large conference room. I felt pretty well insulated. Tony's pale knees stuck out from the holes in his jeans, and he looked like he didn't get to sleep last night.

The senior vice president presided over all of these meetings by standing at the head of the table and barking out orders. The three dozen of us strewn around the table and leaning against the walls looked like the contents of a Friday night subway car headed downtown. We all sat at attention, or as close as we could get, considering this was the music business.

Few among us were dressed "professionally"—mainly the senior vice president and some of the department directors. They were "The Suits." The rest of us were a mishmash of musical stereotypes from the diva to punkadelic. I sat in my place with a red streak in my hair, a black miniskirt, and combat boots.

"First of all," the senior vice president began, "there is something that you are all going to have to deal with. We are getting computers!"

Everyone in the room reacted. Some gasped in horror. Others whooped and applauded.

He waited a moment for the room to get somewhat of a grip on itself and then raised his voice over the remaining din. "Everything is going to be all right. It will take some getting used to, but we'll have a system . . . mail network? . . . Georgina?" He looked over his shoulder at his executive assistant, prudish in her big-shouldered blouse and straight skirt, her ankles crossed.

"Ethernet, I think," she said.

". . . where you will be able to send each other messages. Instead of writing your copy and press releases and letters on the typewriters, you'll be able to use a writing program and save them to a floppy disk."

Jenny turned to the person on her other side and joined in the general mayhem of concerned voices. People in real businesses already had computers in their offices. My cousin, Jessica, even had one at home. Here, we felt lucky we had a copier that worked.

"When?" Tony called out.

"The next couple of weeks." The senior vice president was trying to raise his voice again over everyone. "We'll start having installations and training sessions for people who have never used them."

"Finally!" Tony said, glancing at me and then shaking his head. I did my best to sneer with him as the discussion around us began to ebb.

Then the senior vice president banged his fist on the conference table like a gavel to retrieve our attention. "We are only doing this because the corporate people upstairs are paying." He raised his voice again, this time taking on the tone of a scolding parent. "I'd like to remind you all that we have not been very high on the charts this year. And it's because we are behind the times! Every other label has computers already! While you people are all sitting on your pretty little asses, the music world is passing us by! Do any of you know what else every other label has?" He paused, waiting for the sudden silence to produce a response. "Anybody? Anybody?"

He paused again, this time for dramatic effect, searching for some kind of spark among the blank faces looking back at him.

"Rap!" he bellowed.

He pointed at Michael, one of only two black people in the room. "Do you know what I am talking about?" he demanded. Michael sat still, not knowing what to say.

Then the senior vice president banged his fist on the conference table again. His red tie danced over the gloss of its surface as he leaned toward us. "Run-DMC! LL Cool J! Jazzy Jeff and Fresh Prince! Public Enemy's second LP just hit gold!" he shouted at us. "This rap thing has left the station and we have none! Not ONE rapper on this label. And they are getting more hardcore and mean. They're calling it—" He zeroed in on Tony. "Tony! What is it?"

"Gangsta," Tony grunted, running his beefy hand through his hair. All those speed metal bands that he promoted went nowhere. That was supposed to be the next big thing.

"Yeah, gangster," the senior vice president enthused, drawing out the "errrr." He did a James Cagney move, with his elbows in at his waist, his hands in finger-pistols. "We need a gangster rap kid. Someone young, black, and mean."

He paused and scanned the room.

"Kenny!" he boomed.

All of our heads swiveled towards Kenny Lippman. LaKeisha, the other of the only two black people in the room, made a stifled "humph" sound, and Jenny pushed her knee into mine with an eyebrow wiggle. I responded with an air of equal cynicism.

Kenny blanched. Even as his body stiffened, he could not shed his beleaguered slump. His pale, skinny arms remained crossed around his torso, like he was trying to hold himself together.

"Kenny!" the senior vice president repeated. "You are arts & repertoire! Recruit me a gangster rapper!"

Kenny's last find had been a waif-like, singing girl that nobody seemed to like.

"Right! OK!" Kenny said, mustering up some bravado.

We all knew he was doomed.

"You can take someone else with you." He looked at all of us along that back wall. "Bring in that new punk girl." He didn't know my name, just my outfit. "She probably knows about urban."

My face flushed. I didn't know rap music from a hole in the ground! LaKeisha's hand, which had been situated to hold up her chin, fell to the tabletop with a thud, and I sought out her face through all of the curious expressions now swiveled toward me.

She rolled her large, golden eyes.

THREE DAYS LATER, I ABANDONED MY DESK IN THE ADMIN PIT with a flourish. My box of photos, my stapler, and I made the monumental journey ten feet down the hall.

There had been no specific talk yet about me contributing to the mean rapper search. Kenny came by my half-packed desk after the meeting and grilled me about my résumé. First, there was a long discussion about my studded bracelet and my footwear. He was very impressed that my Doc Martens boots were steel-toed. Then he asked me if I'd ever been arrested and seemed extremely disappointed when I answered that I had not.

Now, I put it out of my mind because I wanted to relish the fact that I was finally sitting in my own office. Making my first set of calls from my own phone on my own desk, I again betrayed my inner Labrador Retriever. I was entirely too thrilled to do the mundane act of picking up the telephone receiver. First, I called my mother.

"Guess where I'm calling from?" I sang into the sieved plastic.

"Did you move into your office? Oh, Jill! How fun!" She was enthused in that way only a mother can be.

Mom's optimism and steady cheeriness was an inherited demeanor I always actively worked on repressing in myself. She had an antiquated and very specific idea of how the corporate world operated. Having your own office was a big deal and she was truly happy for me. She had no idea that I never wore a suit or that most of my coworkers would scare the hell out of her if she passed them on the street. I had no intention of telling her.

"Let me call your father." I could hear her palm muffle the speaker and her blurred voice calling out.

Dad got on the phone and immediately asked, "How's your car running?"

"I don't know," I sighed. "Jessica has it in her driveway in New Jersey. I haven't driven it since the last time we talked."

"It's going to atrophy if it doesn't run," he scolded, using biological terms for the engine.

"I know, I know."

"So how's the view from the upper bunk?" he asked, referring to my promotion.

My parents were fifth-generation Texans, but I wasn't the first in the family to head east. My uncle and aunt used to live in northern New Jersey. While I was growing up, we made at least one trip a year to visit them. I'd hang out with my cousin, Jessica, and we'd see a Broadway show in the city, shop, and generally gawk at the hustle of the city streets. We actually traveled a lot. Because I was an only child, it was probably easy to pack me off to places like France as if I were another suitcase.

As I hung up the phone with my parents, I heard Kenny's pleading voice pierce through my doorway from down the hall. He was following Tony in a zigzag flutter as Tony clomped down the long carpet.

"Tony, please," he was saying, "I can't go into that neighborhood all alone. You're from Brooklyn. That's a tough borough."

"I ain't going to fucking Queens with you. So what if I'm from Brooklyn? Take LaKeisha. She's from the 'hood. She'll know what to look for." He stalked off and left Kenny standing in front of my open door.

Kenny turned and looked at me with a desperate expression. He bolted back in the direction that he came from.

For a second I paused in my victory lap. Maybe it was premature to be so celebratory. I glanced at the still-empty walls of the room and wondered if I'd even get enough time to put up posters before getting kicked out for being a law-abiding citizen. I had to maneuver through this maze and figure out just how tough I was supposed to appear to be. But I was determined to make the best of it while I could. I could do "mean" if it came to it. That was what the boots were for.

My next call was to Jessica. She was working at home this morning.

"Jessica Boyajian!" She answered her phone with perky efficiency.

"Hey, it's me," I said, matching her perk.

"Oh." The sparkle drained from her voice. "Hi, Jill."

I reached into my box of photos from my former desk as I squeezed the phone between my ear and shoulder.

"I'm in my new office!" I told my first cousin and only close relative of my generation, hoping to get some kind of impressed reaction.

"Good. It's about time with all the work you've done for them." I could hear her shuffling papers.

"They painted it and I'm here. All ready for the big time," I said, wondering if she might say something related to *congratulations.*

I picked up the photo of Mom and Dad and placed it in the corner of my bare desk. They were standing on the lawn of our house in the subdivision of Valley Sea Estates —a great name except that there was no valley or large body of water within several hundred miles. Maybe the "sea" referred to the small man-made pond at the entrance.

"That's great. You are planning to come to Easter, right?"

The family of her husband, Greg, included me in their annual Easter hyper-extravaganza. At first, I just went as a buffer for Jessica. She was the newcomer into the tight-knit Armenian American family, which was also crocheted rather snugly into their suburban community. It only took ten years, but she wormed her way into their hearts and was now accepted full force. They embraced me by default as her kin.

"Yes. I bought a silk top that I can wear. No metal studs."

I led a double life when it came to her in-laws. They liked me fine, but didn't get the streaked hair, the punk rock, or even the concept of living in the city.

She sighed, then gave a little giggle.

"You can wear whatever you want," she lied. "Ara is looking forward to seeing you." Ara was my cute nephew.

There was a beep sound on the phone line.

"Oh, that's my office on call waiting," she said. "I've got to go. It's great about the office. I'll talk to you later."

"Okay, I'll—" I said, but she had already hung up.

I replaced the phone in its cradle and stared at it for a moment before picking up the next photo from my box. I sat down and hunched over the photos with my elbows on the desktop, zeroing in on Jonathan, then on My Gordon.

"Gordon," I pleaded, "when is Jonathan going to call me?"

The last time I'd heard from Jonathan was almost a month ago via a pay phone in the back of a dive nightclub. I could imagine the blinking neon beer sign and sticky floor just from the background noise. I never knew exactly where he was in the country. I used to find it sexy that he traveled so much. He was completely in-the-know about the coolest places, because he was always with the coolest people. I was so impressed and he loved to show me around.

But now I had not even been able to get a hold of him to tell him I had my promotion and here I was, already in the new office. It sucked. What kind of a boyfriend was that?

Suddenly, my phone actually rang all by itself. I jumped and grabbed at the receiver.

"Hello?" I blurted excitedly.

"You're supposed to say something like, 'Jill Dodge here,'" Luann scolded through the line.

"Oh yeah. Right." I lowered my voice a little and officially announced, "Jill Dodge, Product Management."

"OK, that's better! It's on for after work tonight!" she said. "All hail the product manager. Joanie and Alyssa can come. Hancock's at seven thirty."

ABOUT AN HOUR LATER, AFTER I HAD MADE MORE PHONE CALLS looking for Jonathan, to Flying Flock's booking people and label reps, LaKeisha came into my new office in her designer high heels and slicked dark hair that seemed to supernaturally shorten and lengthen depending on her mood. Today, there was a long ponytail cascading down her back. LaKeisha, a veteran of the publicity department, always dressed like she just stepped out of the fashion pages of *Essence* magazine. Her light brown skin was luminescent. Her neck was long and so were her fingernails.

She was a good deal older than me and had an intimidating way of looking down her nose at you even when she was sitting down and you were standing.

The publicists had the most obvious access to the artists, after the arts & repertoire department, who signed the music groups in the first place. Once the music was released, the only time the artists themselves showed up at the offices was to do press or to yell at the Suits over something that might have gone wrong.

Fashion people often showed up in LaKeisha's office just to give her accessories and ask her to give this to Diana Ross's people or wear that at the next press event. She knew how to work it. If she was not throwing the party, she was invited to one. She had dozens of gold and platinum records on her walls. She was great at her job. She WAS her job, which I found to be a little scary. It was like she had no personal life at all.

Now, she sniffed at the photos on my desk and the little ivy plant I had set up. She stared at me in something that looked like disgust.

"I've been ordered to take Kenny to Queens tonight

to see this rapper we might sign," she said dully. "You, Michael, and Tony are going with us."

I had no idea what I was supposed to do on this outing. I knew college campus mosh pits, new wave semi-punk bands, and singer/songwriters who played in coffee-houses. "Do you know any rappers?" I asked her warily.

"Not a damn one."

She sauntered up to my desk and sat on the chair placed in front of it. "But it seems that since I am the only black New Yorker here, I guess, it's assumed that I am supposed to." She crossed her arms, visibly peeved.

She sighed and eyeballed me in her unnerving way. "Michael and I are supposed to know the 'blackness' of it, and you and Tony are supposed to know the 'streetness.'"

"Oh my God, I can actually hear Kenny saying that," I snorted.

I examined her expression for a moment. It was a good thing LaKeisha was not my boss, because I would have been fired a hundred times over since I walked in the main doors. We had had plenty of controversial arguments over the past couple of years. Many of them were deep. One time, I referred to her as "African American" and she insisted that was ridiculous.

"I'm black!" she said it like an order. "Don't you go get all 'politically correct' on me."

Another time, I picked up a magazine called *Black Music Today* from her desk. It had photos of Tracy Chapman, George Michael, and Luther Vandross on the cover.

My immediate reaction was to comment, "George Michael isn't black."

She said that his music was considered blue-eyed soul, so he was in.

So I shot back that Tracy Chapman should not be on this magazine cover because her music was folk music and definitely NOT soul. "C'mon," I had said. "She's a chubby girl with an acoustic guitar!"

"Well, she's black, so that's soul," she said.

"What? No, it's not!" I cried. "Then the Indigo Girls and Joan Baez should be on this magazine!"

"We have to promote our own," she retorted.

My political correctness censor fell to the ground. "That's just racist!" I declared.

We went on like that for a little while. It was a regular race war that ended with us staring at each other, knowing we were at an impasse. We were both right and we both knew it.

Now I asked her, "Where is it that we are going?"

"Some place in the projects," she said, waving her hand dismissively.

"Are we going to get killed?"

"Maybe," she deadpanned, without a twitch of a smile. She leaned back on the gray-toned office chair and gently tugged on the hem of her perfectly fitted shirt to make sure it wasn't crinkled, even a little. "If we do, it'll make Page Six, and all our artists' sales will go up. So," she continued, her eyes roaming the small room, "you put in your time and you're in the interior office. I tip my hat. I gotta say, I didn't think you'd last three months."

"Really?" I asked incredulously. That didn't seem very nice.

"Yeah, sweetie punk from the middle of nowhere, Texas."

As I was about to object, defend my savvy background as a world traveler, daughter of an entrepreneur, college graduate, she again waved her well-manicured hand in my general direction. "No, I know. You're no hick—I've heard the speech before." She got up and smoothed down her tan maxi-skirt.

"Meet us in front of the building at nine thirty tonight," she said, looking me up and down. "Dress down, like you always do, but put on a cap or something to cover that ridiculous red streak."

THREE

LUANN, JOANIE, AND ALYSSA WERE SITTING AT A COUNTER-height table in the neon-lit bar when I rushed into Hancock's. We always met here because it was exactly in the middle of midtown and we could each get here within ten minutes in case of emergency gossip moments.

I immediately started talking as they all looked up at me.

"Oh my God! I can only stay till nine. You won't believe this. They are sending me to some rap club in Queens to find a rapper and it's just crazy." I unloaded my jacket and huge black bag onto the back of the barstool and plopped myself down, rambling on all the while. "LaKeisha actually gave me some kind of backhanded compliment this afternoon about my promotion. Jenny said she'd get here in a few after she gets off the phone with some radio guy in Philadelphia . . ." I trailed off, suddenly noticing the looks on their faces and the way that the three of them were casting glances at each other.

"What? Did somebody die?" I asked.

"No, oh no," Alyssa began.

"Nobody died, nothing that drastic," Joanie continued.

Luann was slumping in her seat with a sheepish expression.

"What then? What's going on?" I thought this was supposed to be a celebration of ME for once. They all had had their big moments. When Alyssa got that modeling job for *Seventeen* magazine, we spent the weekend throwing confetti at her. When Joanie's boss sent her on a paid vacation to Aruba with her boyfriend and she came back with an engagement ring on her finger, we took her to the coolest bar in town. When Luann made assistant editor, we made her a door-size congratulations card and had Alyssa's waiter/actor friend pop out of it and sing to her.

Luann reached into her purse and took out her pocket tape recorder, the one she used during interviews with soap actors for her magazine.

She sighed and said, "I didn't want to tell you anything tonight, but then we got this message at home."

I had been toiling in the trenches and hanging on by my bitten-down fingernails for almost two years and finally got the real job. I deserved a fun celebration, but now I deflated. I could see something was about to ruin it, right this minute.

"All right already? What?" I urged.

"Last week, Claudia called me—you remember Claudia? From Austin? Who was up here for the CMJ music convention last year? She's living in Atlanta now and she was at the Flying Flock show there. She met up with them and Jonathan."

I sank into myself slightly. I thought I knew where this was going.

"Well, she called me and said there were a lot of groupie types and that she saw Jonathan being all kissy-face with some girl who was traveling with them."

Now, my stomach suddenly hurt. Somewhere in me, I knew this was going to happen. Jonathan always swore up and down that he was true to me while on the road. I wanted to believe him, but really, what cute twenty-nine-year-old guy traveled around to nightclubs with a bunch of rock star wannabes and didn't get laid?

Alyssa piped in, sweetly saying, "Maybe we shouldn't do this tonight?"

"She has to know this." Joanie flipped aside her long brown hair and shoved a gin and tonic into my hand. "A nebulous 'I saw your man with another girl' isn't enough. This will make it a real break in her head. Freedom from this loser!" Joanie never liked Jonathan. She called him "a slickster." I didn't really know exactly what that was supposed to mean, but obviously, it was not good.

Now, I wasn't just queasy; I was getting nervous and frightened. I turned back to Luann and her recorder.

"So?"

She pushed the green button and I heard the crackly sound of our answering machine playback.

"You have. One. Message. First. Message. 'You fucking BITCH!'" a girl's high-pitched voice shrieked from the little machine.

My jaw dropped and I straightened up, leaning into the table as Luann, Alyssa, and Joanie crumpled away slightly, watching me. They had already heard it. I stared at Luann's quivering palm.

"You think that you are Johnny's girl. Well, you are not!" The girl on the recording was either drunk or high or worse, like crazy. "I see your name in this little black book and your picture in his wallet, but he's been sleeping with me. That's right. ME. I'm the one he's with and I can be there for him. I can travel with him. I have him every night. All night. We . . ." Luann fumbled with the buttons to turn it off as people at surrounding tables began to eye us curiously.

"It goes on like that for a while. I didn't think you'd want to hear the whole thing," she said.

"Oh my God," I said. My eyes started to well up.

"Yeah," Alyssa said in her girlish voice. "'Oh my God' is right."

"There is something definitely wrong with that person," Joanie said, taking a swig of her drink.

"I'm so sorry, Jill." Luann put her hand on my arm. "I didn't know what to do, but they thought we should go ahead and play it for you while we were together."

The tears overflowed onto my skin and down to my pouting lips. But oddly, it wasn't from heartbreak. The feeling was more like relief.

I zipped around the various stages of loss and landed on anger: anger at him, but also at myself.

It wasn't even that I "loved" Jonathan. I didn't want to marry him or anything. It pissed me off that I had been jilted and cheated on by someone that I'd been hanging with out of laziness. I duped myself into thinking that we were a classic boyfriend/girlfriend. At the very least, there was a serial monogamy agreement going on here. Having a serious boyfriend was simply part of the adult package. And he was cute and sexy and full of promises. This arrangement was the best way out of not having a boyfriend. You felt like a loser if you didn't, at least, have a guy to point at and say, "He's my boyfriend." Right?

Either that, or you were expected to be actively and desperately looking for a boyfriend all the time, which was just too exhausting.

I should have been the one to cheat on him! Did I even like him that much? He always smelled like a combination of beer and cigarette smoke. I hated beer and I didn't smoke.

All three girls started to pat me on the back, as I wiped the tears from my cheeks and sighed.

"It's all right. It's fine," I assured them. I took a big gulp of my drink. "I'm going to the bathroom."

The girls did another round of glances at each other and Luann volunteered, "I have to go too."

We headed for the back of the bar. By the time we got back, Jenny was sitting in the midst of the group and had been filled in on the shenanigans.

"At least you didn't get the crabs!" she said, sounding delightedly cynical. She knew Jonathan was low and had tried to steer me away from him, too. "Or did you?" she half-joked.

I WENT UPSTAIRS AFTER ARRIVING BACK AT THE BIG BLACK office building. There were still quite a few people sitting in their offices, phones pressed to their ears or shuffling papers around, even at nine o'clock on a Tuesday night. *Doesn't anyone here have a family?* I wondered.

Kenny was in his office too, so I slunk past his door hoping he wouldn't see me and deprive me of at least a few minutes to myself before this adventure.

Back in my little room, I banged nails into the wall

using the back of my stapler and hung up some posters. A framed photo from *Guitar Magazine* of blues guitarists, the Vaughan brothers, Stevie Ray and Jimmy—I was a Texan, after all. An LP cover of the Clash's *London Calling* —my favorite angst-ridden punk band. The one gold record that I was "attached" to from Gloria Estefan—not that I did much to deserve it. All I had done was help organize the huge record release party that cost more than my annual salary. Then I put up a nice mirror at my face level, which meant others would get a great view of their collarbones if they tried to check themselves out in it.

The mirror reflected the smudge of black eyeliner that had fallen below my lower lashes due to my little crying fit. My straight, bobbed, brown hair with the one wine-red streak down the side looked all right. It had enough pizzazz to be noticed, but was not the neon punker mohawk that had everyone gawking. I touched up my makeup, piling on the black eyeliner and mascara, and pinched my cheeks a little to make it look like I might not be dead, after all. I was cute enough, but I didn't look like a Texan. I looked like a New Yorker. The tall and blond Texan Miss America or the world-famous buxom women on the TV series *Dallas* were a far cry from my appearance. Neither my look nor my personality fit neatly into anyone's Texan stereotype and that drove people nuts.

I sat down at my desk and noticed the photo of Jonathan there right next to My Gordon. The framed Jonathan made a clanging sound as he hit the rim of the garbage can.

Turning back to My Gordon, I sighed.

"It's back to you and me," I told the black and white image. "Where is all the love? You found it, didn't you?"

I softly sang to myself a bit of a song from his last album.

Was there a moment in time when we know we are in love, when it feels like we are truly lying in a field of gold, all shiny and warm? My parents had it and it seemed to work out for them. I knew it existed, so simple yet so distant. We were always searching, thinking that we should be in some sort of eternal bliss, when the truth was that love is something so much deeper than that. We could not fathom it. My buddies and I were all a bunch of fakes, walking around with our hardened masks, all the while hoping someone would see through it and sweep us off our feet like the proverbial knight in shining armor. Was there anyone who actually wanted to love and protect me? Not just appear to be doing that, while underneath, being in it mostly for regular sex?

Jonathan certainly did his part to dash my little fantasy to the curb, while My Gordon was doing his part to build it back up. The fact was that nobody could love us enough to make up for whatever we didn't love about ourselves. We doomed ourselves to Barbie and Ken mythology, then got cynical when confronted with liars and cheats. Living in the fantasy seemed easier, though. At least some of the time.

A knock on the open door snapped me out of my reverie. Michael leaned in, peering at me. His familiar brown face and dark eyes were a sudden comfort.

"Making love to your muse?" he joked, his expression full of mischief. His palm pressed on his yellow diamond tie, keeping it from swinging away from his chest.

I looked up at him. Obviously my face gave away my dejected state of mind.

"Oh man, what's wrong?" he asked, coming in to the office.

I sighed and slumped back on my chair. "Men! Men are wrong. All wrong." I began to tear up again.

"Oh, no, no, no. Don't cry. I'm not trained for the crying." He put his hand across the desk, paused, then patted my forearm, like it was the bell on a hotel check-in desk. "Is it the rockin' soundman?" he asked.

"Yeah." I got up and went back to the mirror, wiping under my eyes to try and save my newly applied eyeliner. "'The rockin' soundman and the floozy groupie.' Sounds like a headline of the *Post*."

"You're all right." He came and stood beside me, looking at my reflection in the mirror. "He wasn't for you anyway." He gave me an assuring shoulder bump.

Everybody seemed to know that for sure. Why was I just cluing in?

I turned to him and suddenly noticed what he was wearing. "Are you sure you want to wear a suit to a dive bar in Queens?"

"Too uptown?" He grinned and adjusted his tie.

"You are going to stick out like several sore thumbs," I told him.

Just then, Kenny came running into the room.

"OK! C'mon." He seemed overly jumpy even for him. "LaKeisha and Tony are downstairs with a car." He was wearing dark jeans and a T-shirt. His black curly hair was all gelled up. His expensive leather jacket was a little too nicely cut, but at least it wasn't a suit. I shook my head. These guys were clueless.

Kenny hustled us down the hall and into the elevator,

fidgeting and biting his cuticles on the way down. Michael and I made eye contact and he did a bug-eyed sort of look at me, like he was saying, *Kenny's an idiot and I cannot believe we have to do this.* I grinned at him.

F O U R

WHEN WE GOT OUTSIDE, WE COULD MAKE OUT TONY AND LaKeisha in the dim streetlight, arguing in front of two cars. One was a hired, sleek black town car. The driver sat patiently behind the wheel. The other was a dented 1965 Ford Falcon, as aqua as the Caribbean Sea.

Tony's long hair whipped around his head in the city breeze. LaKeisha wore some sort of tracksuit getup. She was jabbing Tony's broad, flannel-clad chest with a black baseball cap that had the letters "P.E." emblazoned on it in bright gold. "I am not getting in that tin can!" she announced to him and any pedestrians who might be walking by.

"We are not going to show up in a drug dealer neighborhood in a limo," he told her firmly in his gravelly voice. He squared off his feet to counteract the action of her cap jabbing.

As we walked up, they both turned to face us. Kenny rushed at them.

"What's wrong? What's going on?" he gushed.

Michael and I hung back, looking back and forth at the two cars. I was not about to get in the middle of this scrap. Tony and LaKeisha were the two toughest people I knew.

Michael leaned down to my ear. "Ten spot on LaKeisha," he said with a sparkle in his eye.

I stifled a laugh and waited.

They both turned to Kenny and began talking at once.

Tony's argument was that we could not show up in the worst part of Queens in a shiny town car with a driver. Either we'd come off as dealers trying to take over someone else's corner or the car would get jacked while we were in the club. His Falcon, which was actually his grandmother's car and she lived in Brooklyn, would fit right in and nobody would notice us.

I noted to myself that from our collective appearance, this was not a group that would go unnoticed, no matter where we were headed.

LaKeisha was beside herself. She didn't want to be seen, even in a nasty neighborhood, in that thing Tony had brought. She was a senior manager at a multimillion-dollar company and had a reputation to think of.

Kenny decided that it was a "streetness" issue, so went with Tony on this one.

The drive over the Queensboro Bridge was an adventure in and of itself, with the five of us in the throwback monstrosity of a vehicle. Tony drove. Kenny sat shotgun. Michael, LaKeisha, and I were actually quite comfortable in the grand bench seat in the back. They sure made these old boats roomy. No wonder all of those songs from the '50s and '60s were about making out back here. Michael turned to LaKeisha.

"What are you wearing?" he asked sarcastically.

"Oh," she answered, straightening up and pulling down the shiny jacket slightly, "I made some calls this afternoon to a stylist friend. They did a bunch of photo shoots for Def Jam. She sent this over. It's nice, huh? She gave me these too." She held up the cap and dug a thick gold chain out of her pocket. The chain had a gaudy medallion hanging off the end of it.

"You're not really going to put that around your neck?" I asked, pointing at the huge chunk of metal.

"I don't know," she said thoughtfully.

"So, LaKeisha," Michael said, "you are actually from Brooklyn, right?"

"Yes." She didn't say anything else.

"Well, what part?" Michael suddenly seemed very, very young to me. He was about my age, but had worked at Mega Big Records in his current job for several years. LaKeisha had been around the block and had no intention of going around it again or explaining that block to either of us.

She kind of rolled her eyes without rolling her eyes. "I grew up in the Heights."

"So did I," Tony threw back from the front seat.

"Yeah, but I think that might have been a whole different Heights." She sighed and leaned on her hand, her elbow stationed on her knee. She turned her gaze out the window, officially ending the conversation.

I leaned forward and put my face over the back of the front seat, looking out through the windshield. I had a flashback of being on a family cross-country vacation. "Where, exactly, are we going?"

"You don't want to know," Tony guffawed.

"We're going to a little club," Kenny said. "Every Tuesday is rap night and I got a tape shopped to me by some guy who knows a guy who comes here all the time. We're going there to meet 'MC Doggie T.'"

"What do you mean by 'meet?' Is he going to perform or what?" I pressed.

"Yeah, sure, of course. I think so," Kenny replied and started gnawing on his cuticles again.

I leaned back, watching the street scenes moving past the window and tried to forget that I was feeling sorry for myself.

We pulled off into a side street that had rows of two-story brick buildings along both sides, only broken up by the occasional chain-link-fenced vacant lot. This did not feel good in my gut. The sidewalk widened and there was a series of bodegas and a narrow, blackened building with a lit sign in front that read "Drop Zone Lounge." There were two bored-looking black guys standing in front with their arms crossed.

"Are we supposed to be on some sort of guest list?" I asked Kenny, thinking these men were the doormen or bouncers.

"I . . . I don't think so," Kenny stammered.

Tony let us off in front and said he would park and come back.

We loaded out onto the sidewalk. The beat from inside the building was apparent through the walls. We must have looked like a real motley crew—a skinny Jewish guy, a black guy in a suit, a punk rocker girl, and some kind of African queen in fancy jogging sweats. The two guys at the door immediately perked up upon our arrival.

Kenny made to walk past them, as if he owned the place.

"Excuse me," he started to say, just as one of the guys placed the tip of his finger on the front of Kenny's soft leather jacket. The guy's black T-shirt, pants, and cap were all really, really black. I'd never seen an outfit so dark against skin so dark. His muscles rippled under the stretched pull of his short cotton sleeves. I didn't know why he wasn't freezing in this chilly March air. The other guy was skinny and much shorter. He stepped up, crossing his arms and trying to look stern, but his oversized baseball cap and crooked smile gave off a slightly crazed vibe instead.

"May I help you?" The muscle guy asked in a deep, formal voice, looking Kenny up and down like he was something that smelled awfully bad, yet grinning the whole time. We were an obvious source of amusement.

"We'd like to go inside to see the rappers . . . the guys . . . the people who are performing." Kenny tried to puff up his chest a little bit, but it just wasn't a go.

My eyes darted up and down the street and I inched my way closer to LaKeisha. There was nothing moving on the whole street except a few shuffling newspaper pages at the base of the chain-link fence near the nightclub's door.

"You here to see Reg?" the smaller guy asked, as he looked over our whole, obviously-not-from-around-here entourage. He thought we were here for a drug buy.

"No," Michael chimed in, "we are here to meet a friend. Doggie T?"

"Doggie T?" He turned to the other guy and they both smirked.

"Who're you, the butler?" the muscled guy sneered at Michael. He stepped around Kenny, who shrank slightly, relieved to have the attention off of him.

"Jeeves, step to the mahogany, my man, and fetch me a Cream Sherry," the crooked smile guy said in an odd mix of Brooklyn and British accents.

They both howled at their own hilarity.

Kenny looked stricken. Michael froze. I could see the bitterness rise up behind his eyes. The muscle guy saw it too and the tension went up a notch.

LaKeisha sighed audibly and shifted her weight, jutting out her hip, her hand firmly placed on it.

The muscle guy suddenly stepped right up to Michael, his taut chest inches away from Michael's tie. Michael didn't flinch. They were eye-to-eye, nose-to-nose, though Michael was noticeably narrower, even in his shoulder-padded suit. Kenny gasped. I gasped. The guy still had the grin on his face, but with a more searching look in his eyes.

LaKeisha said, "Oh for God's sake," stepping up to their profiles. Her Brooklyn came flying out. "Open the damn door and let us up in this place," she ordered. Both Michael and the muscle guy looked at her, surprised, but for different reasons. Maybe the muscle guy recognized something in her. I was holding my breath, waiting to see what he would do.

He stepped back and smiled broadly. "Of course, Madame!" he mocked and did an exaggerated bow with his arm moving toward the grimy door. The other guy opened the door as LaKeisha led the way with her shoulders thrown back and her head high. The rest of us scurried inside after her, not looking back.

ONCE INSIDE, THE SUBWOOFER OVERTOOK US IMMEDIATELY. With the lack of lighting, we could barely see in the narrow hallway leading to the back of the building. We moved toward the sound of the heavy beat and some gel-colored light. The hall opened up into a room with scuffed parquet floors and a low ceiling. There was something that resembled a dance floor with a small clutch of people standing around. The stage, if you could call it that, was elevated about two feet. The ceiling, being low, and the height of the stage made it so that the three guys on the stage were all slightly stooped as they bobbed to the beat. One of them stood in the back behind what looked like a folding TV tray with two turntables precariously perched on it. Every time he touched the vinyl, the whole ensemble shook unsteadily. The other two had microphones and were moving in time with each other and loudly yelling a back-and-forth rhyme. I could not make out the words, because the beat and the scratching of the DJ and the recorded guitar riff overpowered their voices. The spot-lights blared in blue and red on their faces.

Out of habit and sheer inner child, I started to bop with the beat. I actually loved this kind of thing. But I also knew that I probably should not bring a whole lot of attention to myself. A few people stared at us. There were probably about fifty people in the club. It was mostly skinny black guys in their teens and early twenties. There were a smattering of scary-looking white guys in black T-shirts and a few black girls with large fake gold earrings, ironed hair, and overly padded shoulders, also in their teens and early twenties.

I suddenly felt very old and very pale. I thought that I was a downtown sort of person, but I'd never been this far downtown. I kept an eye on the exit, tried to act cool, and made sure that I was as close to LaKeisha as she would let me stand.

We all filed toward the bar, where Michael ordered me a gin and tonic that tasted like lime-laced battery acid. After one sip, I held it out, away from my body, in case it might get inside me via osmosis somehow. Michael seemed to be doing the same with his drink, carefully standing a foot from the sticky Formica bar to keep his suit jacket clean. Kenny nervously shifted back and forth on his toes. LaKeisha was looking around with pressed lips, probably in horror at the outfits she was seeing on the girls.

Tony appeared at my elbow. Apparently, he had no trouble getting through the front door.

The music stopped. There was some clapping and yelling. A baby-faced MC came onto the stage. Pretty much every other word out of his mouth was a curse word, so I suspect that the former rappers probably had the same kind of potty mouths. There was some shuffling behind him on the stage as the next group brought out a sturdier table.

"Now we got our old friends from last week, MC Doggie T and DJ Fizz."

Kenny pointed, indicating this was the act we were here to see.

Tony leaned down to my ear. "It's a dog and pony show!" He snickered.

Then suddenly, these two guys came on the stage and the whole attitude in the tiny club changed. The beat that started up was clear and piercing, with a funky guitar riff running underneath it. DJ Fizz was tall and boyish in a wifebeater tank top and sunglasses. He leaned his wiry shoulders over the turntables and actually seemed to be "playing" them, like they were their own instrument. The rapper with the microphone was "on" the minute he made himself visible. He definitely had charisma, although he was not as young looking as the DJ. He was handsome, in a cocky sort of way. His hair was cut in a flattop, not too high. He didn't have sunglasses or a hat or anything, but was wearing a gray hoodie jacket over a plain black shirt, and two gold chains bounced around his neck. Instead of hunching over to avoid the low ceiling, like the previous act, this guy had it all under control. He crouched a little, his strong legs angling in a kind of tae kwon do stance. When he parted his lips, there was a flash of gold from his front tooth, and he started to rap in a mouthy, yet clear voice:

> "We're here to tell you, it's rap class act
> and it's fuckin' nuts that you have to ask
> check the strut and shit and build a big pit
> 'cause y'all 'bout to get stuck in it
> Fizz pullin' down the beat, Doggie T rhymin' out
> girl rockin' in the heat, boy, your chance's timin' out
> The fucker big, bad and cocky, dancin' on the floor
> fell on his ass, now he headed out the door
> Move yo' feet, you just a chillin' in the park?
> In the street, they gonna fuck you, nasty nark
> Doggie T tell you how it is 'cause I know
> brother got it goin' 'cause I got someplace to go
> rankin' fakin' bakin' snake make it big

stinkin' blinkin' freakin' fake take a hit
what you got, I got it bigger, better, bad
what you see, my bitch better than you ever had"
(DJ scratch with a guitar riff)
"that shit crazy,
that shit crazy,
that shit crazy"

Everyone perked up and moved toward the front of the stage. The rap itself was not my taste, that was for sure. It was kind of crass and not exactly deep. Most of the rap out there was all verse, but this seemed to have something that resembled a chorus and a bit of musical interlude. Half the song would have to be bleeped out on the radio, though.

Within sixty seconds, four of the five of us at the bar had caught each other's eyes and nodded in one way or another. This was one of those rare moments when we could all see it pretty clearly. Even if the rap itself wasn't that great, these guys had star quality. With a little bit of polish and packaging, depending on what level of crazy they were personally, we could do something with them.

A little thrill went through me. If I was involved in getting these guys signed, I might make it through this probation intact.

Michael, though, was just staring at the rapper, quizzically.

After the set, Kenny and Tony disappeared behind the stage and came back with a cassette tape and a phone number.

Buff deliverymen stacked up heavy boxes of computer equipment along the hallway and in the cubby outside of the senior vice president's office. Georgina began to look like a victim in an Edgar Allan Poe story, with all of the boxes walling her in behind her desk.

A memo went out to all staff that they should be at the weekly two o'clock meeting that was usually only for managers. We assembled, crowding the space of the room, most of us standing around trying not to touch each other in the close quarters. Jenny and I leaned against the wall and made snide remarks.

The senior vice president strode into the room, trailed by Georgina and four clean-cut young men. They were dressed in tandem, wearing khaki pleated pants, button-down shirts, and ties, and were carrying various computer parts. They placed the TV-like monitor, a large CPU computer tower, and the various wires and smaller boxes on the conference table. Then they stood in a line right behind the senior vice president with their hands behind them and their legs stiff, like some sort of geeky military platoon with pimples.

Everybody crowded in to get a look at the machines.

Some people in the room already had worked on computers in previous jobs or at home. Most, though, had never even seen one up close. Tony, of course, hung back.

"All right," the senior vice president said, his normal cue for everyone to settle down. "Each person here with a desk, admins on up, is going to get one of these state-of-the-art, brand-new 1989 computers. These people"—he indicated the nerd lineup—"are the people who will be in your offices, wiring everything up." He turned to the most starched and least acne-ridden of the bunch. "What's your name again?" he asked.

"Alejandro Alvarez," the guy offered humbly. He was obviously a little shy about having to stand in front of everyone. His thick dark hair was short and unruly as it flopped onto his forehead over his large, even darker eyes. He bowed slightly when he said his name.

I elbowed Jenny in the ribs. The guy's formal gesture was a charming crack up. I almost expected to hear his heels click together.

"Ah-lay-hand-dro"—the senior vice president massacred the poor guy's name—"knows everything about this stuff. He and his men will be setting everything up. First, you all get one of these." He motioned to the array of items on the table. "And the instruction manuals. Don't touch anything until you've taken the class. Corporate has a classroom set up on the fortieth floor. All the sub-labels are getting the classes. You have to take the course within the next two weeks."

He held out his hand and without any eye contact, Georgina snapped to and placed a sheet of legal-sized paper in his hand.

"The schedule is right here," he said, waving the paper around, then placing it on the table. "Sign up now for your orientation class. It's two hours long and I've already taken it. Has anyone here worked with computers before?"

Fewer than a quarter of the people raised their hands. I was among them. I used a computer for the first time during my last visit home at my father's veterinarian practice. He had them installed to make a database of his patients and keep track of billing.

There were some grumbles around the room. In our business, two hours was a long time away from the phones.

"I don't want to hear bitching and moaning about this. Ricardo, here," the senior vice president went on, motioning to the guy who had just told us that his name was Alejandro, "is the guy in charge of this installation. Listen to him and be nice."

He looked meaningfully around the room, then strode out, with Georgina in tow.

Jenny, Tony, and I milled around the sample computers with a few others and the computer guys.

Tony shook hands with all of them, one after the other, and said, "I am so glad to see you people!" He immediately started asking technical questions about how much RAM were we getting and what was the writing software.

RAM? Software? I had no idea what he was talking about.

Jenny asked the lead nerd, "So we are going to be able to write letters on this like a typewriter?"

"Yes," Alejandro replied, "and send each other messages —electronic mail. You won't have to use message pads anymore or paper memos."

"Wow," I said, leaning toward the monitor.

Tony was watching us.

THE MONTHLY POKER GAME USUALLY HAPPENED AT OUR apartment because we had the biggest dining area—that is by New York, worker bee standards. The table could fit five people elbow to elbow, and the fact that you could actually walk behind the chairs without sucking in your gut and pressing your back to the wall was a plus.

Other than Luann and me, our game included Jenny, Joanie, and Alyssa.

Luann acted as the hostess with the mostest. She always fussed over what food to put out. I was content with cheese doodles and a glass of wine.

Sometimes, depending on the nearest holiday, she would string up some kind of hokey decoration, like orange and black streamers around Halloween and American flags in early July.

We called this a poker game, but it was really a sort of drunken group therapy session. One or another of us always had something to moan about: romance, jobs, parents.

This time it was my turn, considering the whole crazy-girl phone call debacle.

Jenny asked, "Did you ever get in touch with Jonathan?"

"No," I replied with a sigh as I dealt five cards to each of them. "Five card stud. I don't think he even knows the girl called me. I cannot believe that I can't even find him! It's like he disappeared somewhere in the Arizona desert."

Within a month of my settling in New York, I met Jonathan. Luann and I were waiting in a line, being inspected by the bouncer at a hot spot club in the meat-packing district. Jonathan got us in. I was in awe of his charm and how he was able to talk his way into almost any club in town. No matter if he was not on a guest list. No matter if it was ladies night. He seemed to know every door guy between Avenue A and 105th Street.

"They are supposed to be in Phoenix tonight," I said. "I have the number of the club."

Everybody picked up and rearranged their cards.

"Oh? What time are they supposed to have sound check?" Jenny asked.

"Probably around five o'clock their time," I said. "Ante up." We all threw plastic poker chips onto the scratched wooden surface of the table.

"So, with the time difference that makes it about"— Joanie looked at her watch—"now!" Joanie seemed to find my little drama way too amusing.

They all stopped and looked at me. I filled up my glass with wine and crammed a palmful of cheese doodles into my mouth to keep from having to affirm or deny if I would be making that call just yet.

Jonathan had been equally impressed by me and the fact that I had a job, albeit not an official one, at a major label. We'd been dating ever since. I had to hand it to him. He was so cool, super good-looking, and fun in bed. But all the touring, months at a time, never seemed to keep him here long enough for us to get serious. Our only arguments seemed to be about which bands were better—the Clash or AC/DC? Beatles or Rolling Stones? The Grateful Dead? Oh please!

When he was in town, we were both busy all the time.

It occurred to me that I really never spent that much time *alone* with him. We always seemed to be surrounded by people—at dinners, at concerts, in nightclubs. The only time we'd be alone was late at night, tipsy and in bed together, and that short time between waking up in the morning and meeting more people for brunch or me running off to work.

Luann was the first to speak up during the pause. "Give me two," she said, handing in two of her cards. "You have to talk to him and make the break. Even if he denies sleeping around, you know you have to make it official."

"No, she doesn't," countered Joanie, waving one card in front of my face and placing it on the table. "Guys always string you along. Why does SHE have to be the one to make the move? He should have an ounce of gentlemanly guts in him and call her!" I handed her another card and took another sip of wine.

"What if he doesn't?" Jenny, the instigator, asked, her Jersey accent suddenly more apparent. "She's gonna let this string out forever? Wait until he comes back? That's, like, months from now."

"Someone here has to have a backbone," Joanie insisted. "And Jonathan has proven it's not him!"

"I'm out," I said. I became very intent on making my stack of cards line up with the rest of the deck.

I watched them sparring about the hows and whos of my imminent and inevitable breakup and refilled my wineglass.

"OK," I announced, "I think I'll just become gay. I really want to start dating girls."

Joanie snickered. Alyssa looked shocked.

"No, you don't," was Jenny's deadpan reply, without looking away from her cards.

"Yes," I insisted, "I do. How do I do that?"

She sighed and rolled her eyes. "Kiss a girl."

"Ugh!"

"Exactly. If that didn't appeal to you before, it's not going to just because you decide to be gay."

"But it must be easier than dealing with guys. At least I understand how girls think."

"Not really." Jenny tossed her cards onto the table. "I fold. From what I can tell from all my friends who are gay, it's all the same kinds of fights. The only difference is that your parents have to go into therapy once they find out you don't date the opposite sex, if, that is, they ever want to speak to you again."

I slumped, draining my glass of wine and pouring another.

"Romance sucks all around," Alyssa piped in.

"Besides, you should never turn gay just because you've had too much to drink," said Luann, indiscreetly moving my wineglass about a foot out of my reach.

"Jonathan doesn't love me and I don't love him, either. What the hell am I doing?" I cried out convincingly. "This city is filled with Euro-trash, gay men, and overambitious Suits who only want to date models—"

"But just as arm candy, for a story he'll tell to other guys," Alyssa added. She should know, I guessed.

Joanie and Alyssa were the only ones still left in the hand and they both put in another chip, their minds obviously not on the game. They put their cards out on the tabletop and Alyssa took the pot. I refilled all the wineglasses and sipped the red liquid thoughtfully. Jenny took the deck and shuffled.

All of the single guys I knew were pigs, even the ones who I considered friends. They either cheated on girls who they called their girlfriends or, the more honest ones, would never commit in the first place. They called it "playing the field." That was what Tony did. He had a different girl on his arm every other week. They'd show up for one concert, never to be seen again. So I supposed that was what I was going to do—play the field. That was what you called it in the Big Apple, but where I was from, that was just another way of saying "slut."

"Right, I'm not going to be gay. Maybe I should just be a slut!" I said, louder than I intended.

Everyone at the table spoke up at once.

"We should take back that word." "We're just looking for true love." "The stereotype of the female being a slut and the male being worldly is just oppression." They all leaned into the table as they reassured themselves, me, and each other that sleeping around was not slutty.

I threw my cards at the center of the table and stood up. My chair clanked over backward onto the ugly linoleum floor. I might have had one too many glasses of wine with my cheese doodles after all.

"All right, I'm calling him now." I catapulted myself the three feet from the table to our secondhand, ultra-upholstered couch, which was given to us by my cousin Jessica's very rich sister-in-law, Taleen. Last month, she redecorated for the umpteenth time since I'd met her.

I reached for the phone and fished the pink memo pad note with the phone number on it out of my jean pocket. I punched the buttons of the phone and waited for the ringing. Someone picked up and I could hear the amplified talking, guitar strums, and occasional bass drum thumps in the background, which indicated that the band was starting sound check. I asked for Jonathan and made the mistake of telling the person that it was Jill, his girlfriend in New York, calling. I waited some more. But Jonathan didn't get on the phone. David did.

David was the bass player. It was always the bass player, the peacekeeper, the middle child of every rock band, who wound up dealing with the disgruntled outsiders, which included—but was not limited to—pushy managers, obnoxious radio DJs, nerdy music reporters, and jilted girlfriends, like me.

I mouthed to my poker buddies that it was David. They all made faces and different motions with their hands, indicating what they thought I should do. Joanie punched her fist into her palm, like a baseball player. Alyssa was mouthing "Hang up. Hang up." Luann was pointing at me and shaking her head. I didn't know what she meant by that. I turned away from them.

"Hi, David!" I was cool as a cucumber. "How's life on the road?"

"Oh wow, man, like, it's been kind of hard this past week. We just got here a half hour ago. The bus broke down in El Paso. Big bummer."

"Oh, that's too bad. Is the Phoenix club OK?" I was making nice.

"Yeah, it's great. They said they've presold almost three-quarters of the house."

"Oh wow, that's great! So they did some media work for you. Great, great."

A cheese doodle hit the back of my head. I deflected

the next one with the palm of my hand. The girls at the table were all about to burst, making faces and exaggerated gestures.

"So is Jonathan with you?"

"Uh, well, you see . . ." He was waffling. He didn't want to lie, but knew he was expected to.

"David, I know he's with you. I can hear the guys onstage."

"Right," he brightened, seeing an out. "We are in the middle of sound check. Really busy right now. He'll call you back after the check?"

"No, he won't," I said flatly and sighed. I then said meaningfully, "Just tell him that I *know*."

The girls all gasped. I glanced over toward the table and they were a still-life tableau, all facing me with open mouths.

"Know?" David croaked.

"Yes," I spoke very slowly and deliberately, "and I know you know WHAT I know."

There was a pause. The aural scene muffled. David must have put his hand over the mouthpiece. Then there was a shuffling sound, like the phone was being moved around on a desk or something.

Jonathan was obviously there in the room with him. I could picture it perfectly—David whispering to him what I had just said, shoving the phone at him, and Jonathan pushing back.

"Oh, for cryin' out loud!" I said. This felt like a girls against boys red rover game from third grade.

I put my hand over the receiver and stage-whispered to the girls, "He's there, but he won't get on the phone? What the hell?"

More gestures and mouthing of words. The consensus seemed to be that I should hang up. So I did.

"Oh. My. God. What a coward!" Joanie practically yelled. The poker game restarted in earnest, with shaking heads and man-hating comments flying around as freely as the rider-back cards.

I lay inert on the couch, my face turned up to the ceiling, trying to keep the tears in my eyeballs.

Jenny dealt me out.

JENNY WALKED INTO MY OFFICE THE FOLLOWING MONDAY and threw an LP cover mock-up onto my desk. It was for Kenny's waif-like singer. The name "Crystal Reneaux" marched across the cover, with a gauzy photo of Crystal herself, her pale pink skin almost fading into the background and her strawberry-blond hair floating outside the frame.

"It comes out in two weeks. Self-titled. All the work is in mass production as of two o'clock this afternoon," she announced.

"Congratulations! She's pretty. Very . . ." I picked up the LP cover and searched for the right word.

"Willowy? Airy? Wimpy?" Jenny offered.

"Well, it's not hard rock. It's supposed to be willowy. That's her thing, right?" I studied the picture. "How's the music? Do you have a tape of the final?"

"It's got some nice songs. It's all very dreamy and poetic. I'll get you one, if you want." She scrunched her nose and waved away the curl on her forehead. Jenny hated dreamy and poetic. I could like it, if it was done right.

"She's also weird," she said.

"As in . . . ?"

"She talks in whispers and is always looking around

the room, like some kind of bird watching for predators. I think the Suits like her because she's probably going to end up in a loony bin. That'll sell records."

She stuck her tongue out at me and then handed me a pinkish glass paperweight shaped like a natural crystal. The name "Crystal Reneaux" in flowery typeface was etched across it.

"You think?" I examined the vapid paperweight, then put it on my desk, under the ivy overflow.

There was a soft knock on the open door. We both looked up and saw Alejandro, the computer guy, leaning shyly in the doorway.

"Is this office 'R'?" he asked.

"I don't know," I answered. "Do these offices have numbers or letters?"

"I never noticed any," Jenny added.

We both looked around, bewildered.

He had a roll of wiring wrapped around his muscular forearm and a drill in the other hand. He leaned back out and looked up and down the hall. "This isn't working," he said to himself.

"Aha!" Jenny joked in response, raising both her arms. "Welcome to the music business!"

We both giggled a little at her inside joke and she waved at me as she brushed past him. "See you later."

I got up and stood in the hallway with the computer guy, and we both examined the doorframe and the wall.

"The name plaques are not marked with anything," I said to him, stating the obvious.

I was able to look into his face without craning my neck. He was only a few inches taller than me.

"These buildings are old," he said matter-of-factly.

He took a small step closer and motioned into my office in a friendly way. He was still a respectful distance from me, but I caught a delicate whiff of musk cologne.

"I saw some of your posters," he said. "I love the Clash." He smiled at me.

"Yeah," I responded, sizing him up a little bit more. He had a cute smile, but starched button-down—check. Pleated pants—check. Loafers—check. The only thing this guy was missing was a pocket protector.

"I'm sure Georgina has some kind of map," I offered coolly and stepped back inside the doorway.

"Oh, yeah." He suddenly checked himself, too, looking down at his wires. "I'll ask her."

He turned and walked down the hall. I peered around the doorframe after him. He did a quick look over his shoulder back in my direction, and I flinched backward into my office.

I didn't even notice Tony in the hallway, witnessing this whole skit. I nearly jumped out of my skin as his wide image appeared in my peripheral vision.

He grinned at me. More like, leered at me.

"You looking for Julio there to work on your hard drive?"

I stuttered, "What? No . . . how rude . . . his name is Alejandro, anyway, not Julio."

"OK. Whatever." His thick city accent and burly demeanor were so coarse compared to my last few minutes near the computer guy that I backed away from him.

"So," he continued, "Kenny signed Doggie T. The Suits are all over it."

"Good, I think he's got charisma."

"Yeah, but there's something too clean."

"What do you mean?"

"Didn't you see how he was dressed?"

"He had on a T-shirt and hoodie."

"But it was a new, perfectly fitting T-shirt. A hoodie that looked like it just came out of a plastic bag from China."

"That's just because he knew we were coming. Trying to impress the corporate guy."

"Right, and if he was really tough and mean, that wouldn't have made a difference." He thought about it. "Who knows? Michael's not into him either. But he is getting that assignment and I am here to let you know that so will you. We don't have any black product managers. Punkette is the closest thing we've got—aside from me."

"Really? They're going to assign it to me?"

"I am booked, baby!" He headed out the door. "I've got six other acts on my roster and you've only got last year's leftovers. This is your test. The one you'll get to go start to finish."

He stopped and let that hang in the air for a second.

"Don't fuck it up," he added.

KENNY AND LAKEISHA WERE ALREADY SITTING AT A TABLE IN the back of the diner when Michael and I got there. LaKeisha was looking at him in her way, with her head slightly tilted back, as he studied the menu. When we walked up, LaKeisha moved over for me to sit next to her.

Kenny put down his menu and said, "Yes. Great. Glad you two are here."

Sitting alone with LaKeisha probably made him nervous.

The rest of us grabbed menus. Once we ordered, we heard a strange buzzing noise. Michael turned to Kenny.

"My man, are you packin' an alarm clock?"

Kenny fished an object out of his backpack. It looked like a beige brick with an antenna.

"What is that?" LaKeisha gawked. Then she started laughing. "You have a car phone in your backpack?"

Kenny started pressing buttons on the thing, obviously not knowing which one would make him able to answer the call. "Which one is it?"

"Give it here," Michael said, reaching for the phone.

Then Michael started punching buttons.

I started to laugh with LaKeisha. "He's joined the CIA!" I said.

LaKeisha added, "Might as well be talking into your shoe, seeing as how big that is to carry."

"Stop it!" Kenny scolded us, but he was smiling too.

Michael put the phone to his ear. "Hello? Hello?" he was nearly yelling, like he was Alexander Graham Bell making the first phone call ever.

He shoved the thing at Kenny, who took it and also called into it. "Hello? Hello?"

There was a pause as he listened and put his finger up for us to be quiet. The three of us leaned in.

"Yes, I hear you. Margaret, I can hear you. You don't have to yell." He was talking to his admin. "Yes, tell him that I will be there in forty-five minutes. I'm meeting with them now . . . Yes. I know . . . yes. OK . . . bye."

He punched some more buttons, stopping to make a face because he knew he had no idea what he was doing.

"Where did you get that thing?" I asked.

"That computer guy, Roberto? He got it for me. Pretty cool, huh?"

"Seems annoying to not even be able to have lunch without talking to the office," Michael said.

"Well, this was about exactly what I wanted to tell you all." He placed the brick-phone on the table, like a centerpiece. "This is all good news. Good, good news. Jill, this is your big break. I signed Doggie T. You're gonna love him. He's a star. I can see it. I know it."

It was now his job to get us excited about this.

Michael turned to Kenny and asked, "Who is he anyway?"

"He's for real. He's scary. Criminal. He's the next Ice-T. Now that guy is mean!"

"Yeah?" Michael seemed skeptical. "Where is he from?"

"He said he's from Philadelphia. South Side. Gang area. That's bad. Which is good? Right?"

"Do we really want to deal with kids in gangs?" LaKeisha asked.

"It's what they ordered up," Kenny answered. "He's young. He's foulmouthed. He's cocky. He's devilishly handsome." He turned to me for confirmation.

"Yeah, a good lookin' guy," I said. "In a dangerous sort of way." I knew that was what Kenny wanted to hear.

LaKeisha crossed her arms. "I need to see his bio."

"No problem. You got it. Actually you'll get more than that. He and the DJ are coming into the office on Monday with their manager. They will be here in the afternoon."

My first artist. That meant I finally would get a say in something. I was going to be there at the recording studio.

Picking out cover photos. Storyboarding videos. This was make-or-break time. I felt a cold sweat break out at my hairline.

Kenny had only eaten a few bites when he put down his fork and announced that he was leaving for another meeting.

Michael let him out of the booth and centered himself back on the seat.

We ate in silence for a few minutes, each of us in our own revelations. I tried to concentrate on chewing, but my mind went in a thousand directions. Should I be afraid of this guy? Was he really in a gang? I would just have to keep my cool and see how this worked out. There was a lot at stake here. I needed this to go well. The air got a little thick among us at the table. Michael kept looking at LaKeisha. Finally he asked her, "Well, LaKeisha, what do you think?"

"What do you mean?" She feigned bored ignorance.

"You know what I mean."

"Well those two in front of the club seemed more like gang members than anyone." She looked between us thoughtfully. "But it's just as well."

I watched Michael. I knew that Michael had gone to college at Columbia University and took the train out to his parents' house in West Orange, New Jersey, on holidays. He was a suburban kid like me. He didn't know anything about real inner-city gangs.

"I feel like I've seen him before somewhere, but I can't figure out where," he said thoughtfully.

"Well, I know I was scared at that club, and you were not at all," I said, pointing at LaKeisha.

"I grew up with thugs like that," she offered. "Hell, I fought thugs like that. Beat one kid down because he messed with my cousin."

Michael and I looked at each other. Neither of us knew what to say to that. I couldn't imagine LaKeisha in an actual physical fight. She was too dignified.

Again she looked at both of us and sighed. "Most of those boys are just stupid. You can stop them with a look like their mama gave them. It's the guys who are *smart* and *mean* and never got a good chance; they're the ones you better stay away from."

She took a sugar packet out of the little holder and slowly flapped it back and forth, looking down her nose at the two of us.

"I hate where this rap stuff is going," she said finally, almost like she was talking to herself.

Michael and I exchanged looks again. I knew she was into R&B and soul. The music that floated from her office was Aretha Franklin and Sam Cooke.

"Did you see that Ice-T album cover that just came out?" she asked us.

"Yeah," I replied.

"Half-naked girl. Brothers, lookin' like they just got out of jail. Just more stereotypes."

"Well, there is still all the pop stuff," I said. "Janet Jackson, Luther Vandross."

She sighed. "Hmmm," she said. "No. It's going to be RAP. And instead of being the fun stuff, like Jazzy Jeff and Fresh Prince, it's going 'gangsta.'" She used her peace fingers to make quotes in the air.

"Frankly, I don't think this Doggie doogie, whatever,

is for real anyway," Michael said, trying to move the subject away from the larger cultural question.

"That's what Tony said," I said.

"Well, look at that, Tony and I agree on something. Amazing."

LaKeisha was inspecting Michael. She seemed to be checking his mocha skin for cracks.

We left the diner and LaKeisha said she wasn't going back to the office, that she had an appointment. She left us at the corner and walked in the other direction. It was a cool, clear afternoon. I watched her swish down the hard pavement like she owned the sidewalk. People parted as she approached, creating a clear path just for her.

"I'll get us a cab back to the office," Michael said, stepping a foot out from the curb into the street. He raised his arm, signaling to the oncoming traffic. I hung back on the sidewalk, digging in my huge black purse for a mint tin and watching him.

I hated to admit it, but I knew nothing about African American culture except what I saw on television growing up. The suburbs of Houston were white. All white. I had a photo of my first grade class and not only was every last kid white, they were mostly blond, blue-eyed people of German descent. There were no blacks, no Mexicans, no Jews, no Asians, no Greeks.

Now, looking up and down the street in this big city, I was in the midst of every ethnic group known on earth.

Several cabs with their top lights on, which meant they were available, passed by Michael and his waving arm. I watched as he stood there, seemingly his calm self, in a pastel shirt and creased suit pants, being avoided by one taxi, then another, then another. He looked back at me and must have seen the horrified look on my face. He dropped his hailing arm in defeat and came back onto the sidewalk.

"You do it," he said and stepped away from me a couple of feet toward the doorframe of the diner. He leaned against the wall and crossed his arms.

I stood on the curb and put out my hand. A cab practically appeared from nowhere within seconds. I opened the back door, placing my booted foot into the seat well and motioned to Michael.

As he got in, all I could do was apologize.

"Oh my God, Michael. I'm so sorry. I can't believe that. I am so sorry," I gushed.

The cab driver, a dark-skinned man with a bushy mustache, turned to inspect us.

Michael talked over my apologies, "It's not your fault. It's OK. But you saw that? Right? It's not your fault."

I felt so bad, even though he was right. It wasn't my personal fault. But I felt genetically guilty. I glanced at the driver. He was doing his best imitation of a man of patience; his large nose scrunched in what I decided was judgment.

Michael responded to the driver's glare in a polite yet firm voice, "Fifty-Second and Fifth, please."

He sat back.

"How do you deal with that?" I asked him. I was really offended for him, but he did not seem to be offended for himself.

"You either deal or you don't. Makes things worse if you get mad about it." He put a hard period on the end of the sentence.

I sat back and crossed my arms in indignation for him, frowning out the window at midtown Manhattan, supposedly the most enlightened place in the Western world.

THE ITEMS OF MY TO-DO LIST TICKED OFF IN MY HEAD AS I marched down the hall toward my office. The Admin Pit was empty as I passed. Everyone was probably still out to lunch. It was quiet. I turned the corner of my office doorframe and fell over a person who was on his hands and knees just inside. I flew toward the scratchy Berber carpet, delivering a girly scream on the way down.

My arms reached out reflexively to break my fall. There was a blur of blue button-down shirt and tan arms also reaching out to catch me. The two of us rolled and crumpled in a heap just short of the desk's metal leg, which surely would have been the instrument of an extremely unattractive gash to my face.

For a second, we lay there, entangled on the floor. Anyone looking in at that moment would have thought the worst. I let another second go by and we both exhaled. This wasn't so bad. The heat of his chest radiated against my ribs. He was staying there that extra second, too, I noted to myself. I scrambled to my feet.

"What are you doing?" I yelled at him.

"Are you all right? I'm so sorry." Alejandro was still

on the floor, reaching for the tools that had gone flying when he tried to break my fall.

He looked up at me and suddenly started laughing.

"What are you laughing at?" I demanded over his amusement. "You shouldn't be in the doorway like that. For God's sake!" I stomped around my desk, straightening my shirt, and ran my hands through my hair.

He got up off the floor and tried to make a straight face. "Really, I am so sorry. You just came in so fast. I didn't even hear you in the hallway. People usually make noise, y'know, when they walk." He was holding back the smile from his lips, but I still saw it there, in his eyes.

I just looked at him, waiting.

"You're like a cat," he offered.

"Humph," I said. "Well, you move pretty fast, like a cat, too. At least you broke my fall before I could get a concussion." I tried to sound authoritative, but was inwardly feeling a slight melt. "So thanks . . . I guess." I was confusing myself. I did a self-reminder that I was in man-hating mode. I had been tracking Jonathan all over the Southwest and still had not been able to pin him into a phone call over the past two weeks. Now, here was another attractive man in my office, laughing at me.

"What were you doing anyway?" I asked him.

He pointed to the wall beside the doorway. There was a small hole at the place where the wall met the floor. A wire forlornly stuck out from it, like a king snake trying to squeeze into the room.

"We're setting up the wiring to get you all connected," he said. "I don't want to put in the CPUs until the infrastructure is complete. I'm trying to sneak around so that I do the noisy drilling when people are out of the office."

I studied him, hoping my cheeks were not flushed after our bear hug mere moments ago.

"All right, all right. Well, do you have a lot more to do here?" I tried to sound businesslike.

"Just pulling in the wire and lining it around to the desk," he said.

"OK. Well. Go ahead and finish up. I just have to go over some stuff and make phone calls. Are you done with the drill?"

"Huh?" He seemed to suddenly notice the drill in his hand as if it had appeared out of thin air. "Yes, yes, no more noise for now." He turned and walked back to the doorway.

I sat down in my chair. "By the way," I said as I shuffled through my lists and memos of calls to return, "I saw that crazy phone you got for Kenny. It's like carrying around a brick. Are a lot of people getting those?"

Alejandro bent down on one knee by the wall with his back to me. I tried not to look at the breadth of his shoulders.

"Some people," he said. "Important people with a lot of money. But I wouldn't buy one just yet. They are going to get smaller and cheaper if you wait."

"I don't think I want to be *that* in touch," I said. "Thank you very much."

I found one phone number of a graphic designer that Jenny suggested using for my first big assignment. He seemed like he might be right for a rap album. I picked up the phone and started to dial the number.

Alejandro pulled the wire through the little opening, but it was not moving easily, so he was flexing his back and arms to get it to move. He glanced over his shoulder at me as I dialed. He knew to pause the conversation. Then he leaned down to get a closer look at what he was doing.

I shifted self-consciously in my seat as the ringing in my ear seemed to fade in and out. I purposefully moved my gaze away from the well-fitted back pockets of his jeans to the opposite wall of the office, my eyes roving over the framed photos and resting on My Gordon's face on my desk. I could swear I saw Gordon wink at me. I shook my head and put down the phone. Nobody was answering anyway.

LUANN WAS BANGING AROUND IN THE KITCHEN WHEN I GOT through the door of our apartment that night.

"Hey," I called out to her, huffing from the climb up five flights of stairs. I flung my bag to the floor by the door.

It was about eight o'clock.

"Hey," she answered from behind the wall.

I grabbed the mail that lay in a pile on the coffee table and sat on the couch examining the envelopes—mostly bills and junk mail. There was a postcard from my mother with a large graphic on the front screaming, "Greetings from Houston," along with a photo of a guy on a bucking bronco. On the flip side, in her loopy yet genteel handwriting, it said, "Visiting the Rodeo & Livestock show. Saw Johnny Spalding, your old classmate. He still plays the trumpet and is in the Livestock brass band here! I'm off to check the cows! Love, Mom. PS—Hi, Miss Luann, Stop reading my daughter's private mail, young lady!"

I smiled and carefully put the card to the side. I missed her.

"Did you see this postcard from my mom?" I called to

Luann. She came out of the kitchen area with a bowl. It looked like she had just finished cleaning up from her dinner.

"Yeah!" she said. "Your mom is a hoot! I miss going to livestock shows. It's weird how we'd always make fun of it, but boy, I miss the smell of cow manure sometimes."

She handed me the bowl. "Here, I had leftovers. I was about to put this in the fridge."

I looked into the bowl at an impressive amount of linguini with marinara sauce on it.

"Thanks. I haven't eaten."

"I miss the smaller ones in east Austin, too," she continued her reminiscing. "Y'know, where those old men would sell whole ears of corn straight out of a roasting barrel, with the shuck pulled down as the handle?"

"With chili powder," I recalled.

"And a thousand local bands would play," she added, sitting down on the coffee table in front of me.

"Yeah, there is nothing like that in the Northeast. That's Texas."

I twirled linguini around the prongs of my fork, feeling a hot pang of nostalgia.

"Y'know what I really miss about being back in Austin?" I said. "I mean besides the clubs and all the local music?"

"Hmm?" she answered while sifting through the pile of mail next to her on the coffee table.

"Just people having backyard barbecues. Y'know, like 'Hey everybody, come on over. The grill is on!' Everyone's so busy and bent on impressing each other around here that there is no such thing as just hanging out."

Luann looked thoughtful, picking up and examining

a piece of junk mail. "I miss that too. But is that a college thing? Or a Texas thing?"

I looked at her. She was from Dallas, another suburban Texan like me. We'd met in Austin at one of those backyard parties.

"I think it's both," I argued. "I mean, we used to have that at my parents' house, too. Everyone in the neighborhood would show up in our backyard with a plate of something to eat. That was a regular Sunday afternoon. No big plans or fancy tablecloths."

"We have some of that with the poker girls."

"Not the same. It's never outside. It's never HOT out. A yard. I miss having a backyard and having people bring their friends over—friends who are not there to pitch me a horrible demo tape because they think I can get them a record deal."

Luann and I had known each other for almost ten years. We'd ended up living together in Austin with a couple of other girls, finishing our college degrees at the University and having a ton of parties at our house. Some of it was crazy!

She moved to New York before me. Timing was right for us to be roommates here. We were really best friends at this point.

"Do you ever think you want to go back?" I asked her.

"All the time," she said, throwing a plumber's ad back on the pile of envelopes.

Neither of us had touched the bills. They lay there, helplessly unopened, on the coffee table. We both stared at them for a minute while I chewed on my pasta.

"So," I said, changing the subject, "what celebrity did you get coffee for today?"

"Well, you remember Tad Martin from *All My Children*?"

"Really? We all love Tad, just a tad!"

"He—Mike Knight is his name—did an interview with Paula today and asked for a cappuccino!"

"Fancy!"

"How about you?"

"No celebrities today, BUT I got my first artist assignment. The rapper."

"They didn't put Tony on that?"

"No. He's got a ton of other stuff," I said. "I called around for some rap albums from the other labels. Someone's sending over this year's Run-DMC. There's LL Cool J, Kool Moe Dee, Ice-T, Public Enemy, N.W.A.—they are all very bad for society."

"Wow." Luann seemed surprised. "You're doing some homework."

"If we're going to sink on this thing, it's not gonna be because of me. Rap may not be my thing, but there is some stuff I like. I had that first Run-DMC LP and the Beastie Boys. You only get one chance in this place."

She got up and went into the kitchen, coming back with a box of Cracker Jacks.

"Your cousin called to remind you about your Easter outing to the 'burbs and to make sure you didn't die last week in Queens."

"Yeah, when is Easter?" I reached for the remote and turned on the TV.

"Weekend after next," she answered and came to sit on the couch next to me.

"Hmmm."

We both went silent to let Sam, Woody, and the rest of the gang at Cheers make the jokes for us for a while.

| EIGHT

When I walked into my office the next morning, a pre-press cassette tape sat on my desk. I assumed Jenny put it there for me to listen to Crystal Reneaux. I turned it over in my hands and opened the plastic case. The boom box sitting on my shelf, next to the turntable, had both a cassette tape player and a compact disc player in it. I slipped the tape in the cassette tray, shoved it closed, and pressed the play button.

The music intro for the first song was full of piano and reverb. The ethereal vibe was kind of hypnotic. I sat down in my chair and leaned back, closing my eyes. I would reserve judgment while I waited for the voice. Sometimes, you love the music and then the singer ruins it. Crystal's voice sort of faded in, floating from a sky-high tone and landing like a tiny bird on a branch. It was very beautiful. This was the kind of music that you listened to alone on a warm summer night, while dozing near an open window. I could envision her in a gauzy dress, singing with a starry night behind her.

I sat there like that listening to her voice, longingly serenading a distant lover in a minor key, searching for beauty in an ugly place, crying out from an inner sorrow. The verses of the first song were:

"And my heart listens for the tide
and I won't hold my breath for a while
but we're not here that long, we're on our own
the bonds we make are strong, vivid and old

I loved you then, I love you now
but you can't get the feeling, it's covered up
and we might break some feelings, we might cry
then we can deliver, we're flying high"

The piano swelled and the chorus repeated:

"We try and try and try
Up and down's our style
try and try and try
and it's worth our while . . ."

Song after song lilted and took me to fragile places. She was obviously a very personal songwriter. It was not pop music. It was hard to tell if anyone would play this on Top 40 radio.

"What do you think?" Jenny's sudden and harshly accented voice jarred me out of my reverie.

I cracked open my eyes and squinted at her sideways. I must have liked the music, because I did not welcome the interruption.

"It's really beautiful. I think I love it," I told her.

"You must be growing up," she answered me. "I know, I can't help liking some of it either." She seemed almost disappointed to have been pulled into the sentimental music.

"You know, since I love it, it will probably bomb. Remember the Great Brothers?"

She grinned. "Who?"

"Exactly."

The Great Brothers were a band that was signed right when I started working here. I loved the music so much that I played their advance tape all day and night. Rock radio wouldn't play them because they said it was too "southern." Country radio didn't like them because they were too urban. MTV didn't pick it up because the lead singer wasn't cute enough. They didn't fit into a simplified marketing niche, so now they were all back in Richmond, selling insurance or something and playing local clubs on the weekends. They didn't sell out.

Nuance was not something anyone in this industry wanted to try to sell. But it was great art. I still exchanged Christmas cards with the guitarist.

"So what do you think of your rap guy's demo? Will it sink or swim?" she asked.

"I think it'll swim. Nothing subtle about it. It's not for me at all."

"Well, congratulations on that much! Then you know it'll be popular."

Kenny poked his head over Jenny's shoulder as I reached to press the "stop" button on my boom box.

"He's here," was all Kenny said. He seemed his nervous self.

I knew that was my cue to take off my "fan" hat and put on my "industry" hat. Jenny backed up and let me out into the hall. Kenny strode ahead of me toward the conference room.

"Good luck," Jenny said and she actually hit me on the butt, like a linebacker encouraging the quarterback in a football game.

When I entered the conference room, LaKeisha and Michael were already sitting at the table. Kenny flitted around the room, trying to decide which seat to sit in. You could tell he was measuring the trajectory of people coming through the door and who they would lay eyes on first. I assumed he wanted them to see him as the big cheese in the room. He stood behind a chair farthest from the door. Then he did his best to spread out his papers on the table to look like he took up more space than he actually did.

LaKeisha watched him with amusement.

"Kenny," she ordered, "would you just sit down already?"

I sat between Kenny and LaKeisha.

"Who are we meeting here? I mean besides this . . ." She looked down at the promo photo on the table in front of her. "Dog E. T.?" She purposefully messed up the emphasis on the name to rile Kenny up.

Michael winked at me from across the table as he grabbed one of the promo photos too, studying the mean grin coming up from it.

"Doggie T is the MC," Kenny told the room. "That means 'Master of Ceremonies,' which in these cases is the rapper. Then there is Whisky Fizz, who is the DJ. He does the scratching in the background. The music, if you will." He was reciting this like it was a college dissertation at Oxford.

"They are bringing their manager, Robert Washington. We already did all of the contracts with the lawyers."

We heard the senior vice president talking in the hall. The usual drill had already happened.

The "new artist drill" went something like this: The new artist would show up at the reception area. Sheila, our favorite Goth receptionist, would call Georgina, who would escort the artist to the senior vice president's office suite. There, they would be invited to sit on a plush couch that was set up in front of her desk, facing the ornately carved wooden door with a bronze plate on it that read, "Senior Vice President."

She would politely ask them if they'd like coffee, soda, or a glass of water. She would get it for them from a small, wood-paneled refrigerator under the window, which had a view down Fifty-Second Street from their perch on the twenty-fourth floor. Then she would take her time walking around her big desk, sit down, pick up the phone, and buzz into the senior vice president's inside office. The senior vice president, who was obviously very busy making multi-million-dollar deals on the other side of the ornate door, would answer the buzz. Georgina would say professionally, "Mr. T, Mr. Fizz, and Mr. Washington are here to see you."

She would listen to an answer that the artists could only imagine. Then she'd put the phone down and smile at them and say, "He'll be right with you. He's just finishing up an important call." Then she would type something on her IBM Selectric III typewriter. It was probably a fake document, like a letter to her mother or her grocery list. She had to do something to look like they were interrupting her very busy workday.

It was all a put-on and it was hard to judge who knew that it was just that. The senior vice president knew that the new artist was coming. He had nothing on his schedule. He was most likely in his office eating a bagel. He just made them wait because that was what important people did. If someone was eager to meet you, it meant they didn't have the power.

So, probably, Doggie T, Whisky Fizz, and Robert Washington sat there, looking at each other excitedly. They might have commented on the view. Or took in the myriad of famous faces posted on the walls or the gold and platinum albums. All meant to make them, or any visitor, feel in awe.

Then, after about five minutes of this, the senior vice president would burst out of his office and greet them like they were his long-lost school chums. He'd re-offer them the coffee, soda, or water, and shake hands all around with a politician's smile on his face. He might slap each one of them on the back, all the while telling them how pumped up we all were, here at Mega Big Records, to have them on the roster.

Finally, he'd say that we had a fantastic team waiting for them in the conference room, ready to get started on their meteoric rise to fame and fortune. He would take the elbow of the one with the most marketable good looks, usually the singer or a guitarist—in this case, probably the rapper—and steer them down the hall, showing off each department as they went by, down to the conference room.

Then the senior vice president would say, "And here we are!" Entering the room where we waited.

And here they were.

According to my briefings with Tony and Jenny, who had been through all this numerous times, one decisive action by the senior vice president was whether he stayed in the room for this meeting or not. If he personally wanted to get behind an artist and had a real feeling there was money to be made, he would stay for this meeting. If not, he would do intros and then leave. I waited for that cue. My career was at stake along with Doggie T and Whiskey Fizz.

They walked in. We all got up as they moved through the doorway.

But something was off.

The senior vice president did not look as jolly as he usually did. He seemed flustered. Doggie T almost jumped into the middle of the room.

"Hey, pea-pole!"

He did a general wave at all of us in a very cocky and affected way. He did not shake anyone's hand. He immediately sat down in one of the swivel conference chairs and put his basketball sneaker–covered feet up on the conference table, crossing his ankles. He grinned at the room in an obvious attempt to show off the gold tooth in the front of his mouth, but without taking in the fact that the room was full of living, breathing human beings.

Bringing up the rear was the manager and the DJ. The manager held out his hand to each of us. "Hi, you all know Doggie here. I'm Robert Washington. It's very nice to meet you. Very nice."

He pumped my hand, then LaKeisha's. She rubbed her wrist afterward. He sort of waved to Kenny and Michael on the other side of the table.

"This is William Fitzgerald or Fizz for short." He motioned to the DJ. "They call him Whisky. Get it? Whisky Fizz?"

I nodded and shook Whisky's long, cool hand. "Hey," he said. He was more reserved, at least compared to the other two, and the only one to look at my face.

The senior vice president sat down next to Doggie T, watching him with a mix of fear and fascination.

Kenny remained planted in his chair. He was measuring the situation. We could all tell that something must have happened to alter the normal "new artist drill."

"OK! So." Kenny tried to start the ball rolling. "The papers are signed and we are here to introduce the team to you all and get an idea of where—"

"Hold up!" Doggie interrupted. He lifted his feet off of the table and almost lay down across it to reach out to LaKeisha, like he had just now noticed her. "Hello there, my fine lady." He took her hand.

Kenny looked horrified. The senior vice president was enthralled by the ego coming off of this guy. So was I. Michael crossed his arms and pursed his lips slightly.

LaKeisha played along. She held her hand out to him like a princess awaiting a gallant kiss on the back of it. He didn't kiss her hand, thankfully. But he did caress it and continued caressing up her forearm, until Robert poked him in the ribs and said, "Leon, cool it."

Whisky had his head down, but on his lips was an obvious smirk.

"All right, all right, my man," Doggie said, putting his hands up like a crook caught by the cops.

Michael broke in, "So that's your real name? Leon?"

Doggie sat back down and leaned back in the chair, draping his elbow over the arm. "Yeah. My given name is Leon H. Thompson. You can add in 'the third' after that—ha ha!"

He looked directly at Michael, sizing him up. "But people call me Doggie, if you don't mind."

This was all very weird and obviously not going as Kenny had planned.

The senior vice president finally returned to himself and became verbal. He said, "Doggie, Whisky, Robert, this is LaKeisha Cunningham. She is our premier publicist for black artists. Michael Johnson will be your lead for radio promotions. And Jill Dodge is going to be your product manager. She'll direct any actual product like album art, photography, video ideas, that kind of thing. She will have your master marketing plans and everything LaKeisha and Michael do will be part of that plan."

The attention of the three black men settled on me.

I perked up and smiled. "I'm sure we can work together to make a great plan," I said, then immediately recoiled. I knew it sounded disgustingly cheerleaderish the minute it came out of my mouth.

The skepticism was obvious on all of their faces.

"Where's Tony?" Robert asked the senior vice president.

"Yeah?" Doggie said, looking straight at me. "What I'm gonna do with some white chick with a degree?"

A flash of angry heat rose up onto the back of my neck.

Michael shot a nasty look around the table.

Kenny responded without missing a beat. "Tony has a full plate. Jill is very capable and knows a lot about the downtown scene. And Tony will always be available to her."

So they did not seem all that keen on having me as the

product manager. In all honesty, it did cross my mind that they would not accept me immediately. I had a double whammy against me—a girl? And white? There was a lot of baggage here. I thought I had prepared myself pretty well, but didn't expect this flush of emotion. I should have this under control. After all, I studied the albums of other rap artists and it was all about being a man—THE man, a big man, a mean man, a powerful man. The girls were exclusively there as half-naked arm candy. The rap world and the executive world had, at least, that much in common. I had to toughen up quick.

I glanced at LaKeisha for solidarity, but she was bemused.

Then my glance traveled to Michael. He did a tight nod at me, which I took as support.

I faced Doggie directly. "I figured you're going for the real gangsta approach. So we'll feature tough photos of you two in most of the product. We want this to come out and be up there next to Public Enemy. They are slated to have an LP out later this year." I hoped to sound like I knew what I was talking about.

Doggie looked over at Whisky. Their eyes locked for a second. I could not glean what was passing between them. But Doggie looked me up and down after that and said, "Hmmmm" in a very noncommittal sort of way. He leaned back again, settling into his chair.

I supposed that meant they would take a wait-and-see attitude toward me. That was better than a full-out rejection.

Kenny moved on. "I've booked studio time at Clinton's starting at the end of next week. Since you didn't have your own producer that you knew you wanted to work with, we chose Jack Pearson. He's done several rap artists from the West Coast and some soul singers."

"He produced a few tracks for Luther Vandross, too," LaKeisha offered, watching Doggie's face for clues of recognition. His eyebrows jumped a little, but otherwise, he was hard to read.

"Hmmm," Doggie said again. More shade being thrown around.

Robert jumped on the Luther Vandross connection. "That's wonderful," he said. "Great. I represented one of his backup singers for several years. Fine, fine singer."

So Robert was a professional manager, not just some guy they knew. At least that was something to keep this ball from racing downhill.

"This is going to be great. Absolutely!" the senior vice president suddenly said and patted Doggie's shoulder forcefully. He was back to his glad-handing self at last. He could see money all over this endeavor. I, on the other hand, envisioned only strife and an uphill battle.

BACK IN MY OFFICE, I CLOSED THE DOOR AND SAT DOWN TO stare at My Gordon. *All right*, I thought, *how did you deal with the black and white thing?* My Gordon was British. He was semi-immune from American history and race relations issues, but not by that much. He somehow managed to transcend all that with the music, jumping from an all-white, working-class punk rock scene directly into Louisiana jazz. How did he get away with that without being laughed out of New Orleans? He had chops and respect. That was how.

"Gordon," I whispered. "Get me through this without coming off like a snobby 'white chick with a degree.'"

Gordon reassuringly looked back at me from inside his frame. He seemed confident that if he could do it, so could I.

NINE

THE REST OF THE WEEK SEEMED TO CRAWL BY. JENNY assigned me to follow up with repackaging some singles for several speed metal bands and a wannabe Top 40 rock band, who could not break into the charts no matter how much press they got. They were all out on the road and needed something to send for tour support promotions. I organized the art department, the printing, the pressing.

The phone was at my ear as I argued with a copywriter from corporate over his use of the word "lofty" in the liner notes of a grubby punk band reissue when Alejandro appeared at my door, weighed down with a huge TV monitor.

I hung up the phone.

"Wow! What is that?"

"This is your computer monitor," he said, landing it on my desk with a thud.

"So you are going to set this thing up here, take up all the space on my desk, but I'm not allowed to touch it until I take that stupid class?"

"That's right." He patted the top of the wide box and said, "This is an eight-bit color monitor. The best there is.

We're only installing four of these. The others are monochrome."

He seemed proud to present it to me, like my childhood cat bringing a dead field mouse into the dining room.

"That's cool," I said, studying the dark screen as if something might appear there.

Tony walked right into the room with a pile of paperwork in his hand.

"Hey?" He pointed at the monitor. "What is that?"

"That is an eight-bit computer monitor and it seems to be mine!" I said, as if I knew what that meant. I made like I was hugging the thing.

Tony looked at Alejandro. "Have you set up any whole systems yet? When are we getting connected here, José?"

I cringed when that last word came out. Really? José? It was getting entirely too embarrassing that nobody could remember this poor guy's name, just that it was probably Mexican.

"Well, Luigi, there seems to be an issue," Alejandro stated as he turned to Tony. "Nobody is taking the computer classes, and we have strict orders that nobody gets any power until everyone has taken the class."

Tony stared at him for a full five seconds before he burst out laughing. He slapped Alejandro on the back, leaving his heavy hand grasping his shoulder. "I don't need a fucking class, man," he said, "but I think I'll take it just to heckle you from the back of room."

I guessed that was something like male bonding. Girls told each other their secrets and boys insulted each other. At least they didn't start throwing punches.

Suddenly, Jenny also stood among us, with yet another Crystal Reneaux promotional tchotchke in her hand.

"Why don't I have one of those?" she asked, pointing at the monitor that was becoming more and more of a trophy to me with each passing minute.

"Because you haven't taken the class," I said.

"Neither have you!" she retorted.

"But I'm signing up right now." I turned to Alejandro. "When's the next class?"

"Monday morning."

"I'll be there," I said.

"So will I," Tony said.

"Me too," Jenny said.

"Boy, are you in trouble," I said to Alejandro. He just smiled at me. His smile was kind of gorgeous. Why had I not noticed that before?

SOMEHOW, WE ALL MANAGED TO GET THROUGH THE MONDAY morning computer class.

It was quite a scene. Alejandro and one of the other guys, Harris, showed us how to use a mouse, how to open a document and save it, which button to push for printing, how to save things on a floppy disk, and most importantly, how to send an e-mail. Jenny caught on quickly. Tony already knew what he was doing. He annoyed everyone by asking questions way beyond the beginner course we were supposedly getting. Some of the others in the room from the corporate departments were a mishmash of confusion, especially the guys from the art department.

With each passing instruction, Alejandro just got cuter and cuter. He put his hand over the back of mine to show me how to move the mouse around, and my reaction to that was chemical. I tried to not think about it. Was I still "with" Jonathan? I decided that I was definitely NOT. But wouldn't it be good to just be single for a while?

Despite the distraction of hormonal attractions, I thought I understood all of the computer jargon. Even if I didn't, it certainly would be a good excuse to get Alejandro back into my office to smile at me some more!

I stopped in the cafeteria on the way back to grab a sandwich. Going out was not an option today, since we all had to catch up on whatever we missed from being in the class. I carried my turkey and cheddar perched on the thick computer-skills handout to my desk, where my shiny new computer sat, taking up too much space.

The second my butt hit the chair, my phone buzzed. It was the receptionist, Sheila, on the line.

"There's a woman here who says she's your cousin?" she said skeptically.

"Does she look like a character from *Who's the Boss*?" I asked.

"Yeah," she answered with distain dripping from her voice. That would mean that Jessica was standing in front of her in full Lady Executive garb: the shoulder-padded suit, the silk blouse with a weird tie thing at the neck, the large aerosoled hairdo.

"There's a kid, too."

That did not bode well.

"OK." I dropped the phone and did a speed walk to the reception area. Ara, my cute little Armenian nephew, saw me from halfway down the hall and began to jump up and down.

"Auntie Jill! Auntie Jill!" Jessica prevented him from running toward me by keeping a vice-grip clutch on his wrist. He waved wildly at me with his free hand.

As I approached, I saw that Jessica was in a state. She was obviously freaked out. I could see how Sheila might be taken aback by this agitated Wall Street type standing in front of her when she was used to laid-back jazz musicians and grunge rockers.

"What's going on?" I asked.

"Oh, Jill!" Jessica began. "She just didn't show up! The nanny didn't call or anything. She just didn't show up!"

"Hi, Ara, hey!" I bent down and gave him a hug.

"Mommy took me to work. It's 'take your son to work day'!"

"Is it?" I asked him, while looking at her, my eyes widening. "I bet that's been fun!"

"There were a lot of TVs and a man was yelling! It was so fun!"

"Where did you take him, the stock exchange floor?"

"It was the ticker room at work. The stocks went nuts this morning! My boss was having a fit. He set up a special meeting at a client's for this afternoon."

"And?" I asked.

"Can you just keep him with you for a couple of hours? He can stay in your office. He's really good. Just give him a paper and some crayons."

She let go of Ara's hand and fished into her oversized purse and produced a large baggie filled with crayons, cards, Legos, and a variety of other small items. I thought I even saw a few Cheerios in there too. She must have swept breakfast playtime into the bag on her way out the door.

"What?" I stared at her in shock. I looked over at Sheila, who had been watching this whole scene with her black-outlined eyes, round and prominent against her alabaster skin. She didn't even pretend to be busy.

"Where is Greg?"

"He had a trial today! He can't take him into a court-room."

"Grandma Sona? Taleen? Taleen is home, isn't she?"

Ara began to reach for a mouse figurine on Sheila's desk. Jess bent over and slammed her forearm on the edge of the desk between him and the little plastic rodent.

"Sona's working, and she's taken him so many times, it's getting embarrassing. Besides, she's always driving him all over the place, in iffy neighborhoods, sometimes with her clients in the car." Sona was in real estate.

The frustrated tears began to stream down Jessica's face. "I cannot believe these nanny women. There is nobody to trust! And I couldn't even reach Taleen. So I had to bring him into the city."

"Oh, Jess." I put my arm around her shoulders.

Sheila butted in from her spot behind the desk. "Don't cry. It'll be all right." Her voice had softened. She handed Ara a rubber stress ball without even looking at him. He grabbed it eagerly.

"Jill will take him," she declared.

"Excuse me?" I said.

"What can she do?" Sheila asked. "Dick husband, busy mother-in-law, out-to-lunch friend? All the execs are at a big luncheon downtown. We won't see them until after three. I'll cover for you. "

"Just three hours! I swear!" Jessica faced me and put her hands on my shoulders.

"All right, all right."

"Thank you, thank you, thank you. I owe you so much." Jess turned to Sheila and said, "You too, thank you. But my husband's not a dick. He's a gifted litigator."

Sheila shrugged. "What's the difference?" she said dully.

"OK, ARA," I TOLD HIM ONCE WE WERE BACK IN MY OFFICE with the door closed. "Here's the deal. The door stays closed. This is going to be like a spy game. We are hiding out."

"Cool!" he said, his dark eyes looking around at the walls and the shelves. I nervously scanned the shelves for breakable items and realized that there was really nothing in here that I cared that much about, except the photos on my desk.

My shelves were lined with various promotional items from heavy metal to Muzak. There were tapes and albums and some CDs on the floor and the shelves, too. A stack of magazines crowded the corner. I didn't know how I could have accumulated all of this in the few short weeks I'd been in this office.

I grabbed a copy of *Rolling Stone* magazine from the top of the stack and handed it to him. "Here, you can look at this if you want."

He stared at it for a second.

"You can read, right?" I asked. I knew he was in first grade, but wasn't sure if you're supposed to be able to read by then. I recalled him reading out loud at Christmas, but it was from some Dr. Seuss book. *Go, Dog. Go!* might be at the same intellectual caliber as most of the music articles in my office.

"Of course I can READ!" he said with indignation, his hands on his hips. "I've been able to read since way back in kindergarten!"

"Ah." I tried not to sound sarcastic. "That long ago?"

"There are only some words I have to ask about!" he defended his intellectual prowess.

"OK, OK. That's great. You can read! Here! Read!" I thrust the magazine at him. "Ask me if you need to figure out a hard word."

He ignored my offering and went over to the wall where a bunch of LPs and singles were leaning against the plaster. "Can we hear some of the music?"

I knew there was a reason I liked this kid.

"Sure, look through that stack and let me know what you want to listen to." I pointed at the newest stack that a friend at Capitol/EMI Records sent to me. There was a Crowded House LP on top. I figured it was relatively benign stuff. EMI was known for classical music.

"I have to finish something at the desk." I pulled out the marketing charts for the grubby punk band. "Let me know if you want to hear something," I told him.

A few minutes went by as I ate my sandwich and studied the chart. I almost forgot he was there, sifting through all of the LPs. He'd stop once in a while and study a picture on one of the covers, then move on.

"Aunt Jill?"

"Hmmm?" I said, marking on the chart in front of me.

"What does this word mean?"

I looked up and to my horror, he was holding up the N.W.A. single, with its title "Fuck tha Police" emblazoned across the front cover in two-inch-high lettering.

Of course, he was pointing at the f-word.

"Fff. Uh . . ." He was sounding it out!

I practically yelled over his voice to stop him from saying the whole word. "Oh, I think that's French . . . uh, for . . . not sure what it means."

I held out my hand to him to give me the vinyl. Instead, he cradled it closer to his chest.

"My teacher is French. I could ask her."

"Did I say French? Umm, no, I think maybe it's Polish."

"Oh, then I could ask Irena. She's from Poland."

"Who's Irena?"

"She's in my class," Ara answered.

I reached for the LP. "Where do you go to school, the United Nations?"

He held fast, with his big brown eyes taking in and enjoying my flummoxed reaction. He was no dummy. Regardless of how cool I tried to be, he knew there was something up with this word.

"Look," I leveled with him. "That is a bad word. Don't try to sound it out and don't say it to your French teacher OR your Polish classmate OR, God forbid, your mom."

"What does it mean?" he pressed.

"It doesn't matter." I wrenched the thing out of his hand and held the offending typeface up against my belly. "It's just one of those words that is very, very bad to say."

"Then why is it on this music? Is the music bad?"

"I think the people who wrote this song are very angry

at the police. They don't like them because they feel like the police pick on them and are mean to them. They don't think it's fair and they get mad about it. That's why they say that word. It's very, very disrespectful, though. So don't say it."

"Oh." He looked at my belly and the back of the cover like he was trying to sound out the letters through the vinyl. I hoped and prayed that this would blow over.

But then he turned back to the rest of the stack. I quickly opened a drawer in my desk and put the single facedown inside it. He pulled the Crowded House LP from the top and asked if we could hear that.

I put the record on the turntable that sat next to my boom box and played it. We both bobbed our heads to the rhythm as he kept looking through every last item of music in my office. I made lists of things I needed to follow up on with other departments and questions to ask Jenny.

After a few more songs went by without incident, there was a quick knock on the door and before either of us could move, the door opened. I held my breath. If it was the wrong person, I could be in trouble.

It was Michael.

I sighed in relief.

Then the door opened wider and Doggie T came into view.

I panicked.

They both stood in the doorway, shoulder to shoulder, a study in fashion contrasts. Michael in his suit. Doggie in his ribbed tank top. But they both had the same confused expression on their faces as they took in the little scene in my office.

"Come in and close the door!" I said in a barely

audible voice, frantically motioning them in as Ara jumped up and plastered himself against the wall, trying to inch his way behind the door. He knew that he was not supposed to be here and did his best.

Doggie walked across the threshold with his eyes squarely on Ara, as the poor boy stiffened against the wall in some kind of kid attempt to become invisible. I jetted around the desk and pulled Michael's arm to get him inside the office, too. I poked my head out the door to look both ways and make sure nobody else was in the hallway.

When they were finally inside, they both stood there like they forgot why they came.

Ara grabbed his plastic bag filled with Legos and crayons and moved from the wall to behind my right arm.

"Yes?" I said to Michael and Doggie, acting like nothing was off. "May I help you?"

"Who is this?" Michael demanded.

"Is that your kid?" Doggie asked.

"No, he's my nephew." I tried to sound assured, like it was totally normal to have a child at the office.

"Ara, this is Michael and this is . . . uh . . . Leon," I introduced them. I didn't know if I could explain the whole "Doggie T" thing.

Michael nodded at Ara like he was the maître d' at a fancy restaurant. "Ara."

Doggie put out his hand and familiarly asked, "Hey, little man, how you doin'?"

Ara shook hands tentatively. "OK," he said nervously.

"Jill, what is this?" Michael asked.

"Don't tell. Please. My cousin had a nanny problem and he ended up here just for a few hours. I didn't know Doggie was here. Are we supposed to have a meeting or something?"

"Not exactly, but he came to talk to Kenny and he wanted you to talk with us about some of the songs." He took a step away from Ara and Doggie.

"What you got there?" Doggie said to Ara, pointing at his bag.

"Legos." Ara looked down at his hand.

Michael continued, "We have a concept idea that he's come up with."

"That's great!" I said. "What is it?"

"Well, it's not the 'party, party' thing. It's more political." He handed me a cassette tape. "This is the demo with two more songs. You need to listen to it and get an idea of where they are going to go."

I opened the tape cover and looked at the label on the tape. Written in gold letters across the top, it said "Rapper Doggie T & DJ Whiskey Fizz." Then there were song names listed. "Walk Like You Mean It"—not bad, lots of swagger. "You Got My Gun, Bitch"—didn't like that one. I closed the cover so there was no way that Ara could see it and then I put it into my pocket. I'd wait until I got home to listen to it.

"Are these going to get radio play, I mean, y'know, as in the FCC won't yank it off the air or bleep the whole thing out?" I asked Michael.

"Good question. That is part of what we are here to discuss."

"I mean I know it's supposed to be all 'gangsta'—" I mimicked the senior vice president's stupid Cagney move —"but do we have to go that far?"

"Well . . ." Michael's voice trailed off as he looked around for Doggie.

We both realized that we were having this conversation without any input from the person who this was supposedly all about.

Doggie and Ara had moved and all of the Legos were out on the corner of the desk. Doggie had a Lego in his hand and directed Ara where to put the next one. They were building something.

Michael and I both stared. Doggie had crouched down to be at eye level with the boy and talked to him in a low voice. Ara nodded. It was like Doggie transformed into a whole different person than the one we had met at the club or in that crazy first business meeting.

He felt our eyes on him and suddenly stood up. He crossed his arms and cocked his head, sort of checking himself back into a street thug.

"Look, man, I ain't got nothin' against a kid, but can we do this another day? I gots somewhere to be."

With that, after a sly wink at Ara, he turned and strode out of the room.

Michael did his bug-eyed look at me and followed Doggie into the hall.

"Wow," Ara said. "He's smart."

"What do you mean? What was he telling you?" It seemed odd that "smart" would be the adjective Ara chose to describe Doggie T.

"He showed me how to make a bridge." He held up the small set of Legos that were formed into a simple pattern that created a half circle and a bridge.

I took the little clutch of plastic in my hand, turning it over. I looked at the doorway where Doggie had just made his exit.

ALEJANDRO HAD TRIED TO CONNECT ALL OF OUR COMPUTERS through his network and it was not working, so he set up a science fair project on the table in the conference room. Several computers and monitors hummed merrily as I entered the room to wait for Kenny and the others to get there to discuss the direction of Doggie's recording.

"Hey," I said to Alejandro as he popped off the back of a computer unit and began to fiddle around with the wires inside. I looked over his shoulder into the mass of tangled wires.

"Did you ever read the book *1984*?" I asked him, staring at the mess inside the computer box.

"Yeah," he said. "Don't be afraid of it. This is going to be something we all use in the future."

"Until it starts to use us," I said.

He smiled. "You think I could control your mind through the monitor?" He wiggled his fingers, allowing the small Phillips screwdriver to wave around.

"You wish." I leaned toward him and smiled back. Why could I not help myself from flirting with this guy? It was definitely his smile. His whole face smiled when his full lips curled up.

Tony poked his head into the conference room. "Hey, what's the deal, man? Why can't I send any e-mail?"

I jumped from my perch on the table and put distance between myself and Alejandro. Tony gave me a questioning look. Was that a tinge of concern I saw in his face directed at me? He turned his attention to Alejandro.

"Hey, *Paco*, how come nothing's working?" They continued to call each other by different Hispanic or Italian names, now out of humor instead of ignorance.

"I don't know," Alejandro replied. "That's what I'm trying to figure out."

Tony peered into the CPU box and frowned, as if he could make sense of what he saw. Alejandro pointed to the wiring racing around the table to the separate computers on the table. "The issue is with the networking. The connections are there, but they are not talking to each other. It might be the software, but I have to make sure the hardware is right first."

"Huh," Tony grunted as LaKeisha and Michael walked into the room.

"Are we having a meeting in here?" LaKeisha exclaimed.

Alejandro jumped up. "Oh, I'm sorry. I didn't know you were having a meeting right now."

Kenny came in and LaKeisha immediately started complaining to him about the mess on the table.

"Upper management told us to give them whatever they needed to get the computers working, so he'll stay." He turned to Alejandro. "Just move this stuff to one side of the table, so we have enough room. You can keep working—quietly."

As Alejandro and Tony moved the computers to one

end of the table, Kenny said, "Also, you all need to come to Crystal Reneaux's record release press party next Friday."

Tony groaned.

"I mean it," Kenny insisted. "You can come too," he said, pointing to Alejandro. He was not even trying to remember his name. "Jill, bring some people. We need to make it look like there is a ton of interest."

Doggie T and Robert Washington suddenly stood in the doorway. Tony walked up to Doggie T and they did some kind of secret handshake.

"Hey man, how you doin'?" Doggie said to him.

Robert moved into the room and looked around at all of the technical equipment. He spoke to LaKeisha, "Good morning, Ms. Cunningham."

"Mr. Washington," she said simply.

"OK, why don't we all sit down," Kenny called us to order. "Tony, you're not in this meeting, remember?"

"Oh yeah, sorry." He patted me on the shoulder and walked out the door, looking back like he wanted to stay.

Everyone settled into seats at one end of the long table while Alejandro kind of hunched down in a seat on the other end, trying to be inconspicuous. Doggie stood studying the wiring on the table from the doorway.

Kenny called to him, "Join us, Leon, please." He motioned for him to sit.

Doggie walked in his affected strut to a seat at the middle of the table, closest to Alejandro and his gadgets. "The name is Doggie T. Only my mama calls me Leon." He paused and grinned, pointing at Kenny with both hands. "And you don't look like my mama!" He laughed at his own corny humor, his head bobbing back and forth and his gold tooth sparkling. Michael and Robert joined in the laughing. The rest of us gave our own versions of constrained chuckles. Again, not the best start.

The discussion began with the direction they wanted to go with the music. The sticking point was curse words. Kenny and Michael argued against them, saying that would limit any hope of radio airplay. Robert and Doggie argued that it was part of the language of the street.

The rest of us were not really supposed to say anything. But I couldn't resist. There were two sides to the issue. One side: it was a real and universal expression of frustration. The other side: it was not acceptable in polite society.

"This music is rebel music, not charm school," I told them. "We have to consider who our audience is. Without the cursing, the rap is less credible to the people we are trying to sell it to. It's controversial. And controversy sells."

"Yeah, girl!" Doggie exclaimed. He turned to Kenny and Michael. "You think the street is 'polite society'?"

Kenny gave me a withering look.

Michael voiced surprise. "It's all about airplay, Jill!"

"Not 'all.' There is word of mouth. There are night-clubs," I told him.

Robert chimed in, "Look, he can keep it to a dull roar. His rhymes are not all cursing. It just has to be judicial."

LaKeisha remained silent, leaning back in her chair with her arms crossed.

Finally, the talk turned to the logistics of studio time and if they needed to hire musicians.

I noticed that Doggie kept looking over at Alejandro and his computers. I wondered about Doggie and why the others felt something was "off" with him. I studied him while the others bickered.

My gut feeling was that there was nothing dangerous about him. Kenny talked him up as a stereotype, based completely on his physical presentation—the hair, the arrogance, the gold tooth. But angry? Thuggish? Criminal? He did not seem like those things. That was what was missing. During this meeting, he was much more subdued than when we first met him. At least I won him over a little bit.

FROM THE OUTSIDE, IT APPEARED TO BE A DEAD WAREHOUSE IN THE middle of Hell's Kitchen. Ten more feet west and you'd be in the Hudson River, catching some deadly bacterial disease. But the location was something of a cover-up. A lot of the buildings in this area of Manhattan were TV or recording studios because they used to be real warehouses, with huge rooms and tall ceilings. This studio was very discreet with a blacked-out metal door in a plain brick facade. Only a small bronze sign screwed to the wall indicated what went on inside. It read "Clinton Hits."

It was nine o'clock at night, but you'd never know it by the number of people in the posh reception room. After telling the receptionist that I was on the list for studio B, I wandered down the hall, which had carpeted walls lined with gold records. This was not the biggest or most famous recording studio. There were only about six studio suites, but it had its share of stars recording here. It sure impressed me and I wondered how a newly signed artist would feel walking down this hall—how Doggie T felt just last week when he came here for the first time to start recording.

When I entered the studio suite, I didn't see anyone in the production booth. So I walked down toward the studio doors. I heard a piano playing. Every studio had a stand-up piano in it. Someone was playing a beautiful set of chord progressions and arpeggios. Just as I cracked open the door, a man's voice began to sing a soulful song. The first words were drawn out and his voice was clear and strong. I froze in the doorway, listening.

"The silence here has been stolen
and I hold your thoughts in my heart
you cannot return what you have taken
earth and sky come back with time

"There's a circle around my heart
the more you know, the less you see
the circle around my heart
The motion through a life should be
the circle around my heart . . ."

I peered around the door and scanned the room for the source of the singing. The room was a tangle of wiring, guitars on stands, DJ turntables, and drums. It was void of people, except on the far side, behind all of the mayhem of equipment, a person sat at a piano in the corner.

As his voice silenced, his shoulders relaxed and I clapped a couple of times.

He suddenly stiffened and turned toward me.

It was Doggie T.

An expression of panic briefly passed across his face when he saw me, and he quickly rose from the bench, fumbling to get away from the piano.

"I'm sorry," I said. "I didn't mean to freak you out. That was beautiful! I didn't know your voice was so . . ." I paused and felt awkward all of the sudden. I wasn't supposed to know he could really sing.

"Aw, hey baby . . ." He put on a swagger to walk toward me, grabbing his cap from the piano top and cocking it sideways on his head. I could tell I—as one of the people working at the label—was the last person he wanted to know that he had a sensitive side.

"Hey, here I am! We all need a ballad once in a while. Piano ain't my thing. Where are your people?" he asked, peering around me, probably hoping that I, alone, had heard that emotive vocal. He sounded weird. I was getting more and more of that feeling that Michael and Tony kept harping on about how Doggie seemed to be laying it on a little thick.

"Kenny's on his way over." I eyed him cautiously. "Where are *your* people? Wasn't the recording session supposed to start at nine?"

"Yeah, well, I think this producer guy you all hired is on LA time, y'know what I mean. He's showing up with his homeys late every day." He looked around, then seemed to decide he was supposed to be angry about it. "I done told Whisky to come back at ten. I want me some words with homeboy."

"Who is the producer, again?"

"Jack Pearson. He seems to like spending my money!"

"Well, it's not money you've made just yet," I warned as I glanced back toward the door. I was not supposed to have this kind of conversation with an artist. Where was Kenny?

We heard the outer door open and harsh voices. Whisky walked in. There was a girl and another guy with him, both black. I did not recognize them. The girl had a downtown Brooklyn look with big hair and even bigger earrings.

"I'm tellin' you, it's no big deal! You're making a big deal," Whisky was saying to her.

The girl argued back. "You don't seem to get it," she told him forcefully. "These guys ain't messin' around. They think you look at 'em funny and they pound you. Do you hear me?"

"What's up?" Doggie studied them.

Whiskey answered before the girl could, "Cookie and Tyrone's outside. Cookie's all bent up on something. I don't know what."

Doggie was visibly affected by this news.

"What is it?" I asked him. "Who's Cookie?"

"Just some guy from the club," Whisky answered for him.

I could see by looking at Doggie that Cookie was more than just "some guy" from the club. His dark eyes went even darker. There was something going on here that was way off.

The girl elaborated for me. "He's one of the rappers at Drop Zone. He's got some rhymes, y'know? And he ain't happy with Doggie here, y'know?" She paused and smiled at me, putting out her hand. "You're Jill, right? Oh, hi, I'm Shandra. This here is Jackson." She indicated the other guy, who just nodded coolly.

"Hi, Shandra, Jackson." I shook the girl's hand, then looked back at Doggie, my eyebrows lifting up to my hairline. "What's Shandra talking about?"

Doggie turned to me, smiling. "There is nothing to worry about. I got this."

I turned to Jackson and asked, "What do you think? You know this Cookie?"

"Yeah, he's my cousin. He all right. He just don't like getting pushed, you know what I mean?" he said thoughtfully.

Just as I was about to press Jackson on this statement, Kenny walked in. He looked around at the five of us, standing in the middle of the studio, apparently doing nothing.

"What is this?" He peered through the glass into the production room, where the absent engineer and producer should have been. "Why are there no tapes running in here? Where is Jack?"

"Man, I was about to ax you that, Kenny G!"

Kenny rummaged through his backpack and pulled out a little black book and his brick phone. "I'm calling him, right now. We've got deadlines here."

He headed back out the door with Doggie and me trailing behind him. "Where are you going?" I asked.

"There's no signal inside. It only works in the lobby."

We were headed down the carpet-lined hallway when there was a commotion at the lobby door. Suddenly a large guy burst through the door into the hallway. It was the same muscled guy who had messed with us in front of the Drop Zone all those weeks ago. I assumed this was Cookie, a deceptively cute name for the bulk of man that was barreling toward us with a very angry look on his face. Coming through the door behind him was the skinny, scary sidekick that was also with him that night. Presumably Tyrone.

I took a couple of steps backward, looking around for a doorway or something to back into for cover.

Kenny was summarily swept aside and Cookie went straight for Doggie, shoving his forearm into his collarbone and easily pinning him against the carpeted wall. A framed gold record jumped off its peg with the force of Doggie's back slamming into it. It fell to the floor, twisting and cracking on the way down.

"What the fuck!" Doggie yelled. "Get off of me." His voice croaked off with Cookie's wrist right at his Adam's apple. Kenny looked stunned. Whiskey and the others came out of the studio suite and were running up to the scene.

"Who you think you are, nigga?" Cookie demanded. His nose was almost touching Doggie's. Doggie was trying to keep from losing his balance. He pushed up on Cookie's strong arms without effect.

Whiskey rushed up, bumping past me and going to Doggie's rescue, grabbing Cookie's shoulder. Seeing that, Tyrone also moved in. They were all suddenly in a stagnant bunch, trying to push against each other. Nobody was able to move anybody else. Cookie was the obvious pillar of strength in an almost Herculean stance of immobility.

"Guys, take it easy," I said, dancing back and forth on the periphery, scared to death.

"Cookie, man, whutchu doin'?" The concerned voice came from behind me. It was Jackson.

"Man, you think you can waltz in from fuckin' nowhere and steal my rhymes?" Cookie growled into Doggie's face. "Then get a cushy deal with pasty boy, here." I assumed he was referring to Kenny with the "pasty boy" comment. "You ain't nobody. Nobody ever seen you 'round before a month ago. Then you come on saying you down with Schooly D? You so full o' shit, you stink from down the block!"

Kenny recovered himself as he took in what Cookie was saying. He took on the air of a CIA interrogator, with the convenience of someone else to muscle an interviewee.

"Doggie, what is this guy talking about?" he asked, still standing about a yard away from them and not moving to possibly help —like maybe to keep Cookie from cutting off Doggie's air.

Meanwhile, Shandra silently inched around us all against the opposite wall. She got to the other side of the knot of men and walked at a quick speed to the lobby door. I hoped she was actually getting security and not just ditching us.

I remembered to start breathing again.

"Aww, geez," Jackson said from behind me. I didn't quite understand whose side he was on.

Cookie reached his hand around to his back pocket of his

black jeans, still pushing into Doggie's chest, and pulled out a cassette tape. It was Doggie T's demo. I recognized the writing and color graphic. He held it between his thumb and forefinger, bringing it around to dangle in front of Doggie's eyes.

"This," he said, "track one. 'Walk Like You Mean It.'" With each word of the title, he tapped Doggie's forehead with the plastic tape.

"Hey, all right," I said, with my hands up in front of me. "Let's all calm down." I took a tentative step forward.

Cookie looked over at me. He looked at all of the others, frozen around him. They all stared at him, waiting for his lead. He also seemed to suddenly realize that Doggie was unable to talk due to the arm jammed into his neck. He eased up slightly and shed a small amount of the tension.

He turned back to Doggie. "Whatchu gotta say?"

"Man," Doggie rasped. "I don't know what you're talking about. You got a copyright or something?"

"What?" Kenny boomed. "You didn't write this?" Now Kenny was moving in.

The lobby door flew open and the owner of the studio, a guy who appeared to be some kind of mob boss, with slicked-back hair and a five o'clock shadow, came running down the hall. Two other men with slicked-back hair followed him. They looked like the Secret Service. I wondered to myself, *what is the deal here? Is everyone a character out of a movie?* They were followed by my hero of the day, Shandra.

They immediately got in the middle of all of the black guys. Cookie allowed them in. If he had not, we'd have all been in trouble. Each of them stepped back from each other several feet, while Doggie bent over and caught his breath. He searched out his neck with his hands and coughed.

Cookie was not done, though. He pointed at Doggie as he let the studio G-man push him away, saying, "If I hear any of my rhymes on your stuff, you a dead man."

Tyrone trailed after them as the studio owner started yelling at Kenny.

"What is this? We can't have this kind of thing going on here."

Kenny assured him that everything was all right. Just a little disagreement.

I went up to Doggie and asked him if he was hurt. He shook his head, but remained doubled over, his eyes toward the ground. I looked around for Whiskey, who stood off a couple of feet away, his arms crossed, also shaking his head, but obviously for a different reason.

He looked over at Jackson, who returned the look with a tight nod. Jackson then sauntered after Cookie and Tyrone, who were being escorted down the hallway back out to the lobby and hopefully on to the street. There was obviously some underlying understanding going on there.

Once they were out of the hallway and the lobby door had closed behind them, Kenny turned to Doggie and ordered, "Stand up and get in there."

He hustled him back down the hall. We all moved in a shocked trance back into the studio as the studio owner bent down to gather up the broken glass and frame on the floor. "Come see me when you're done," he called to Kenny.

Kenny kind of waved at him as we walked back into the studio suite.

"OH MY GOD. OH. MY. GOD!" I STUMBLED INTO THE STUDIO IN FRONT of everyone else. I had never been that scared in my life. People in my world did not shove each other against walls. My heart was still in my throat. I trembled, even though I was not really in any danger.

Doggie and Whiskey both slunk into the studio with their heads down, like a couple of seventh graders on their way to the principal's office. They both walked slowly all the way over to the far wall and sat side by side on the piano bench.

They knew what was coming. We all knew.

Shandra hung by me. I looked at her and said, "Who is this Cookie guy? Is that really his song? What are we dealing with?"

She looked at me, wide-eyed. "He hangs out with Reg at the club. You see how big he is! I tell you, he be like the 'Hulk.' You don't wanna cross him."

Kenny stepped up in front of Doggie and Whiskey. I stood behind him in a punk rock stance, my feet more than hip-width apart, arms crossed over my chest. I was the girl punk henchman backup.

For a second he just looked at them. Then he paced a few steps one way, then the other. The frustration wafted off of his shoulders as he began to chew on his cuticle. He paced and paced.

Finally, he stopped and faced them, or rather the tops of their heads. They were both studying their shoelaces like their lives depended on it.

"What the hell was that?" he yelled at them.

He paced again.

"Yeah?" I echoed anxiously. "What the hell?"

"If that rap is his, you can't use it!" Kenny scolded.

"No way you can use it. He'll kill you," I echoed again.

"What you're doing is not only personal suicide, it's gonna kill this contract!" Kenny said.

"What were you thinking?" I was still shaking and finally

noticed that neither one of them had moved a muscle. They sat like stones.

We all stood there in tense silence for what felt like forever. Shandra was obviously holding her breath.

"We got other words," Doggie finally said.

"Not as good, though," Whisky said. It was a challenge.

Doggie shot him a look of daggers.

"What do you mean?" Kenny almost screamed. His voice had gone up about a half an octave. There was a vein popping out on his forehead. "You gave me the one on the first demo tape and two others last week. We have to come up with at least twelve tracks here. Are ANY of them yours?"

"They are all mine! That's the only one that isn't."

"Look," I interrupted, "this is not going to get us anywhere. Kenny, just go talk to the manager guy and tell him we are booking out for tonight." Kenny looked at me. This studio time was expensive and we had this place booked for the whole month. He was not going to budge.

"No!" he yelled into my flustered face. "He's going to put something down tonight. He's going to sit here with Jack and come up with an angry rap about THIS."

He turned back to Doggie. "You are locked in here until 3:00 a.m."

With that, he turned on his heel and strode out of the room.

I stood there dumbfounded. This was insane. I ran after him.

I caught up with him in the production room doorway. "You can't have him leave at that hour . . . not with that Cookie guy out there, probably waiting for him!"

"He's a liar!" Kenny shot back at me.

"I know, but if something happens, you do not want that on you! Do you?"

He snorted through his nose.

"I'm calling Jack and finding out where the hell he is, anyway."

"Let's just cool off. Maybe we need to get him some security?"

He paused.

"Fine, I'll have a car come pick them all up and take them back to Queens and tuck them all in their little beds."

It took me a second to figure out how much of that sentence was an offer and how much was sarcasm.

"That would work—I mean the hired car part, not the tucking them into bed part."

LUANN AND I SAT ON THE HARD PLASTIC SEAT OF THE EXPRESS subway train. We were on our way to meet Claudia, our college friend from Atlanta. She was in town to play with her band. We had just had a bill-paying affair at home before leaving.

"We need to turn off the lights more!" I told Luann, referencing our astronomical electric bill.

"No, you need to turn off your radio. You leave it on when you go to work and it plays all day."

"The hair dryer uses a lot of amps, too." I jabbed at her coiffed hair.

The subway was packed at eight o'clock on a Wednesday evening. I looked out the window at the dark tunnel wall, and watched the lighted platforms race by.

Luann changed the subject of the conversation that was moving into roommate-fighting territory.

"Claudia's been working with this band for over six months. They performed in Austin last Thursday at the South by Southwest Music Festival."

"That's cool." I was still gazing out the subway window.

"I worked at the first one they put on a couple of years ago, remember? It was fun," she said about the conference. "So many bands. . ." Her voice drifted off as we arrived at our stop and jumped up to exit the train.

We came up on Houston Street and headed for the Knitting Factory. It was a hole-in-the-wall and famous for booking weird art bands.

The entrance was dark and the interior was darker. The whole place had a grimy feel to it, like the floors had never been mopped, ever.

Claudia was on the stage closing her saxophone case when we walked in.

"Hey!" Luann bounded up to her and they did a hug and kiss thing. I trailed behind, feeling tired.

"So how was South by Southwest? Did you go eat a ton of Tex-Mex in Austin?" Luann asked. I perked up a little at the mention of the memorable food.

"Yeah, great enchiladas," Claudia chirped. "Can't get 'em like that anywhere else."

Her bandmates were out getting something to eat and would be back later to do the show.

We grabbed a drink from the bar and sat at a table in the corner of the small room.

"So what kind of music is this band you're in?" I asked.

"Totally avant-garde," she answered. "Jazz."

"Cool."

Claudia had been a music major at college. She was one of those people who took piano lessons since birth, played in the school band, and seemed to be able to play any instrument she happened to pick up. She was into what she called "experimental music." All this basically meant she was too talented for her own good.

"Hey, what's this about South by Southwest?" I asked her. I knew that Flying Flock was also scheduled to play there last weekend.

"Yeah, we got in this year. It was a lot of fun. I went and hung out with your Flying Flock guys again."

Luann and I eyed each other.

"Well, was the crazy girl still with them?" I asked.

"I didn't see her, but the whole thing was weird," she said, sipping her drink. "The band, like, fell apart."

"What do you mean?" Luann asked.

"Well," Claudia sighed, searching for the right way to tell the story. "They were all set to perform at one of the clubs on Thursday night. They go in, they have their gear with them, but the stage manager wouldn't let them have a sound check because the band playing before them had some big set on the stage. They left for a while, then came back without Kevin."

"The guitarist?" I was confused.

"He just got lost in the streets of Austin."

Luann said, "Well, I could see how that could happen. That's sort of the rite of passage for every musician in town."

I laughed at that comment.

"Then Jonathan had some kind of fight over the soundboard with a woman from the *Austin Chronicle*."

There were only a few women who would be considered "from" that paper. It was a grand opera of male testosterone over there. I had written a few show reviews for them when I lived in Austin. The women's bathroom had some interesting graffiti. The most memorable quote said something like, "Welcome to the *Austin Chronicle*! Where men are MEN and the women must have a good sense of humor."

"Was it Cindy Widner?" I asked.

"No, I don't think so. A name with lots of *m*'s. A large blonde."

"Margaret Moser?"

"Yeah! That was it."

"Oh, good!" I replied, recalling an image etched in my mind of Margaret, standing backstage at a Stevie Ray Vaughan show, lips red as a fire engine, and taking up just as much space as a fire engine with her aura. She got mad at the lead singer of the opening band for some offense involving Stevie's guitar strings and a Twinkie. She verbally took his cute ass, kicked it black and blue, and handed it right back with a searing smile. "I'm sure she tore him apart and I'm even more sure he deserved it!

"Anyway, they never performed. I don't have the whole story, but they met up with some girls. Kevin went off with one of them and never came back to the van. Last I heard, the others were crashing on one of the girls' couch until he shows up . . . or they can find him . . . or whatever."

"I hope he's all right?" Luann sounded concerned.

I, on the other hand, was completely unconcerned. "I'm sure he's fine. He's probably off smoking pot and having sex and doesn't even know that days and days have passed," I said.

Claudia continued, "I went over to the girls' house before I left. Jonathan was having a conniption fit. They were supposed to play in New Orleans last night and they have other dates scheduled later this week. It's all canceled. He left. He decided to go home."

"So he's on his way back to New York," I said, just to confirm.

"Great," Luann added sarcastically.

"Does he even have any money? How's he getting back?" I wondered.

"I don't know," Claudia said. "He said something about hooking up with this other band that is touring and heading to New York. So there is no telling when he'll show up in the city."

"Not that he'd call me and tell me any of this," I sighed.

"It's a fiasco," Luann added.

"What a fiasco," I echoed.

"Definitely a fiasco," Claudia agreed.

We were all silent for a minute. Luann and Claudia watched me for reactions. I wanted to change the subject.

"Well, that's rock 'n' roll!" I said, trying to sound snarky.

I went on to relate the story of what had happened at the studio with Doggie T and Cookie.

They stared at me with wide eyes.

"Oh wow," Claudia said. "I think that's even more drama than I can handle."

A FEW DAYS LATER AT THE OFFICE, LAKEISHA HAD HER HAND ON HER hip as we stood in the hallway between the stairwell door and Kenny's office, waiting for him.

"This guy is taking up all that studio time doing what?" she asked me impatiently.

"Well, they are putting down some tracks. I heard a little of it. There is . . . uh, they have potential."

She made her trademark "humph" sound.

I had no idea why I felt the need to defend Doggie and Whiskey. They were floundering. After that episode with Cookie, they had some kind of fight with each other. Now, Doggie was in the studio with only the producer, a drum machine, and a hired guitarist. I didn't know how anyone could get wired up in a soundproof room and create rap music that way. It seemed like an oxymoron. Angst needed feedback. There were plenty of bands who did great when they played live in a nightclub and fell on their faces once they got into the studio.

"We keep signing all of these duds," LaKeisha grumbled. "We

don't need these teenybop rappers. We need some crooners. People who can sing! And write a song!"

"What other duds?"

"That Crystal woman!" she announced. "That girl can't sing her way out of a wet paper bag."

"What do you mean? She has a great voice. It's just soft, that's all."

"There is no such thing as a 'soft' great singer," she snapped. "That pale girl singing is so lame. I fall asleep just thinking about it."

"LaKeisha, that's not fair."

"No, the only white women who can sing do it because they're singing like black women."

I rolled my eyes. Here we go again.

"Anyway," she continued. "We have this cotton puff girl on one hand and the goof-off gangsta boy on the other. We are resting on the catalog right now and all of upper management knows it." She looked off down the hall, presumably for Kenny. Where was he? We had a meeting scheduled.

"Just because we have some jazz artists and a few bands with black people in them, they think we can pull out a rap act and sell it?" Now, she was complaining to herself.

"Yeah, I guess that's why they pushed so hard," I said. "We just don't have the connections."

"And I don't like everyone around here thinking that I should know people," she lamented. "I mean street people—drug dealers and pimps? What do they think I am, some kind of gangland mama? I live uptown!"

"Yeah, I know," I said. It was true, that just was not her.

She sighed audibly, but didn't say anything. Her face softened a little bit and she did her look-down-the-nose at me. Maybe she just needed glasses.

I slumped against the wall.

People passed us on their way to the copy machine while we stood there sulking in silence for a few minutes.

Suddenly, we heard singing.

We both froze under the florescent lighting, listening for where it came from.

Yes, it was a fragile, beautiful woman's voice echoing through the stairwell door.

"Out into the rain, out into the night
You can't explain your desire or your fright
you're only a man, you cannot stop time
if God had a plan, we would always feel fine. . ."

Both of us rushed to the door of the stairwell. LaKeisha eased it open, as if she was trying to not scare the voice away. We peered into the stairwell. The person singing could be anywhere up or down the scaffold of stairs. The concrete walls created the perfect reverb. The voice bounced toward us from all directions.

"and you drink your whisky and you stare at the floor
waiting for something to break into your world
I am your mirror, only your mirror
I am your mirror. . ."

I tiptoed out onto the landing and looked down the open well of metal banisters. Two floors down, I could see the heads of two men sitting on a step and the unmistakable hair of Crystal Reneaux standing in front of them.

I motioned to LaKeisha and she did a comical stealth walk across the landing to where I was.

"It's our cotton puff," I mouthed to LaKeisha.

"What is it like when you are alone?
Oh every night, your fears falling cold?
I'll hold you hand, but I won't lead you on
I understand when you want to go home . . ."

Crystal's voice was full, even while coming off as being delicate. The words were full of emotion and sadness. I looked at LaKeisha triumphantly. She responded with a roll of the eyes and did a little wave as if she was saying, *all right, all right, you win this round.* And then she shushed me as the song was reaching a crescendo.

"I'll drink your whisky and I'll stare at your floor
I will break into your private world
I am your mirror, only your mirror
I am only your mirror."

We held our breath as the last note of her clear voice dissipated through the forty-five stories of the building.

"Wow," LaKeisha whispered.

Below us, the two men got up from the step and were saying, "That was wonderful, amazing," their voices muffled as someone above us clapped their hands. Then there were dozens of hands clapping. Others up and down the building had done exactly what we did, quietly snuck out into the stairs to listen.

The voice of the senior vice president called up the stairwell, "Ladies and gentlemen, Miss Crystal Reneaux."

Crystal's mousy speaking voice followed, breathily saying, "Thank you, thank you?" as they hustled out of the stairs back into the posh offices of upper management, where they had obviously come from.

LaKeisha and I walked back into our dank, beige hallway and stared at each other for a moment.

"Can't sing her way out of a paper bag, huh?" I said, crossing my arms in front of my chest.

"Wasn't he supposed to be here already?" LaKeisha looked around, avoiding my gloat.

I saw Kenny approaching us. He was chewing his fingernails and reading something, using only his peripheral vision to maneuver down the hallway.

He almost bumped into me before he stopped to look at us, one face to the other. "Hey, come on in," he said.

He opened the door to his office and we trooped inside after him. We stood around the mess of paper that constituted his desk. Although there was an orange couch directly in front of it, there was also no place to actually sit. It was filled with boxes of product, demo tapes, and magazines.

"You just missed your redheaded sign singing in the stairwell," I told him.

"What? Really? How did it sound?" he said.

"Better than the album we're about to put out," LaKeisha said.

Kenny made a face at her.

"OK," he said, as we both stood there staring at him questioningly, "so here is the list of publications for rap press." He handed LaKeisha a piece of paper.

"This," he said, handing me a different piece of paper, "is some rough drawings of what they want for the album cover. We need a red Corvette convertible and about three busty women. African American, light skin."

Yuk! But that was what I was being paid to do, find the busty women.

I shot a look at LaKeisha to see her reaction to this assignment. If she bit her tongue any harder, she would wind up a mute. I could almost see steam coming out of her ears.

"Where is the music!" she cried, attempting to divert her real feelings. "I can't start talking this kid up until I know what I'm promoting."

"Yeah, what happened after Whiskey left the other night?" I asked.

Kenny started to gnaw on his cuticle again as he looked back and forth between us.

"He didn't put anything down yet, did he?" LaKeisha sounded amazed.

"He's working it out."

"Oh, come on," she said. "What is he doing in there night after night? He's been in there for weeks and you don't have one song?"

The phone rang from somewhere under the pile on Kenny's desk. He shoved the papers around until he found the source of the sound, relieved for an interruption.

"Hello?" Pause.

"Yeah." Pause.

"They're right here." Long pause. He looked up at us again, listening to the person on the line. We had not moved from our positions in front of his desk.

"Hmmmm," he said in a resigned voice. "Fine, just get back here as soon as you can . . . all right."

He hung up the phone and sighed in a way that obviously meant that the caller had not given him news he wanted to hear.

"What is it?" LaKeisha demanded. "Who was that?"

"Michael and Tony are in Philadelphia."

"Why?" I asked cautiously.

"To find Doggie T."

"Is he missing?" I asked, alarmed.

"No, he's in the studio. But he said he was from South Philly, but the club owners say he just showed up there last year."

"Maybe he went under a different name before?" I ventured.

"Well, that was Tony. He went down there with pictures and he said the kids in the neighborhood didn't know him. He's not from there."

LaKeisha and I exchanged worried looks.

LaKeisha said, "What is up with this kid?"

Kenny didn't know how to respond.

"He's a player," LaKeisha affirmed, as if we didn't know that. "I could tell that from the start, but he's too . . . too . . . cute."

"Too cute?" Kenny seemed astonished. "You think he's cute? With that gold tooth in front?"

"Anyone can buy a gold cap," LaKeisha snapped.

I said, "What difference does it make if he isn't from Philly? Maybe he moved there recently?"

"Yeah!" Kenny agreed. "He scares me to death. He's got street gang and drug deals written all over him."

"Uh, huh," LaKeisha said, crossing her arms. "And what do you people know about it?"

She looked at both of us accusingly. She was right. We knew nothing about it.

She wrenched open the office door and stalked out into the hallway as Kenny's phone rang again. I followed her, leaving Kenny behind to his phone.

She stopped halfway down the hall and turned to face me. "I don't know why I keep putting up with all this crap!" She pointed a finger up in the air, as if that might make her bitter point more obvious.

"This is not why I got into the music business!" she orated. "I used to love to listen to music. Now, it's this rap crap. I can't stand it. They're not singers! They're criminals! And now we even got guys pretending to be criminals!"

I sighed, but I knew what she meant. We all got involved in this industry because we were moved by some kind of music. It was like breathing for most of us. We needed to be inside the song, inside the voice. If it didn't speak to us anymore, there was no reason to be here. I didn't respond to her speech.

She deflated slightly, turned, and marched away, leaving me alone on the stained, beige carpet of the hallway.

THIRTEEN

THAT SUNDAY WAS MY YEARLY TREK TO THE SUBURBS FOR EASTER. Jessica's extended family never went to church on Easter. Instead, they partied and called it brunch. Sometimes it was at Sona's house (her mother-in-law) and other times it was at Jim and Taleen's (Greg's brother and sister-in-law). Taleen was the original owner of my infamous fancy couch.

It had been drilled into Greg's head since birth that he was supposed to marry a nice Armenian girl, preferably one who came from a good family and was smart enough to graduate from an Ivy League school. Unfortunately for his parents, especially Sona, he met Jessica during his freshman year. They fell hard for each other. They sometimes took breaks from dating, always because of the fact that she was not of his "tribe." During their off-again times, Greg worked the Armenian "Sports Weekend" circuit to find this elusive good Armenian girl.

Under the auspices of sports, the community would organize whole weekends full of social events in resorts up and down the Eastern Seaboard. It was a hotbed of hookups. The whole purpose was to get young, single Armenians together—near hotel rooms. This would hopefully lead to Armenians marrying Armenians. They didn't even try to be subtle about it. From what I understand, it worked for a lot of people. But it didn't work for Greg.

He tried, for his mother's sake, but nobody clicked with him the way Jessica did. He loved Jessica and she loved him.

Jessica waited it out. After a decade of proving she was smart, respectful, and generally socially acceptable, Sona had to admit that she might be OK as a daughter-in-law. Finally, they set a date and she became part of the family.

And this family knew how to throw a party.

Any holiday when I didn't go to Texas as well as christenings, birthdays, weddings, even funerals, and always Easter was spent at one of their parties. This entailed me trading my leather jacket and Converse sneakers for a silk blouse and heels, plus a headband to hide the red streak. I rode the rails under the Hudson River, through the hell of Newark, and out to the greened, suburban neighborhoods of New Jersey. Jessica awaited me in a car and drove me even deeper into Jersey to one of the huge homes of her affluent relatives. This time, it was Jim and Taleen's.

As I stepped out of the train onto the platform juggling my bag and a cake box from a midtown bakery, I looked around for her in the little lot of the suburban station. She sat behind the wheel of her BMW, staring out at nothing as I approached the car. I had to bang on the passenger window with my elbow to get her attention.

"Wake up, lady!" I yelled at the closed window.

Her face jumped from sullen to bright when she saw me.

The doors unlocked and she reached across the front seat to open the door. I wedged my foot in to open it all the way and shoved the cake box at her. She took it, turning to place it in the back while I settled myself into the plush passenger seat.

"What's up? You looked like you were way faraway."

"Just thinking."

"Thinking?"

Her face went back to sullen as she started the car. "I'm just tired," she said.

She and I had been close once, but since she had gotten married and moved to the suburbs, she didn't confide in me so much anymore. She was extra busy. I was extra busy.

I figured that she didn't have as much to worry about anymore now that she and Greg were married. They both made good money. He was there for her to talk to. She didn't need me for that like she used to. Then when Ara came along, it became harder to talk. She literally did not have the time to leisurely chat, even on the phone, like we used to. We used to talk for hours. Now, I was lucky if I could get in ten minutes before either Ara or Greg interrupted, or another mom or her work beeped in on call waiting.

Otherwise, we'd mainly see each other at these large parties where the conversation was not exactly deep.

Now, we remained silent in the car as she pulled out of the parking lot. I stole glances at her. She seemed overly distant.

"So who's going to be there today?" I asked.

"The usual crowd. Taleen and Jim, their kids. Greg's first cousin and her kids. They live in Philadelphia. Don't know if you know them. We only see them once or twice a year. But now, I think they want to come more because the two kids are boys right around Ara's age. Seven and nine, I think. At Thanksgiving they had fun together. Sona's friend and one of her adult kids with their kids. Some neighbors, too. I think." She was rambling. "There are always so many people," she went on. "I don't know why Sona would invite the neighbor with more kids. I think he just got a divorce or something. It's going to be a madhouse. She actually went out of her way to insist that Taleen invite the neighbor. We need more kids running around like a hole in the head."

"Sounds like a lot of fun," I said, hoping to lighten up the air in the car.

She stopped at a stop sign and turned to me. "Fun? Fun? Who do you think is going to be cleaning up after all of those kids? And the dishes? And if I try to sit down for two seconds, how do you think Greg and 'Mayrig' Sona will react to that?" She was suddenly crying, AGAIN! She covered her face with her hands.

"Oh, Jess." I instinctively reached out and put my hand on her shoulder. She angrily shrugged me off, so I just sat there and watched her cry, not knowing what to say or do.

There were no other cars anywhere, so we sat at the stop sign with the car idling.

"What did I get myself into?" Her sobs began to subside.

"Put the car in park," I told her.

"We've got to go," she said. "They're expecting us."

She began to drive through the intersection.

"Let 'em wait. Come on. Pull over," I gently insisted. "You can't even see and your eyeliner is running."

She could not help letting out another sob and she finally pulled over to the shoulder on the barren street. She shifted the gear into park.

"That is the second time in a week that I've seen you cry," I said. "You're not a crier. What is going on? Really?"

She slumped down in the seat and screwed up her lips to keep another sob from escaping.

For a few minutes, we just sat there as she calmed down.

"Do you want to tell me what is going on?" I finally asked.

"I'm just overwhelmed. You wouldn't understand."

"Oh my God! Stop saying that without even trying to explain it to me. Do you think I'm an idiot just because I'm not married or have a kid?"

"No, of course not!" she retorted. "Greg and I had a fight right before I left to pick you up, but it's so much more. I don't even know where to start."

"First thing at the top of your head. How bad can it be?"

"Greg doesn't help like he said he would," she blurted out. "I know I shouldn't complain. I should be happy. I have a professional man, a house, a child. We're all healthy. But all I do is run around like a crazy person, then I get home and he's sitting on the couch with a beer while the kitchen looks like a tornado went through it. Now, we have to find another nanny or deal with extended care after school. I don't want to even consider daycare." She spat out that last word like daycare was akin to condemning her only child to the fiery pits of hell.

Now, she was on a roll.

She listed out everything that she had had to do since I had seen her four days ago. Everything from cooking and doing the dishes to placing an ad for a nanny to getting up in the middle of the night to clean up Ara's throw up, while Greg just went to work, then came home, watched TV or fiddled with his computer or stereo system, then slept through the night.

I nodded in best-friend-listening mode. Although I thought she might have been exaggerating a little bit, I didn't say so. I knew Greg was not a complete macho creep, but if I had to do half of that and get through the tasks of work every day too, I'd be exhausted.

Finally, she paused and took a deep breath. "Hmmmm," was all I could say.

She took that as encouragement and launched into a companion tirade against the school PTA and the snotty moms who gave her "the look" for not volunteering and the fact that she didn't carry a Louis Vuitton bag nor did she have a French tip manicure.

Finally, she wound down and slumped back into the seat, expended.

"Have you talked to Greg about all this?" I asked.

"Some. Not really. I don't know . . . No! By the time we both get home from work and through dinner, we don't have time or energy to talk about anything but the latest thing in the house that needs repair. He has no clue. He is clueless."

I ventured to ask, "What are you doing for fun?"

"There's that word again." She was frustrated. "Life is not all fun! I don't have a fun-loving, not-a-care-in-the-world life like you!"

"What makes you think I don't have a care in the world? I can barely make rent? I do have responsibilities, you know—at work, paying bills? I'm trying to survive on my own in the meanest city in the world. I don't have a loving husband."

"I don't have one either!" she practically shouted.

There was a pause while that sank it. I tried to gauge just how deep this really went.

"When was the last time you just let the dishes stay dirty until the next morning?"

"What? I can't do that!"

"Don't you think if you did that a few times, Greg might notice and start washing them himself?"

"He leaves pieces of rice stuck to the plates. It's gross," she threw back at me.

I tried really hard to sound neutral. "So it's not that he's not doing the dishes. It's that you don't like *how* he's doing the dishes?"

"Sometimes," she said tentatively.

"What happens when you all talk about it?"

She remained silent.

"Do you ask him, point blank, to do certain chores?" I pushed.

"I yell at him all the time to help me!"

She caught herself in her own words. A shocked look came over her face.

"Oh God! I'm a nag!" She began to cry all over again. "I'm a shrew. I'm one of those uptight, bitchy wives from a bad chick flick. The one that gets left for the cute, young secretary!"

"Are there tissues in this car?" My hands flew around under the seat.

Jessica flopped her pointer finger toward the glove compartment, while her other hand covered her red eyes. I opened it and plucked six tissues in succession from the box and handed them to her.

Gently, I said, "Remember when we were kids and Mom and I would come up from Houston and stay with you for a whole month in the summer?"

She nodded, still sniffing.

"I thought you were so grown-up. You were already wearing a bra and had a diary with a lock on it. You didn't want much to do with me that one summer before fourth grade."

"Yeah." She was wiping under her eyes with the tissue. "You were a pipsqueak. I didn't want a little kid hanging around my middle school friends."

"I know. You had a crush on some boy. What was his name?"

"Josh."

"Yeah, he was cute and his mom dropped him off at the pool in a Mercedes. Josh Posh, I called him. You did all this stuff to make him think that you were really sophisticated. You worked yourself up trying to impress him. You wore a ton of mascara to the swim meet and it ran during your freestyle race. It looked like an octopus had inked in the water."

She smiled sheepishly.

"You were so worried about what you were supposed to be, what was expected." I paused for dramatic effect. Then I said, "No matter that you tried to pretend like you were a woman and wore heels and all, I knew that you still slept with your pink teddy bear every night."

She sighed.

"And, when none of your friends or the boy you wanted to impress were around, you'd play Barbies with me and make up all these crazy things for Barbie and Skipper to do, like skydiving and saving ships of children from sinking."

"That was the only time I felt relaxed."

"Exactly, you had wind-down time. Nobody to impress. I didn't need to be impressed because I was just your pipsqueak cousin."

"Ara's my pipsqueak now." She looked out the driver's side window. "But I don't even get to spend much time with him."

After a moment, she said, "Greg was my pipsqueak. We used to lounge around. We don't lounge anymore."

I brightened. "I know what you need! A night out, totally outside your stuff. Friday night, we're having a record release party for one of our artists, Crystal Reneaux. It's a celebrity party. Drinks. Press people. People from my office. You can forget all that stuff and sleep over with me! It'll be like when I first moved here. You used to sleep over all the time."

"I can't do . . . I don't know." She looked doubtful. "Leave Ara alone with Greg for the whole night?"

"Why not? Do you really think he can't handle it? Is he that bad?"

"No, I guess not. I don't know."

I handed her more tissues. "Here, blow your nose. There is something right there." I pointed just above her lip.

She grinned. "You're the only person I know who has no qualms about pointing out my snot."

"That's what family is for!"

I grabbed a soccer water bottle from the backseat, dipped a tissue in the water, and handed it to her.

She shoved the rearview mirror in her direction and cleaned her face. Then she sat back and sighed.

"Yeah!" she said finally. "OK, I'll come to your party and spend the night."

She put the car in gear and we headed toward our leafy destination.

FOURTEEN

WHEN WE ARRIVED AT JIM AND TALEEN'S HOUSE, IT WAS COMPLETE chaos—high-class chaos, but still chaos. I thought things got crazy in rock 'n' roll, but this was beyond. Their front hall opened into a huge living room.

"Who are all these people?" I asked, gawking at the festive and highly decorated atmosphere. People were laughing. Children were running around. There were platters of hors d'oeuvres on every surface.

"Like I said—mob scene," Jess said out of the corner of her mouth, then turned, smiling broadly. "Hi, Taleen!"

Taleen strode toward us with a smile on her red lips, in her curvy body-skimming dress, high heels, and dangling earrings. How could she look so good after preparing a house for an all-day party for sixty where the children outnumbered the adults?

"Jessica, what took you so long?" She gave us both the European kiss greeting, barely missing lips-to-skin on both cheeks. "Jill, you look great. Here, give me that box. Is this a cake? Wonderful! What will you have to drink?" She led us around a group of little girls in frilly Easter dresses playing jacks on the glossy floor. I watched them as we headed toward the wet bar.

"We're doing mimosas to start," Taleen announced and handed us shimmering, fluted glasses with orange juice and champagne.

We took the drinks and I looked around to take in the scene. I did not recognize half of the people here. Mayrig Sona was holding court in a large chair by the even larger fireplace. She was Greg and Jim's mom and the undisputed matriarch of the family and probably the entire state of New Jersey. Even Jess's father-in-law and Taleen's parents, powerful people on their own, deferred to her. Everyone here under fifty-five years old called her "Mayrig" because it meant "Mother" in Armenian. Although, nobody here spoke much of the language otherwise. They just threw in certain nouns of their heritage tongue, which I found to be funny, because often they were the unmentionables in English.

This, I learned from Ara. He knew how to say words like "underwear" (vardig) and "ass" (eshegg) and "that's bad" (gesh-eh). His favorite one, and a word that always cracked us both up for no good reason, was "cucumber" (var-oonk). These words all sounded like sci-fi Martian names to me.

Ara, his cousin, and some other boys I didn't recognize came snaking through the room in a chase. He called to me in passing, "Hi, Aunt Jill!" and gave me a quick hug, then disappeared through the basement door.

That was probably the longest conversation we would have today.

"Those are the boys from Philly," Jessica informed me.

"Ah yes," Taleen said, fluttering her impossibly long eyelashes. "The cousins from Philly spent the night last night!" She leaned into us, shielding her face with her diamond-studded fingers, and grimaced.

"Oh, no, were they bad?" Jess asked.

"The worst," Taleen said simply, trying to be nonchalant before heading into the kitchen. Jess shot a worried look at the basement door.

Jess and Taleen, despite the outward differences, were very good friends. Taleen did not have a job outside her home and had a maid that came in three times a week. She seemed to always be going somewhere, planning some event, and extremely busy. Her husband, Jim, owned his own business, but I never could get a handle on what, exactly, his company did. I didn't think I'd ever had a conversation with him that lasted more than sixty seconds and the few lunches in the city that I'd been invited to with Taleen never seemed to cover that topic.

Greg was standing in the kitchen with Taleen's oldest son and another woman I didn't know, as we walked in. They hovered over the appetizers on the kitchen island.

I noticed how Greg looked hopefully at Jessica. She walked over to him and touched his arm, settling in to peruse the appetizers too. Whatever they had fought about was done for now.

"Look what Jill brought from the city," Taleen said, opening the box to reveal the chocolate ganache cake with Easter eggs etched artistically into the icing. They all oohed and aahed.

"Thank heaven, you brought CHOCOLATE," Greg joked. "We didn't have enough on hand today!"

"There is no such thing as too much chocolate," the woman said.

"Jill, this is Sarah. She's my cousin from Philadelphia."

"Hi." We shook hands.

An hour of eating and drinking ensued. I did not even meet half of the people in the house. I might not have even seen some of the children, since they were all running back and forth, like an army of ants. After the appetizers, more mimosas, and chatting, dinner was served at a variety of tables in the dining and living rooms. None of the kids seemed to eat or even be able to sit still. They'd been eating Easter candy nonstop since 6:00 a.m.

I was at the "grown-up" table with family. Mayrig Sona sat to my left and Greg sat to my right.

"So, Jill," Sona began, "how are you doing? Tell me every little thing."

"Jill just got a promotion," Greg helped me out. I seemed to be able to hold my own with world-famous rock stars, but he knew I sometimes got tongue-tied around his mother. This woman ran most of Bergen County with her real estate business. She wasn't just a realtor saleslady. She owned her own company and commercial buildings. Although her husband was an executive in a pharmaceutical company, she was a powerhouse in her own right. She really looked at you. Most people in my industry looked over your shoulder to see if someone more important was coming in behind you while they talked about themselves. You were the audience.

Mayrig Sona expected *you* to perform for *her*. What is your million-dollar business plan or how have you solved world hunger?

"Oh, that's wonderful!" She seemed genuinely excited for me. "What's your title?"

"I'm a product manager now."

"She keeps rock stars upright!" Greg said, always putting down the fact that I worked with musicians, who he saw as a bunch of druggy freaks with weird hair. I often pointed out to him that he was the one who worked with criminals.

"A manager! And so young!"

I knew that she was being overly kind. There were plenty of people my age with the title of "manager." A little red flag popped up in the back of my mind, but I was too full of mimosas and Armenian string cheese to notice it.

"So are you seeing anyone?"

"Maa," Greg warned.

Sona ignored him and looked at me with penetrating brown eyes. I noticed the laugh lines around her mouth and the heroic amount of gold jewelry she wore. She seemed to have no end of energy.

"Well, I sort of just broke up with somebody," I volunteered, recalling the sting of my non-conversation with Jonathan.

"Oh, I'm sorry."

She obviously was not.

She smiled. "More wine?"

It was only two in the afternoon and my head was already swimming. As I shook my head and began to say, "No, thank you," she was already refilling my glass.

I glanced at Greg, who was eyeing his mother with suspicion.

The chatting and eating continued for what seemed like forever.

The kids' table disbanded, and when they began pestering their respective parents at the dinner tables, Taleen stood up and announced the egg hunt would begin outside. She produced twelve baskets, like a magician, and handed them out. Some of the adults ran after the kids out the gorgeous French doors to the deck and beyond to the backyard. I always loved seeing little kids do this sort of thing, so I took my perpetually filled wineglass and wandered to the patio. Jessica fell in beside me. I felt more than a little drunk.

"You feeling better?" I asked her.

"Yeah, I'm sorry I lost it in the car."

"It's OK."

"I talked to Greg about coming to your party on Friday and staying over in the city. He's all for it."

I glanced at her sideways. She seemed a little blurry, but otherwise, my same old older cousin.

"Are you all for it?" I asked.

"Now I kind of have to be, or he'll think I don't trust him with our only child."

"Well you trusted me. Why not him?"

We stood in the doorway to watch the egg hunt, which was happening in earnest on the lawn. The kids chased around, trying to beat each other to the hiding places, with some of the parents trailing behind them. I could see Ara and one of the Philly cousins jockeying around the base of a promising pine tree.

Suddenly, Sona popped up at our side with a man in tow. I recalled seeing him earlier among the crowded dinner tables. He had the Jersey mafia look: dark slicked hair and a double-breasted suit, a little like the security guys at Clinton's.

Without ceremony, Sona said, "Jill, this is Ronald Focarino. He lives down the street. That's his daughter out there in the pink dress." She pointed at a gaggle of little girls—all in pink dresses. "Ronald is single," she added meaningfully.

"How ya doin'?" He shook my hand and held it for just a moment too long before letting go. The red flag from dinner began waving around wildly in my head now and suddenly, I felt extremely not drunk.

Jessica took a step backward and disappeared.

"Ronald is an entrepreneur," Sona began her sales pitch. "He's in and out of the city all the time."

"Sona and Taleen told me all about you. So you live the wild life, huh?"

"Wild life?" I asked.

"Yeah, the high life," he said. "With all the rock stars?"

I opened my mouth, but I didn't know what to say, so I closed it again.

"Maybe you two could meet for a drink sometime," Sona interjected enthusiastically.

I panicked and looked around for help and caught Jessica frantically gesturing to Greg inside the living room. Greg had been on his way into the kitchen with a spent platter of pilaf. He practically threw the platter on the nearest counter and headed in my direction.

Ronald said, "I could give you a call. What's your number?"

Sona leaned in closer. "Oh, I have her number. I can give it to you."

"Umm, I guess . . . I don't . . ." I managed to mumble.

Greg, my savior, appeared at my elbow.

"Hey, Ronald." He inserted himself between us. "Long time, no see! When did you arrive?"

Sona's smile stiffened. "Greg, I was just introducing Ronald to Jill. They have so much in common."

"Really, Ma? Like what?"

Her eyebrows twitched slightly, but the smile remained plastered on her face. There had apparently already been words between them about this matchmaking. "Well, they are both single," she offered.

Ronald was checking me out, up and down. I suddenly felt the need to inspect my shoes.

I glanced back and forth between the mother and son and felt a bizarre combination of affection, resentment, and utter horror. They both had good intentions for me in their own ways. I had no idea what would make Sona think this guy was my type, but then again, what did I know about "my type?" Jonathan was supposedly "my type" and he was a jerk. And now, I found myself attracted to the geeky computer guy at work, so why not a mob wannabe from Jersey, too?

World War Three was about to break out over my non-love life.

Greg and Sona engaged in an intergenerational staring contest.

Meanwhile, the children had been yelling and calling to each other in the yard this whole time, swooping up colored eggs. Suddenly, the timbre of the yelling changed and we all looked up in time to see Ara shove one of the Philly cousins to the ground.

The boy bounced back up like a rubber ball and went for Ara. They both wound up on the grass, fists flailing in a little boy fight. Before any of the adults could get there, Ara yelled, "You're a stealer! Fuck you!"

I froze.

"Ara!" Jessica reprimanded from halfway across the yard.

But Ara was in a rage. He looked at his mother, wild-eyed. "He's been stealing all afternoon and cheating on the games. He hit me in the basement. I hate him!"

The other boy pointed at him and taunted, "You said a bad word!"

"You and your brother have been picking on me all day. You stole that green egg from my basket. It's not fair!"

Jess had reached him, but he darted away from her grasp and ran toward us. Greg was ready to intercept, but the small boy zagged around our little clutch of messed-up matchmaking.

"Ara, they are your cousins!" Sona began a pursuit too, but was hampered by her high heels.

Ara ran around us in a circle. He was beside himself with rage.

"Fuck the cousins!" he screamed.

I hung my head and stifled a guilty snort.

Ronald saw my reaction and started laughing. The others looked on like shocked statues. Greg chased Ara into the house as the new mantra of the day repeatedly echoed off the marble floors and paneled walls. "Fuck the cousins! Fuck the cousins! Fuck the cousins!"

"Where could he have heard that word?" Sona pondered.

I held my face in a perfect mask of bewilderment.

Jessica stopped on the edge of the deck and braced her hands on her hips. I could feel her glare penetrating right into my soul.

The only good thing about Ara's outburst was that it deflected Ronald's attention from me. Soon after, Ara crumpled in a crying heap of diving blood-sugar levels and was carried out to the car. We made a hasty retreat from the party.

Greg drove directly to the train station after we left the house. The thick silence coming from the parents in the front seat hurt my head. Ara and I sat in the back staring at each other like we were both on death row, awaiting the executioner. I didn't say anything and I was not sure if the boy would rat me out once they got him home. As I opened the car door at the station, Ara grabbed my arm. The tears still shone in his eyes.

"I'm sorry, Aunt Jill," he said plaintively.

"It's all right." I hugged him.

Jess told me she'd call me about Friday.

I pecked Greg on the cheek through the open driver's side window and said, "Thanks for a memorable day."

He shook his head and chuckled.

"Yeah, right," he said. "Don't think it's over for you, Miss Jill."

I stared after the car as he pulled away from the curb. What was that supposed to mean?

FIFTEEN

THE WEEK AFTER EASTER DRAGGED INTO VIEW. MY HANGOVER LASTED well into the middle of it. It only got worse when Jenny came in one afternoon and told me that Jonathan had been seen in New York.

"He never did call you back, did he?"

"No. The jerk."

"Well, what are you going to do?"

"What am I supposed to do?" I replied. "I'm not going to leave messages all over the place like some lovesick puppy."

"Yeah. He'll be around here at some point, y'know."

This had happened before. Or something similar. Jonathan was really cute and sexy. When he was gone, it was easy to put that out of my mind. But when he was standing right in front of me, I was putty. Jenny knew this.

"You have to steel yourself," she ordered.

"Oh, please." I wrinkled my nose. "What do you think I am? A wimp?"

"No!" she exclaimed. "I think you're a pushover for a cute face and broad shoulders. Look how you are fawning all over that computer guy."

"That's just flirting. A distraction. I'm through with men. Remember? I'm going gay."

"Oh yeah, right. I forgot. Anyway," she said, changing the

subject to work, "the press party for Crystal is Friday. We are supposed to bring people. Who can you bring?"

"I'm already bringing my cousin. I'll bring Luann. How about Joanie and Alyssa? Kenny said to invite the office people. I'll invite the broad-shouldered computer guy!"

"None of those people are industry!"

I gave her a shrug. "Nobody else seems interested. It's a Friday night! There is lots to do in the big city."

"Fine, whatever," she spat. "Just tell Leah or her intern in publicity to put them on the guest list."

She walked away.

I got up from my desk and put a Stone Roses tape in my tape player, then sat back down, laying my head on the desktop. I didn't feel like working. I closed my eyes, listening. The song was called "I Wanna Be Adored."

Was that what I wanted from a guy? Adoration could only come in fleeting moments. Or in hindsight over a lifetime. Teenyboppers adored a singer. Fathers adored their little girls. But that was not something that could last for more than a little while. The teenybopper moved on. The little girl grew up and wanted to do her own thing. You couldn't function in a state of adoration. It was an immobile state.

I looked over at My Gordon.

"What do you think?" I asked him. "Can a family be real if they don't hate each other now and then?"

He seemed thoughtful over this one. A little perplexed.

The phone startled me by ringing at that moment.

I sighed as I picked it up.

"Mega Big Records," I paused. The receptionist had already said that to this caller. I had graduated from that. I said, "Hello, this is Jill."

"Hey there, Jill," a male voice came from the phone. I tried to place it. "This is Ronald . . . Ronald Focarino."

My mind reeled. I had not even recovered from the weekend's hangover.

"From the Boyajians' house?" he continued.

"Uh, oh, yes," I said cautiously. "Hi, how are you?"

"Good, good," he declared.

Damn, why did I answer the phone? I didn't think to ask Sheila to screen calls.

"You left so fast the other day," he went on, "after, uh, the thing with the kids. We didn't get to talk."

All right, my semi-genteel upbringing kicked in. This was a family reflection moment. I had to be polite, evasive, Southern. There was a way to brush him off without being rude and having it get back to Sona and her brood.

My mother would never let me forget the time when I was fifteen and I insulted one of her aunts. The woman spent twenty minutes at a family picnic telling me that I should only wear knee-length or longer skirts. "Nice young ladies never wear pants or shorts!" she said to me, pointing at my bare knees. I told her she was an old biddy. My mother was mortified.

"It's nice to hear from you," I lied to Ronald. "Have you recovered from the party on Sunday?"

"Yeah," he chuckled. "It was good. Long day."

"Uh huh." I had no idea what to say to this guy. I looked at My Gordon. He smirked at me.

"It was a *Children's Crusade* that day. Like some kind of war for candy," I said.

"Yeah, your nephew sure took it that way."

"He was *Driven To Tears*," I mused, still looking at the photo on my desk. "He turned into a *Demolition Man*."

"I used to get that way as a kid. Y'know I remember one of my birthdays. I threw a big tantrum over a Howdy Doody puppet," he told me. If he was playing with Howdy Doody toys as a kid, that meant he was much older than me.

"*Born In The Fifties*?" I asked, amusing myself at his expense. I put my index finger on My Gordon's mischievous eyes.

Ronald paused.

"That Taleen is quite the hostess," he tried to change the subject.

"Yes, *Every Little Thing She Does Is Magic*," I replied.

"I just happened to bump into her and her mom last week. In the mall. I never usually go there."

"*Synchronicity*!" I exclaimed.

"Huh?"

Geez, he didn't know what that word meant. I explained, "What a coincidence that you were there at the same time." *And are single and need a woman*, I added in my thoughts.

There was a beat of uncomfortable silence.

"So I got a lot goin' on in the city. I'm coming in this Friday. You think you might want to go have a dinner with me?" Ronald finally ventured.

"On Friday?" The press party was Friday. I had to work! I could get out of this honestly!

"Yeah, the rest of the weekend I have my kid."

"*On Any Other Day*," I said. "This weekend, I have to work that night."

"They work you on a Friday night?" He probably thought I was lying.

"Yeah," I attempted to sound disappointed. "Big mandatory event. That's corporate life. And of course, you have to be there on your visiting days with your daughter. I'm sorry you only get weekends with her."

"Yeah. My luck ran out with my ex. Things fell apart a few years ago, but I still take my kid to the park."

"*When The World Is Running Down, You Make The Best Of What's Still Around*, I guess." He didn't seem to hear my comment.

"I've opened a couple stores in Manhattan and Brooklyn. Dry cleaning in the city is booming."

I had to cut this off. He was going into impress-her-with-money mode.

"Uh, Ronald," I tried to sound sincere. "This weekend isn't going to work. I'm sure we'll see each other at the Boyajians' sometime."

"What about next week?"

"Oh, probably not. Work is awfully busy."

"Well, I'll give you a call later in the month? We can get together." He sounded overly confident, on the verge of cocky.

"*We'll Be Together*? I don't know," I answered.

"Yeah. Is it all right if I call you for a date later on?"

"*It's Alright For You*." I would have that talk with Sheila about screening my calls better.

"All right, then," he said, as if I had agreed to something.

"Well, bye-bye."

"Bye," he answered. "We'll talk soon."

I hung up the phone and said to it, "No, we won't."

I looked back at My Gordon, relieved that I avoided something. He seemed a little dismayed at my behavior. Maybe I was not being very nice, but really, there was nothing about this guy that appealed to me. Sure Sona was technically family, sort of, but I had no duty to go out with him just because she tried to set me up.

I walked out into the hall and stretched my arms over my head. Checking out who might be around. I didn't feel like staring at production schedules.

Tony was lumbering down the hallway.

"Going to lunch. Wanna come?" he asked.

SIXTEEN

THE PRESS PARTY WAS IN THE BACK OF A THEATER. I INVITED JOANIE and Alyssa to meet us there, but neither of them committed, so I did not really expect them to show up. Alejandro, Jessica, and I stood at the door to the private VIP room, waiting for the publicity intern to finish arguing with a journalist. She told him that he was not on the guest list. I knew this guy. He wrote for a major magazine. His round glasses, bearded face, and wrinkled shirt were the unofficial uniform of all music writers everywhere.

The interns always messed this up. When people read eloquent words printed with photos of the beautiful people beside them, they thought the writers were slick, cosmopolitan New Yorkers directly out of old Technicolor movies. Little did they know that these powerful pensmen were the ultimate nerds of rock 'n' roll. First of all, they were all guys. And, these were the guys who were bullied all through grade school and picked last in kickball. They weren't nerdy enough to be good in math and science. Yet, they all seemed to have photographic memories and could tell you who played bass on every Muddy Waters blues recording, who produced every album from 1960 on, and probably a whole bunch of baseball statistics, too.

If the intern blocked his entry, sparks would fly. I could see Leah, Crystal's publicist, flitting around inside like a butterfly. Tony was also just inside the doorway. I waved at him and pointed to Leah, making the internationally known semaphore flag signs for "Get her over here now!" Finally, Leah showed up at the door and freaked out that the ignorant girl had been keeping the music editor of Spin magazine out of the party.

"Oh, I've been waiting for you!" Leah excitedly strained, like there was no oversight. She swept him past the red-faced intern and handed him a glass of wine. "There is someone you absolutely must meet." She threw a stabbing glare at the intern behind the editor's back.

Then this same girl started to give us a hard time because Alejandro was not on the list, even though he was here with me, and she had seen him every day for weeks at the office. Some people take their jobs way too seriously.

Finally inside, Alejandro and Jessica both looked around in something that resembled amazement. There were more than a hundred people in the room. Crystal's music piped in the background, and posters of her and the LP cover papered the walls. Every table had several of the fake pink crystal giveaways on them. Also, everyone had a drink in their hand. There was a pretty good cross-representation of the music industry here. I suddenly felt like the tour guide at an animal park.

"That's the senior vice president of our label and his wife." I nodded in the direction of the elevated area to the right. The wife was a well-coiffed, attractive woman in her forties. She came to most of the opening VIP parties and was on all kinds of charity and museum boards all over New York. LaKeisha loved her.

"They are sitting with the president of corporate and his wife. That guy just redecorated his office—the whole fortieth floor of our building—to the tune of something like $3 million!"

They both stared.

"The guy they are talking to is from MTV. Some big muckety-muck." I nodded toward the other side of the room. "And there is the guitar player in Gloria Estefan's band."

They stared some more.

Jenny bounded up to us with Tony trailing behind her.

"Isn't this great! Leah got all the musicians and the producer to show up and call in all their favors!" she said excitedly. "There are tons of radio people here, too."

Tony wore an annoyed expression. He positioned himself in our midst like he was trying to shield himself from the rest of the room.

I introduced my cousin to Tony.

"I hate these things," he mumbled.

"Really?" she asked him. "The networking opportunities here for people like you and Jilly are outstanding."

He shook his head and shot me a questioning glance.

"Yeah, making nice with a bunch of stuffed shirts, needy press, and radio nerds," he retorted. "It's a blast."

"It's your job, you idiot." Jenny punched him in the arm.

Kenny strode up to us in his jittery way.

"You guys! Mingle!" He pleaded. "You have to talk this girl up. Jennifer, she's your artist. Get in the mix here and sell, sell, sell."

Tony rolled his eyes.

"I am. I am. I've talked her up to everyone in this room at thirty-second pops, just like you said."

"What was that?" I asked.

"The thirty-second pop!" Kenny said excitedly. "You have a product. You have to sell it in less than one minute or you completely lose the sale. I learned it in college."

My look bounced around the group. Jessica was about to second this remark, I could tell.

"Oh look, there is John from BMG," Kenny exclaimed. "He'll love her." With that he was gone.

"Product?" Alejandro said. "She's a person, isn't she? Not a bag of potato chips."

"Except she is a bag of potato chips!" Tony said. "To the Suits, she definitely is a bag of potato chips. Doesn't matter if the potatoes are rotten, as long as the package looks good and you can sell it!" He was dripping with sarcasm.

There was a flurry of activity at the corner of the room where Leah and the senior vice president stood at a doorway on the raised area. Leah took a wineglass and was tapping it with a fork, like the maid of honor at a wedding.

"Everyone, everybody!" she called for attention. "Please welcome our rising star, Miss Crystal Reneaux!"

The senior vice president opened the door with a flourish. Crystal stood sheepishly there in the doorway. The people who worked at the label or were part of her band or production team all applauded wildly and made hooting noises. The press and radio guys watched like she was a B movie on late night television, clapping politely.

The senior vice president took Crystal's hand and led her through the doorway. The girl was short, like me, but probably less than half my width, and I was not exactly fat. Her flowing strawberry-blond hair was meticulously messy in long loose curls. She wore some sort of flesh pink chiffon getup, which also flowed around her skinny, little body, intertwining with the hair. She looked like a lost child.

Her huge eyes darted around the room as she was led to the table with the MTV execs, Leah talking in her ear.

"What'd I tell you," Jenny said. "She's a sparrow."

"Is she all right?" I asked Jenny.

"That girl needs some food," Alejandro said.

"She's gonna fuckin' lose it in five minutes," Tony predicted.

"She's got a strong image," said Jessica, ever thinking in business terms. "But, yeah, she doesn't look very healthy."

Tony sighed and leaned back on his heels. "What do you do for a living, Jessica?" he asked.

"I'm a financial analyst."

"A financial what?"

"I analyze businesses and make sure they are worthwhile to invest in."

"And then you take other people's money to invest? Hmmm," he said. "Sounds like some hooey."

"Right, and metalhead rock music is steady work."

He shrugged, but smiled at her.

We all stood there chatting for a while and drinking. We listened some more to the banter between Tony and Jessica. It was like a game. She held her own, though.

Alejandro and Jessica probably thought this would be a whole lot more exciting.

Eventually, Leah escorted Crystal around the room to the more important press people who had the power to write up good articles about her. Leah was the pusher and protector at the same time. As they got closer to us, we could overhear her pitch.

"Anthony! Darling, how are you?" she crooned. "That interview with Keith for *Rolling Stone* was marvelous, simply fantastic! Crystal here should be next on your list, I am sure of it," Leah gushed as she practically shoved poor Crystal into the balding journalist. Crystal smiled demurely and tentatively put out her hand. Anthony gently took it, but didn't really look at her. He looked at Leah.

"Right, Leah, you put on a great party as usual," he said. "Hello, Crystal. It's a pleasure to meet you."

"Don't you love the music?" Leah pushed. "I'm telling you,

this girl is going to take over the airwaves. I know you want to be the first to publish how great she is."

He simply nodded, glancing at Crystal and giving an uncomfortable smile.

Crystal looked even more uncomfortable, but was about to speak when Leah went into protection mode.

"Well, I'll give you a call to set something up." She pulled Crystal along with her as she turned toward another writer. "Chris! I'm so glad you are here. That cover story on Jon was absolutely perfect . . ." They moved away as Anthony walked across the room to talk with someone else.

"I feel like I want to kidnap her and take her to my mother-in-law's kitchen," Jessica said.

"She does look a little bit lost, doesn't she?" I said.

Leah turned toward us with her fake smile on and then immediately frowned that we were not writers from a well-known national publication or television show. She pulled Crystal in a different direction as Crystal waved meekly at Jenny.

"This is not good." Jenny was getting upset.

Tony had stepped up and leaned into Jenny's ear. "Hey, you want to head to the back?" he asked her.

I sighed. I knew what was coming now. He fished a film canister out of his pocket and flashed it in his open palm for a moment. I was sure that it had some illegal substance in it. So was Jenny.

Jenny looked around at me. She knew I didn't do that stuff. She went out of her way to act cool about it. Everyone I'd ever known in this business or in college had smoked, snorted, or ate some kind of pharmaceutical enhancement at parties, except me. I stuck to my gin and tonics.

Jessica noticed this transaction and perked up. "Wow, it's been a long, long time," she said.

Tony reacted with surprise. "Aha! I knew it. You like to party. I wasn't sure of how stuck in the mud you were, being related to the goody-goody punk." He was, of course, referring to me.

Alejandro remained silent through this exchange. He glanced at me sidelong.

I sighed. "If you want to go with them, I'm fine with that," I told him.

"No, not really, I don't."

"OK, then, more for us." Tony headed toward the door that Crystal had come through and the others followed him. Alejandro and I stayed where we were, sipping our drinks.

"So you don't 'partake'? I thought that was what all people in rock did." He gestured after Tony and the others.

"I guess I'm not 'all people in rock.' Never have. Nobody believes me, though."

"Not even a joint?"

"No. Not even a clove cigarette."

I could not read his expression.

"What?" I asked him. "Is that a good thing to you or a bad thing?"

"You are a wise person," he answered. "Very wise."

I felt a sudden blush rise to my face. I had been called a lot of things over my refusal to do any kind of drugs. The adjectives usually ran around the general area of uppity, geeky, puritan. I didn't feel that I was judging anyone else. My choice was not even based on morality or that won't-somebody-think-of-the-children mentality. I simply didn't like it. People seemed to want me to say I was a recovering addict. In this business, that would have made me much more acceptable than someone who had never done any of it in the first place.

"What about you?"

"High school." He shrugged. "Makes people stupid."

"Hmmm and where was high school?" I tried not to smile at him.

"California. San Diego. My parents work at the base. My father used to be in the military. That's a long way from here." He took a sip of his drink and looked around the room.

"Then how did you get to be living here?" I asked him.

"My uncle teaches Latin American Studies at NYU. He's putting me up."

I could see there was a lot more to that story.

"What about you? Why are you in New York all the way from Texas?" he asked.

"Music. I wanted to make a living being in music." As I said it, I looked around the room at all of the cynical people. The senior vice president always yelling at everyone. Leah, lying to the journalist about loving his article. She probably didn't even read it. The little clutch of writers, only talking to any of us for the story. Kenny, with his thirty-second schmoozing. Even Tony and Jenny were always so cutting and nasty all the time. I was working here for a reason that I had not forgotten. I had to prove something . . . to them . . . to Dad . . . to myself.

"Sometimes you think you want something so bad, then when you get it, it's not all it's cracked up to be," I said. "Let's go find the others. Maybe we've made enough of an appearance here and can go out to dinner or something."

We made our way to the mystery door, where people appeared and disappeared.

THERE WAS A LONG HALL BEYOND THE DOORWAY. THE MUSIC AND clinking of glasses faded as we ventured down it. At the other end of the hall, we came out into a larger foyer that wrapped around the backstage of the theater. All along it were VIP party rooms.

"This is like a maze," Alejandro said.

"It's the backstage labyrinth. They rent out different rooms for business parties, nightclub after-parties. All kinds of things."

"They could be in any one of these rooms," he observed, moving a little closer to me.

"Yeah." I grabbed his hand and headed toward the first door, creaking it open. "I love checking these out."

It was silent inside. It was a large room with a pool table on one side and a bunch of seating areas and plush couches on the other side. On the plush couch side, a long wooden bar dominated the wall. Behind it was another door and a lineup of hundreds of bottles of expensive booze.

"Are we allowed . . ."

"Yeah," I said, walking into the middle of the room. "In this room, Bob Dylan could have gotten drunk. John Lennon might have had a deep talk with his guru. A lot of talent has been in these rooms."

He wasn't looking around. He was looking at me.

"You are really passionate about it."

"Well, yeah. You asked me before why I came here. This is it! Haven't you ever wanted to be one of those musicians? Filled with all that talent and expression and just able to put it out there and have other people get it?" I did a little whirl with my arms out.

I suddenly felt very free. I didn't usually feel that way. He walked over to one of the overstuffed couches that backed up to the middle of the room. He leaned on the arm. He watched me and I liked it.

"I guess," he said. "But there is so much hype. Lots of pretty faces with nothing behind it. It seems kind of hard to figure out who is for real."

I walked around the couch he was leaning on and sat in it, facing the bar.

"That's true," I said. "But think how cool it would be to find that one artist who is going to speak to a generation? That person needs the pushers like Leah and LaKeisha and Kenny. All that talent needs a way to get out to the public. That's what I want to do. Help the ones who might be able to make a difference."

He slid down to the cushion part of the couch next to me.

"You didn't want to be the singer? Play in the bands?" he asked.

"I can't sing and I've got a bunch of thumbs when it comes to playing. I can play a few chords."

I looked at him. He was an arm's length away.

"Wasn't there a song on the radio that changed your life?" I asked him. "An album? A band that opened your mind up?"

He thought a moment. Then looked right into my face.

"Pink Floyd," he said simply.

"*The Wall*?" I moved a little closer to him.

"*Dark Side of the Moon*." He moved a little closer to me.

He leaned toward me and there was that moment when your

eyes lock. He kissed me softly. I felt it all the way to my toes and we both kind of crumpled down into the cushions.

Just at that moment, the door banged open. Instead of popping up, though, we both instinctively ducked lower behind the tall back of the couch, startled.

"You are just so beautiful," a man's voice said heavily.

"Thank you," a woman's high voice replied.

They were obviously already in the throes of groping each other.

"I can really make you a star, you know."

"Oh, yes, yes."

There was the sound of the pool cues being hastily shoved aside on the pool table and the rustle of clothing. Now, they were on the green felt, whoever it was.

Alejandro and I both remained down, hidden behind the back of the couch. We stared at each other wide-eyed, barely able to contain the laughter bubbling up inside.

I slowly raised my head high enough to peer over the back of the couch toward the pool table.

All I could see was a mass of pink chiffon and tangled strawberry-blond hair. It was Crystal. The man's back was to me. He was wearing a suit. Then they moved slightly and he leaned back to fumble with the buttons on the front of her dress. His red tie swung and his expression struck me as grotesque. My stomach plummeted. It was the senior vice president.

"You are going far, very far. I'll make sure of it," he told her.

I squeezed back down into the cushion, suddenly avid to get out of this place. Alejandro, seeing my abrupt change from glee to disgust, was doing his own reconnaissance to see who it was. I wildly looked around for an escape. There was another door on the other side of the bar behind the couches.

"It's my destiny!" Crystal said dramatically.

I pulled on Alejandro's shirtsleeve as the horrible sounds of unzipping seared into my memory banks. We both slid off the couch onto all fours on the floor. We scrambled toward the bar. I prayed that the door was unlocked and not a closet.

Alejandro reached the door first and gingerly slid his hand up to the doorknob. It turned. What a relief.

He opened it without a sound and pushed it only wide enough for us to get our bodies through. I scrambled through the opening with him following. Once inside, I stood up, waited for my eyes to adjust to the darkness, and saw that we were inside some kind of butler's pantry. I could see a crack of light under another door at the other end. Lining both walls were shelves filled with glasses and napkins and other bar items.

I made a beeline for the other door, feeling like I was underwater.

It was a service door out to a hallway that led back to the main hallway and the kitchens.

Alejandro followed me.

I didn't stop until I was back in the main hall, where I began to pace back and forth.

"Oh God. Yuk. Ewww," I was saying.

But Alejandro was laughing. "Amazing. I always thought that was just a bad stereotype. Sleeping your way to the top!" He thought it was hilarious.

I stared at him in disbelief. "This isn't funny!" I scolded.

"Yes, it is."

"This is that girl's LIFE!"

"Hey, she looked like a willing participant to me," he answered.

Damn. He was right. But it was so wrong.

"Ugh! It makes my skin crawl. His wife is in the other room! In the same building!"

"Oh yeah. I forgot about that."

"Forgot about that? Not to mention, she's like, what? Nineteen years old. He must be pushing fifty," I said with disgust.

"Cute and young," he replied. He leaned against the wall, calm as a deep river.

I stared at him again, this time with my male-hatred antenna up.

"Just like another man."

I strode away from him, hoping that I was going in the right direction to an exit or back to our party room.

He followed.

"Hey, that's not fair!" he objected, catching up with me, matching my stride.

"No, I know. Really. I know. Get it while you can. That's the man's mantra." I kept walking.

"Hey, I'm not like that."

"Really, then what was that back there with you and me?"

"That was me trying to get to know you better."

I looked at him, slowing slightly. Was I being too harsh? After all, I didn't know him at all, really. He was not Jonathan.

"Prove it!" I challenged.

"OK," he said without skipping a beat. "Will you go out with me on a date?"

I stopped. "What do you mean 'a date'?"

"Haven't you ever heard of a 'date'? It's a thing where a man and woman go out to dinner and a movie or dancing? Just the two of them? To get to know each other?"

I had a sudden realization that I had never been on a real first date. Every romance I had ever had came from splitting off from some group event—football games in high school, keg parties in college, industry events here in New York. And now, I had been asked on two "dates" within a week.

The concept of a "date" seemed like some ancient ritual that was so far from my actual life that he might as well have asked me to build a pyramid with him.

"Fine! I'll go on a date with you," I said. It came off as more of a threat than a gracious acceptance of an invitation. My mother would have cringed.

"Fine! Great," he replied with equal feistiness. "Next Saturday. A week from tomorrow.

"OK."

"OK, then, next Saturday night. I will pick you up . . . at your apartment."

"Fine," I curtly responded.

We both began to walk again, not speaking. I glanced over at him. He was looking straight ahead and I recalled the feel of his lips back there on the couch. I hadn't had time to register how nice that had been. I remembered now.

"What about them?" He jerked his head back to indicate the sex romp we had almost heard.

I was silent.

It was all very sordid. If I told Jenny or Tony or even Michael, they'd probably just laugh in their cynicism and say, "So?" But eventually, it would get back to the wife, who I didn't even know. Did I want to be the purveyor of heartache?

"The only one who would care is the wife. I don't even know her," I said.

"Or she might be the type who already knows."

"Already knows? You think this has been going on a while?"

"No, but this can't be the first singer he's made promises to."

"Yeah," I said, deflated. "No. What for? We should probably just keep it quiet."

"Yeah."

| EIGHTEEN

MONDAY MORNING WAS A SERIES OF PRODUCT MEETINGS. TONY, Jenny, and I sat with hangdog expressions while art directors and graphic designers from the corporate production floor went over every last bit of paper that was attached to this quarter's catalog reissues. We were fed stale sandwiches and floundered in the thirty-second floor conference room well into the afternoon. I sat in the back, picking lint off of my unbuttoned flannel shirt, which was flaking from the faded tank top underneath. Tony checked his watch over and over while Jenny doodled in the margins of her notepad. I still had Alejandro on my mind and wondered if it was really possible that he was that nice of a guy or if he was just putting me on to get me into bed. I was anxious to get back to our floor and look for him.

But right as I got back to my office that afternoon, Michael charged in like he had been lying in wait for me. He firmly but quietly shut the door. The back flaps of his gray suit jacket and his maroon tie flew around his body as he swung to face me.

"Look at this."

He plopped an open high school yearbook down on my desk, covering my release schedule for Doggie T and nearly knocking over my coffee mug.

He whirled his long dark finger over the open page until it

landed on a portrait row of very well-scrubbed seniors. They were all clean-cut, had sparkling straight teeth, and wore various Izod and Polo symbols on their front pockets. This was obviously a well-off bunch of kids from a hoity-toity school. They were also all white, with one blaring exception. And I immediately recognized the cocky smile of Leon H. Thompson, *my* "MC Doggie T."

"Oh my God!" I gasped. "What is this?"

"This, my dear friend, is the 1986 high school yearbook of Nathaniel Academy."

"Tell me that's a school for delinquents in South Philly," I cried.

"No." He began to pace in front of my desk like a lawyer in a TV trial show. "It's basically one of the oldest and most prestigious private schools on the East Coast. I knew I recognized him. That stupid gold tooth on the front of his mouth didn't cover up his perfectly straight teeth. He's not from Philly. He's from New Jersey—and not even urban Jersey! This place is way out in the suburbs!"

"How did you get this book?"

"I went to this school too. This is my little brother's yearbook. My little brother was a freshman when he was a senior, which would have made Mr. Doggie T in the lower school when I graduated."

I tried to do the math on how many years was in between and around that bunch of connections, but quickly gave up because of the more harrowing issues of this situation.

"You went to a private school?"

"Yeah-es," he said with two syllables. "How do you think I got into Columbia University?"

Michael was an enigma, in his simple suit. I still couldn't

figure out his draw to this industry. Even though I considered him one of my best friends at work, I really did not know much about his background.

Right now he was staring at me incredulously.

I blinked back at him. I wasn't sure how to answer that question without insulting him in one way or another.

"OK," he said, letting me off the hook. "Don't answer that! The point is, if this gets out, we are toast! Look, look at this. He says he was MCing all through high school in some tough clubs in Philly? We cannot seem to find anyone who ever saw him. Check this out." He rifled through the pages. "He was MCing all right, at the Student Awards Ceremony for all the mamas and daddies, where, by the way, he got the award for Highest Advanced Calculus Scores."

"Shit!" I nearly shouted through a clenched jaw. I couldn't believe it. I stared at the horrid book in front of me as my stomach turned into a knot.

"How did you remember it was him? I was afraid to even look at a senior when I was an underclassman."

He paused and took a breath, leaning on his fists on the edge of my desk. I could tell that whatever he was about to say was weird for him—a black man—to tell me—a white woman—in an office on Fifty-Second Street, midtown Manhattan.

"Look, the nearest to black there in my own grade was Amit Patel, and he was Indian. From Delhi. Had the craziest accent I ever heard. You think I didn't notice the other black kids in that lily-white school? Altogether, I'd say there were probably about nine of us in a school with thirteen hundred kids. I was up to my butt in SATs and college applications. I didn't know his name, but I knew he was there."

My mind flashed back to my own high school. I breezed

through public school in a cow field and then went to University of Texas, where basically anyone who came up with $500 a semester could attend. I didn't recall any black kids in my high school.

The kind of money needed to go to this type of private school was ridiculous. No rapper worth his salt could come from that kind of money, and especially suburban money. If he didn't grow up in the projects, he had no street cred. I supposed there were scholarships, but if that was the case, that would be even worse! A gangster rapper that got a math scholarship to a private school? No way! We were so screwed.

I threw my pen onto the desk and slumped in my chair.

"Well, everyone knew something was off. What the hell are we supposed to do now?" I leaned forward. "Did you tell Kenny?"

"Not yet. I wanted to see you first."

I felt a small swell of pride that Michael might admire me a little bit to clue me in first to this revelation.

He sat down in my side chair and did "The Thinker" pose.

"We have to tell him," I said.

"I know. But we need a plan of action first."

"Maybe we should tell Leon first. I mean, that we know. Not that he's a stinking liar. He already knows that."

"Maybe."

My phone suddenly rang. I held up my finger for Michael to pause.

"Hello, this is Jill," I answered it. I had finally gotten the hang of not saying "Mega Big Records, Product" like I did for years in the Admin Pit. Someone else was finally saying that.

"Jill!" a woman's voice crooned. I didn't place it at first. "Oh my! You have an assistant to screen your calls. I am so very impressed, dear." It took me a second after I heard the word "dear" to realize that it was Mayrig Sona.

"Sona?" I said, somewhat bewildered why she would call me at work. "Is everything all right?"

"Of course, everything is wonderful!" There was honey dripping from her voice. "I know that you are very, very busy working on your, uh . . . work, but I wanted to let you know that Ronald is going to be in Manhattan this afternoon for his dry cleaning chain. I told him that you would meet him for a drink after work."

"What?" My voice caught in my larynx.

Michael gave me a questioning look and stood up, flipping through the yearbook and walking back and forth in front of my desk.

"I don't know what time I'll be done today," I stuttered into the receiver.

"Now, Jill, I know you may think Ronald is too old for you, but he is a catch. And he likes music."

My curiosity was piqued. "How old is he?" I asked.

"Only forty-six. A very youthful forty-six," she claimed.

"That is a lot older than me, Sona," I said impatiently. That was almost twenty years older. What could I possibly have to talk about to a divorced dry cleaner from New Jersey with a kid?

"Now, Jill, you are both adults. Age should not matter when it comes to love. After all, my husband is fifteen years older than me. You are an open-minded girl. Maybe you will get along? Who knows? Isn't it worth a try?"

I paused. She might be right about the age thing. But there were so many other issues with this idea that I couldn't even land on just one.

"I guess," I ventured, rubbing my aching temple and looking up at Michael.

He took the pause as an opportunity to shove the yearbook under my nose again and point to Leon's face in the group photo of Nathaniel Academy's Thespian Society and the companion photo of him in Shakespearian costume, complete with tights and a feathered beret. I waved the book away.

The moment of objection with Sona had passed, and she was already congratulating me on my willingness. "Wonderful, then it is a date." She told me that Ronald would be at my office at six tonight to pick me up.

"But . . ." I tried to say. I looked down at my outfit. It was a far cry from how I presented myself to the in-laws at family dinners. The tank top and flannel shirt were old and worn. My bottom half was just as downtown in a miniskirt with black leggings underneath and Doc Martens boots. I had on thick, black eyeliner, like I usually wore, not the light stroke I did at Easter dinners. My red-streaked hair was out in full view, not hidden under a wide headband.

"He is looking forward to it very much. You'll have a great time, dear. Talk to you soon. Bye."

"Wait! You already told him?" I protested into the phone, but she had already hung up. How pushy!

I put down the phone and stared at it in disbelief.

Michael was looking at me.

"What was that?" he asked. "You don't look too good."

"*That* was a force of nature!" I exclaimed. "You know who that was? That was my cousin's mother-in-law! She set me up on a date without even asking me!"

Michael started to laugh.

"This is turning into a weird day." I leaned my elbows on the desk and put my head in my hands.

"You gonna go?" he asked.

"She told him to come here after work! Even if I had said no, he's already on his way."

"Ah, you gotta love old aunties!" Michael said, pronouncing the "aunt" in the British way with the vowel as "on" instead of "an."

"One time, my aunt set me up with a girl. It actually worked. She was my girlfriend for about three years."

"What happened?"

"She went to medical school and I got a job in the music business. It didn't mix," he said wistfully. Then he went back to the original subject. "But what about this?" He shook the yearbook in his hands.

I shrugged, suddenly feeling very overwhelmed. "I don't know. We have to tell Kenny."

"Fine," he said. "Let's go now."

He got up with his yearbook and marched to the doorway. I didn't move.

"What about our 'plan'?"

"What plan? You got a plan? I'm not hearing any plan. You're more worried about your love life."

"All right. Fine." I got up and followed him to Kenny's office.

Kenny was there. We both charged in and Michael repeated the scene that he had presented to me a few minutes ago.

Kenny stared at the page for a good thirty seconds. Michael and I stood in front of his desk—me with my standard punk rock stance and Michael with one hand in his pocket. Kenny just sat there and stared at the book with a shocked expression on his face.

"Is he still breathing?" I said to Michael out of the side of my mouth.

"I think so." He leaned down over the desk and looked directly into Kenny's eyes. "You all right, my man?"

Kenny slowly looked up from the book at Michael and an odd, guttural sound came from deep inside his belly. "Aurgh!" he said. The sound got louder and louder, and he stood up as the sound became an all-out yell. "AAAAUUUURRRRRGGGHHH!"

We both stepped back from the desk, looking for the door in case it got worse. Kenny's face flushed and that vein was sticking out on his forehead again.

"This guy!" Kenny yelled breathlessly. "This guy is killing me!"

He moved around jerkily, like he wanted to punch something, but there was nothing close enough to his fists.

"OK. OK. All right." He began to take deep breaths and pace behind his desk. "We can kill the contract if he lied in it."

"Was there something in the contract that said where he grew up?" Michael skittishly pondered.

Kenny stopped pacing. "This could end my career! That guy I signed two years ago tanked and wound up joining the army, never to be heard from again, and everyone seems to hate Crystal!"

"Well, not everyone—" I began.

"She's nuts!" he snapped at me. "How come I get all the crazies? They flock to me!" I had not even thought about that side of this. Kenny had signed Doggie T based on the look and a few raps. He didn't do the real homework of what gangsta rap was all about.

"I was already out on a limb and now this." He sat back down and did that jerky punching move again.

"Who else knows?" he asked.

"Just us," Michael said. "And of course, Doggie. I'm wonderin' now what Whiskey and Robert know?"

Kenny searched the air around him and landed his gaze back on us. "Don't breathe a word!" he hissed.

"What?" I said.

"No, you cannot tell a soul!" He gathered up the yearbook and shoved it into the bottom drawer of his desk. "Especially not

LaKeisha! Nobody in publicity! They cannot keep their mouths shut! Nobody is going to say or do anything."

"You can't put him out there if he's lying about this!" I cried. "They'll eat him alive."

"It's going to come out eventually, even if you burn that particular book," Michael pointed out.

"Yeah, maybe, but not right now and not until he's a hit." Kenny rummaged in the top drawer of his desk and produced a key to the bottom drawer. He locked it and put the key in his pocket.

"Sit down," he ordered us.

"But," we both objected.

"Sit!"

We sat.

He then searched the clutter on his desk for the phone and punched the intercom button. "Margaret! Did we have Doggie T in studio time today?"

"Yes, he's supposed to be there now," she replied through the speakerphone.

"Call over there and verify that he—HIM, personally—signed in."

"OK." She sounded a little miffed.

He started to pace again, thinking out loud. "We know now, yes, but if we all agree not to tell, he could be in the Top 40 by the time the public finds out. Then it'll be good publicity."

"Are you kidding?" I said. In my mind, that would be worse! Someone would kill him, literally. He might be a bookish brainiac, but he sure was a real-life idiot if he thought he could pull this off forever.

The intercom buzzed, then Margaret's voice announced, "He signed in about an hour ago and is booked until midnight."

"OK, thanks. Get me a town car," he told her.

"What are you going to do?" Michael asked.

"We are going to see him, right now. We are going to tell him we know and that we are keeping his secret, but there will be stipulations."

I shook my head.

"It's the only thing we can do at this point," Michael said to me.

WE RODE TO THE WEST SIDE IN THE BACK OF THE LONG BLACK CAR. The town car company only had a limousine available in the middle of the afternoon, so instead of the standard shoulder-to-shoulder seating in a sedan, we were in a triad formation in the luxurious seating area of the limo. I faced the two men with my back to the driver.

I was sitting in stunned silence as Kenny rambled on.

"There is only one way to make it in this business, Jill," Kenny was saying. "Hits. The green." He rubbed his thumb and forefinger together in the sign for money.

Michael had his head down. I was not sure what he could have been thinking. Was he in on this idea of trying to keep it secret, or was he just being quiet at the moment?

I decided that I could not say anything either until I had some time to think about it. I crossed my arms and looked out the window. I studied the sidewalk on Fifty-Fourth Street and saw a familiar gait in one of the people walking along the sidewalk in our direction. It was Doggie T, a.k.a. Leon!

"Oh my God! There he is!" I cried, pointing out the window.

Kenny did a double take. "Pull over! Pull over!" he yelled at the driver.

Kenny jumped out of the car and walked up the sidewalk to

meet Leon. I leaned forward and positioned my head to the side of Michael's ear.

In a stage whisper, I said, "We can't do this! This is not just a matter of money. The gangsta rap thing is called 'gangsta' for a reason."

"If Leon is willing to put his life on the line, why should we stop him? He already made that decision."

"You don't believe that, do you? He's young and stupid. He's from your school. Leon H. Thompson is your . . . 'homeboy.' He's your . . . peer."

He sat back and studied me. A look crossed his face that was a mix of resentful and flustered. I hit a nerve, but I couldn't tell which one.

The door opened and both Leon and Kenny got into the car. Leon looked around suspiciously.

"What's going on?" he asked.

Both Michael and I stared at Kenny. Kenny paused, then opened his hands in some sort of preparation.

Leon noted our collective agitation.

"You people are whack!" Leon said.

"'Whack,'" I guffawed. "That's the exact right word."

There was a beat.

"We know you're not from 'the 'hood,'" Kenny finally said. "The clubs in South Philly say you appeared there just last year. This Cookie kid says you just showed up in Queens a few months ago. You're not from Philly. You are not from Queens."

"So I move around. So what?" Leon answered, but he nervously glanced at Michael, who was shaking his head.

"We're not going to rat you out, though," Kenny went on.

"I don't know what you're talking about," Leon insisted, but we could all see his face heating up.

"You're not from the 'hood at all, man," Michael chimed in. Then he pumped his fist listlessly and did a soulful version of a football cheer: "Fight, fight, Nathaniel High. Eagles, Eagles, we can fly!"

Leon sucked in some air and leaned back. He looked out the window, but didn't say anything. He was obviously freaking out inside and didn't know what to do now.

This whole scene was getting surreal.

"The flying is the easy part. It's the landing that hurts," I said, again acting out the role of the hench-woman sidekick or maybe now, I'd turned into a Greek chorus.

There was another beat of silence as we all looked out various windows of the limousine.

"So, all right, my parents have money. I grew up in New Jersey and I went to a prep school." His coarse tone sounded hollow. "Is that it?" He reached for the door handle defiantly. "Are we done?"

"You are one cocky son of a bitch!" Kenny raised his voice. "We are in no way fucking 'done.' We have a contract and neither of us can get out of it that easy. Bottom line, my career is on the line and YOU started this whole thing with your act. You are going to keep on acting and we are going to keep this little secret and make some money because you actually have talent."

"You serious?" Leon asked. He gave both Michael and me a dismayed look.

"But you have to tell us your whole life story and who else knows. And what the hell are you doing walking around telling people your real name at all? Nobody, but nobody should know that and LaKeisha is already talking about you to her publicity friends."

Leon's face brightened. He thought he was about to be kicked to the curb and instead he wound up with a posse of co-conspirators.

"Does Whiskey know?" Michael asked.

"He doesn't know it all. He knows I was going to U. Penn in Philly when I showed up at the rap clubs. I asked him to keep that quiet." He turned to me. "That's why he knew I didn't have anything against 'white chicks with degrees.'" He gave me a fleeting puppy-dog expression, which I took as some kind of backhanded apology for that crack during our first meeting. "He got scared after that run-in with Cookie."

"I'm scared about that too," I said.

"What about Bobby Washington?" Kenny asked.

"No. He doesn't know. We found him through one of the club owners in Philly," Leon said to Kenny.

"Then it's just us!" Kenny sounded relieved.

I had to jump in.

"And every person who knows his family!" I said. "And everyone he went to high school with! Any of those people see his face on *Yo! MTV Raps* and that's it! What are you people thinking?"

They all turned to look at me. I was the loose cannon.

"Those people are not in the biz," Kenny said.

"He's right," Michael agreed. "Even if he makes it to gold, that doesn't mean anyone in those circles will even see him. You say yourself that your Jersey family members don't know anything about what you are doing or the bands that you promote. And we are selling this to a black audience. I already told you there were only a dozen black kids in that whole school."

"Fine. Fine." I put up my hands. I leaned back into the seat, unconvinced. Was I the only person who thought rap music was becoming a cross-cultural thing? How else could these other groups be selling double platinum? I saw that this was not the time to argue about it. They were all on board and I had to go along with it, at least for now.

NINETEEN

By the time we got back to the office, it was after six. My head was absolutely pounding and I wanted nothing more than to go home, down some ibuprofen, and complain to Luann. The three of us didn't talk much in the car after we dropped Leon off back at the studio. I practically had to bite my tongue in half to keep from saying what I thought about this whole scheme. When it backfired, we'd all be out of jobs and I would definitely be back with the dogs—real ones at Dodge Veterinary Services, not grown men pretending.

We piled out of the backseat of the roomy yet claustrophobic limousine and into the roomy yet claustrophobic elevator. It was like all the fun had been sucked out of my heart. As we rounded the corner to the reception area, I felt my chest constrict even further when I saw Ronald, the guy from New Jersey, sitting on the couch in front of Sheila's desk. He was talking, moving his hands in an animated fashion, to the unseen desk and presumably, to Sheila. The desk was blocked from view by the open doorway.

Ugh! I thought to myself. I had completely forgotten about my shanghaied date with mob-boy. I grabbed Michael's arm and pulled him over to the wall, putting him between me and the reception area.

"What're you doing?" he protested as I hid behind him and

silently pointed the twenty feet down the hall where Ronald could be seen chatting away on the black vinyl couch.

Kenny walked on, chewing on his cuticles as usual, and breezed right by the couch without looking back. Thank goodness for his hyper-stressed-out rudeness. He was already on to the next thing and, I'm sure, wanted to put space between all of us as soon as possible.

Michael turned around and looked me in the face with his back to the reception area.

"Is that your in-law's setup?"

"Yeah, what should I do?"

He casually and deliberately scratched the back of his neck and peered over his shoulder at Ronald to get a better look.

"Well, I don't know. He doesn't look all that bad."

"Of course you'd say that. You're both wearing the same tie," I hissed at him. "He's from Jersey!"

"What you got against New Jersey?"

"Bergen County!" I reiterated.

"Oh." He looked over his shoulder again.

"Can you go get my big black bag from the chair at my desk and meet me downstairs?"

"Nuh uh." He shook his head. "Your mama didn't raise you like that. You have to talk to him, at least."

With that, he turned and walked into the reception area. Before I even had a chance to straighten my rumpled miniskirt, he was talking to Ronald.

"Are you waitin' for Miss Jill Dodge?"

"Yeah." Ronald seemed taken aback.

Michael opened his arm toward me like he was introducing a nightclub act.

I tried to keep my head from exploding as I walked toward them. I glanced at Sheila behind her desk. She raised her left eyebrow at me. The blackened arch seemed a little too in focus. Or maybe it was the rest of her face that was out of focus.

I turned to Ronald, who was regarding me with a shocked expression.

"Hi, Ronald," I said, leaning slightly toward him.

He looked me up and down, taking in the lack of suit, silk blouse, and sexy pumps that he was probably expecting. By the time his eyes reached my face, I thought he might pass out.

"Ronald?" I asked, gaining a little of my own power back. "You all right?"

Michael had stepped back and I was aware that both he and Sheila were enjoying this little show.

Ronald shook himself. "Yeah, yes, I'm fine. I'm good. Jill?"

By the time he recovered and I had taken a few deep breaths, Michael had somehow gotten us packed off back to the elevator with instructions to go to Arnold's Cafe at the bottom of our building for a drink. I certainly needed one.

Just the elevator ride was uncomfortable. This day seemed to be never-ending. But Michael was somewhat right. I was still my mother's daughter and could not be rude to the guy, especially not with Jessica's family involved. So I endured the ride on the elevator, trying to make some kind of small talk about driving in the city.

"So you don't take the bus or the train? Isn't it hard to find parking?" I asked.

"Nah, I park in a lot real close to here. I know a guy," he answered.

Somehow that sounded ominous.

We spent a half hour in the bar with appetizers and drinks going over all of the things that we did not have in common.

"Ronald," I started when we sat down, "I have to tell you that I'm not really looking to be set up. I know that Sona means well, but she doesn't exactly have a clear picture of my life."

"Obviously," he said, looking at my hair. "Is that color permanent?" he asked, pointing to the red streak.

"Yes, it is. This is how I normally dress. What you saw at the Boyajians' was me dressed for the in-laws."

"Huh," he seemed confused. "Where I come from, that's a Halloween costume. I mean, y'know, no offense."

I tried to not take it as an insult. "Right."

We stared at each other, probably both wondering how we got here. As my gin and tonic kicked in, I relaxed a little bit. The conversation moved to the fact that Sona seemed to think we "had a lot in common" because we both liked music. It turned out that his favorite group was the Bee Gees. And he liked "that singer, Madonna." He had never heard of the Clash, the Ramones, or Midnight Oil, to name a few bands, if not whole genres of music. It seemed he basically stopped listening to new music a good ten years ago, when his kid was born.

"You get too busy to do much of anything after that," he said, resigned. "And fighting with my ex. I spent a lot of time doing that."

He went on to talk about his dry cleaning business and how much money he made. I thought he was trying to impress me with that. If money were a high priority for me, I certainly would not be working in this industry. Just as my eyes were glazing over, he abruptly said, "We are obviously not on the same wavelength here." At least we both agreed on that much.

"You seem like a nice enough guy, Ronald. We can tell Sona that we met and, ya know, no spark?" I asked him.

He agreed. "Yeah, I'm a businessman. You're a rocker chick."

"Yes, that I am," I agreed. "A rocker chick."

He offered to drive me back to my apartment, so we went back up to my office so I could get my bag. It had been a long, tiring day, but I had eaten a little and had my drink, so I wasn't feeling as tense as before by the time I opened the office door. I didn't notice that Ronald came in after me and closed it behind him. I bent over my desk to pick up my bag from the chair.

Suddenly, he was right next to me. He leaned into me as I turned to face him. I was backed up against the desk.

"What are you doing?" My semi-relaxed state disappeared.

"Just 'cause we don't wanna date don't mean we can't have some fun," he said.

He put both his hands directly on my butt and tried to kiss me. For a second, I froze, not quite sure what was going on here. He took that as some kind of invitation to move one of his hands up under my shirt and feel my breast. I grabbed his wrist with one hand and twisted it away. I jabbed the forefinger of my other hand forcefully into the middle of his sternum. I pushed.

"Ouch!" he said.

"Didn't we just agree that we have nothing in common?"

"So?" He leaned back in.

I panicked, wondering if he was the kind of jerk I could just say no to or the kind of jerk that I'd have to knee in the balls and punch in the nose. Subtle difference. I kept pushing on his chest until he finally took a step backward.

"What?" He was actually confused. "You're a rockin' chick. Isn't that all about the sex?"

My heart raced and my blood pressure shot up.

"Get the hell out of here!" I shrieked, shoving him farther away from me with both hands.

I marched around him and opened the door.

"Sorry, I just thought—"

"I don't care what you thought! Out!" I raised my voice so that I could be heard in the hallway.

He looked hurt, as if I was being mean to him for no good reason. "Just because I'm wearing a miniskirt and into rock music doesn't mean I'd sleep with just anybody!" As if I should have to explain that.

He adjusted his suit jacket and walked out of the office. I followed him into the hall.

"Geez, you don't have to get so huffy about it," he said in a low voice as we reached the turn into the reception area.

I stopped. I could see LaKeisha's head pop out of her office in my peripheral vision. Thank God.

My anger now had a safety backup.

I scolded him, "You see this area?" I moved my hands in a motion that circled my torso back to front in a foot diameter. "This is what most people call 'personal space,' you idiot. You don't touch unless invited. Just for your future reference."

"Okay, okay," he exclaimed. Now he was holding up his hands, palms toward me, as if *I* was the person out of line.

I saw Tony appear at the end of the hall. He stood there curiously watching with his arms crossed.

I sighed in relief.

"Goodbye, Ronald. Don't call me. Don't think about me. Don't let me ever cross your mind again," I said.

He didn't say another word. He noticed LaKeisha standing in the doorway behind us. He turned toward the vacant reception area and blanched when he saw Tony standing in the hallway just beyond it. Looking at me with a dejected and almost forlorn expression, he walked toward the elevator banks. His jacket tail flipped as he turned the corner.

The minute I felt that he was actually gone, I burst into loud tears, right there in full view of both Tony and LaKeisha.

––––––––

THE NEXT MORNING, I SHOWED UP MORE THAN AN HOUR LATE TO work. As I approached my office, Alejandro was hovering outside the door with a paper bag in his hands.

"Hey," he said, trying to sound nonchalant. "How are you?"

"Hey," I said colorlessly. I was in man-hating mode before, but after the Ronald incident, I had entered feminazi territory, not only because of the assault from Ronald, but also because of the way Leon, Kenny, and Michael were so ready and willing to perpetuate their big lie. All this piled on to the vision of the senior vice president leering all over Crystal and the Jonathan fiasco. Enough was enough.

I opened my office door and walked in with him hot on my heels. I heaved my black bag onto the desk.

"I didn't see you yesterday," he said.

I sighed. "No, you didn't."

I walked around my desk and sat in the chair.

He felt my coolness and seemed to get a little nervous over it.

"Well, I brought you a bagel and cream cheese." He put the paper bag on the desk in front of me.

I looked up at him questioningly. I knew I *should* feel comforted. He was being thoughtful, nice. But instead, I was suspicious.

"Tony told me what happened last night." He leaned over my desk, peering into my face.

"I figured."

"Are you all right?"

Ronald didn't get beyond copping a feel, but I still felt violated. I was tough, though. I handled it. What was I supposed to do? Crawl into a hole and blubber? Run into the arms of some cute Latino who seemed all set up to "save" me?

"I'm good. Fine." I reached inside the paper bag for the bagel as a diversion from his searching gaze.

"I've got a lot of work this morning and I'm already sort of running late," I said. It was a cinnamon raisin bagel.

"Oh. Right," he responded. "Well, there is another training class to teach in a few minutes. I'll catch you later."

He backed out of the room in a tentative way.

"Thanks," I said to him. "I mean, for the bagel. Cinnamon raisin is my favorite, really."

"You're welcome."

He was so polite.

I turned to My Gordon once Alejandro had disappeared.

He gave off a reproachful expression. He seemed a bit insulted about my coolness toward Alejandro.

What was I supposed to do—fall all over him for a bagel? Like I was expected to do for Ronald because he bought me some fried mozzarella and a highball? Alejandro and I didn't have much in common, either. He was so clean-cut, by-the-book, scientific. Just because I didn't do drugs didn't mean I was some kind of nerd. Why should I be interested in him? Besides the tight buns and the broad shoulders and the melting smile? And that he just brought me breakfast to help me feel better?

I bit into the sweet bread. There was a quick rap on my open door. I looked up to see Jenny.

"Can you come over here a minute?" She took off down the hall toward her office. I followed.

"Look at this," she said, pointing to the wall opposite her desk where a bunch of papers with stick figure drawings were tacked up. Each drawing had a line of a song written across the bottom. It looked like a wall-sized comic book page.

It was a video storyboard for one of Crystal Reneaux's songs —one I had liked, "Try and Try."

"Did you do this?" I asked.

"Sort of. She had the idea and then we went over it together. It's weird. Really artsy-fartsy and she dies in the end."

"Dies?"

"Yeah. Suicide." She reached over to her desk and handed me an open magazine. "The reviews are mixed. They are comparing her to Kate Bush, just like we wanted, but only by saying she's not as good."

"I like her voice better. She's lighter."

"Well, this isn't 'light,'" she replied, indicating the video idea on the wall.

"What does Kenny say?"

"He thinks she's a nutcase. Radio is turning up their noses. She's only getting some play on college stations. It's all too deep."

"College is good. They buy records."

"Even the senior management can't seem to sell her to MTV," she told me. "And they are really pushing." I held my breath for a second. "Pushing" was the perfect word.

"They want a mainstream hit from her and they're not going to get it. And this video won't see prime time. They may not even play it on *120 Minutes*—that alternative music show. It's too depressing. I'm trying to convince her that the girl should run away instead or move on to get strong in the end. Like walk away toward a sunset or something."

I noticed Jenny was really emotionally involved.

"You seem to be warming up to her, though."

"She's all right. Still a little daffy, but her heart is in the right place. Y'know, the music is real."

Real. That word gave me a sudden headache.

Tony poked his head into the office. He handed a paper to Jenny. "Here's the thing on the video production company," he said to her, while pointedly looking at me.

Jenny observed the meaningful look.

"What?" she asked. "What? Is something going on?"

"Are you OK?" Tony asked me.

"I'm fine."

Jenny's arms stiffened to her sides and she mugged at me.

I relayed the events of the night before with Ronald.

Her reaction was to immediately make me sit down and give me a piece of chocolate from a bowl on her desk. "And you let me drone on about the video?" Jenny chided me. "That's horrible."

"Luann already pampered me last night at home. Lots of ice cream and complaining," I assured her.

"We could wait for him at one of those dry cleaning huts of his. One punch. Take him down," Tony kindly offered.

"I'm never going to see him again anyway. I think he's more an idiot than a threat."

"Idiotic men are the worst threats there are!" Jenny exclaimed.

"Look, I have work and Doggie T to worry about right now," I said, trying to stop this conversation. "The video is great, Jen, really. I like it." I headed out the door and back down the hall.

Tony followed me.

"Y'know, you don't seem to be heading in the right direction here in the dating department."

"Ya think?" I retorted sarcastically. "Men are creeps. You know that. Even you become a creep with girls, yourself."

"C'mon, Jill, LaKeisha and I picked you up off the floor last night. And I don't assault my dates!"

I stopped walking.

"I know, of course you don't."

He bent down to look into my face, like I was a child. "Seriously," he said, "I'm lookin' out for you."

"Yeah, thanks."

He put his beefy arm around my shoulders and gave me a quick squeeze. Then he walked away.

I stood there listlessly for a moment. Why were guys so great to me when they were *not* interested in me romantically? I was either their little sister or a welcome mat. It sucked. Wasn't there something in between?

| TWENTY

I STOPPED IN AT LaKEISHA'S DOORWAY AND PEERED INSIDE. SMOOTH jazz floated around the room as she sat at her desk with a red pencil in her hand, apparently editing the press release in front of her.

The brand-new computer rested complaisantly, shiny and unused, next to her elbow.

"Y'know, you're supposed to actually turn ON the computer in order to use it," I said to get her attention.

She looked up at me with her golden eyes and did her sound. "Humph! That thing is more trouble than it's worth!"

"Why? Did you take the classes?"

"It keeps freezing up on me. I write three sentences and it stops and makes all these whirring noises. I don't like it."

She reached over and picked up a square floppy disk from its place next to the CPU. "And what the hell am I supposed to do with these?" She tossed it back down. "Nuh uh, I don't think so," she said with disgust.

Then she leaned her elbows on the desk and appraised me from head to foot.

"Come in here. You put yourself together?" she asked. "After last night?"

Her tone was almost motherly. Not *my* mother, but some-body's.

I took a tentative step over the threshold. "I'm fine," I told her. "I am so glad that you were still at work. Thanks for being there for me and calling the car to take me home."

"Girl, you cleaned out my Kleenex box. You need a lesson in men."

"So I've heard."

"But you told him, so that's good, too." She clucked her tongue, which somehow veiled the approval she just gave me, and reached over to an in-box on her desk, pulling out an interoffice envelope.

"You should tell Alejandro that stuff about the computer making noises. It's not supposed to do that," I said. Then I looked down at my feet, suddenly feeling self-conscious by saying his name out loud. Obviously, Tony and Jenny already knew there was something up between the two of us, but for some reason, the idea of LaKeisha and everyone else being in on it did not sit too well.

The number one warning regarding romance was to never get involved with coworkers. But once you were out of school, where else were you supposed to get to know people before being subjected to a "date" like I had last night?

LaKeisha watched my face flush and she sighed.

"You don't have a lick of sense at all, do you?"

"What do you mean?" I tried to act like I didn't know what she was talking about.

"How about just being single for a little while? You just started this job, and from the looks of it, you might be about to lose it, too. How about concentrating on that?"

"I can't help it if he's cute," I gave a lackluster defense. We regarded each other and it dawned on me that she flew solo at all the perk concerts and press parties or she brought her sister. She never talked about a husband or a boyfriend or any person of the opposite sex at all, even though she appeared to be a grand flirt when the opportunity arose.

"Office romance will bite you in the butt," she offered. "Been there, done that."

"Aha! So you are a girl after all?" I tried a joke, possibly to get some of *that* story!

Her expression cooled, lips tightened and eyes leveled on me. She was not sharing squat. I should have known better.

To avoid my own squeamish reaction to myself, I changed the subject.

"I wanted to ask you something about Doggie T."

"Yes?" She looked at me expectantly.

"Well, last week, when you got mad at Kenny and me about what we knew about rap and the inner city, I think you were right."

"Of course I was right."

"So do you think that someone who is not from the inner city can know anything about rapping?"

"I grew up in the 'hood, little girlfriend," she snapped at me. "Kids been doing that kind of thing for years and it's just now getting to the recording studio."

"Right. And this year, rap was even a category in the Grammys. That's good, though, isn't it? I mean, it's getting popular."

"Yeah, but look what happened to funk and the blues once it got popular."

"What do you mean?"

"You seen any black guys playing blues guitar lately?"

I scrunched my nose and tried to conjure up a blues guitarist in my mind. My first thought was Stevie Ray Vaughan, and his brother, Jimmie Vaughan, and the Fabulous Thunderbirds. Not black. All I could think of was all the bar bands who played in Austin, pretty much all white guys. Then I conjured up the classic bluesmen—B.B. King? Buddy Guy? Albert Collins? They were old men.

LaKeisha watched me scour my mind for a minute, then she spat out, "Johnny Winter? Eric Clapton? Stevie Ray? The only one out there now? Maybe Robbie Cray. Black guys don't play the blues no more. They started it, but they don't wind up with it. Same thing happened to R&B and mark my words, it's gonna happen to rap."

"But what about authenticity of the original? I mean, in the '60s, the black singers in Brooklyn were into doo-wop, right? It worked for them, because that is where it originated. So then, everyone from all over loved it and could relate. Groups sprung up from everywhere doing it. Aren't people happy that it gets popular?"

"Not if they're pretending to be a black guy from Brooklyn. And if the copycat groups make more money and get all the credit? It sure as hell don't make the boys from Brooklyn happy." She studied me from her throne behind her desk. I thought she was getting a soft spot for me after all this time.

There was no way to be sure if our Doggie T/Leon problem was an actual problem. LaKeisha seemed to be saying it was definitely a racial thing, but there was more to it—neighborhoods, privilege, money, class.

"But, if you wanna know what the '60's was like in Brooklyn? Not fun, but it's gotten worse. They're out there selling crack and cocaine now, not a little bit of pot. Used to be some fool kid had a knife—now they all carry around guns!"

"Yeah," I trailed off. "Guns!"

"What are you worrying about? Being on the Doggie T team?" She eyed me curiously.

"Kinda," I said noncommittally, even though my mind was crowded with lists of the worries.

"You're all right. You're not the rapper, anyways. You're the saleslady. The saleslady is supposed to be white. So don't worry about it."

There was a sudden boom of a voice behind me. "Jill!"

The voice belonged to Kenny. He came into LaKeisha's office like a bolt of lightning. He searched both our faces. "Just happened to be walking by. What are you all talking about? The computers? I just love these computers. LaKeisha, are you using your computer?"

She opened her mouth to answer the computer questions when he suddenly switched gears and turned to me. "Jill!" False enthusiasm oozed out of every pore. "Yes! I am glad to find you here. You are just the person I needed to see. Can I talk to you for a minute, please?"

With that he grabbed my elbow and hustled me out of LaKeisha's office. I looked back over my shoulder to see her confused face watch us leave.

Once we were down the hall, Kenny twirled me to face him.

"What are you doing in LaKeisha's office?" he demanded.

"What do you expect me to do, hide from her?"

He gave me a meaningful look that said all I needed to know.

"All right! OK!" I exclaimed, holding up my hands in the universal sign for "I give up." "I'll just get back to my other work now, if you'll excuse me."

I turned to go back to my own office. He watched me walk away, making sure he stayed between me and LaKeisha's door.

I plopped back down on my own chair and looked around my office walls.

My Gordon looked up at me with questioning eyes. How was

this going to play out? I shrugged my shoulders at the photo. Should I just stay in my office for the next few months until my probation period was over? I did not see how I could keep up this kind of charade unless I stayed very, very far away from every person involved. I had to feign total ignorance and distance myself.

What about the fact that Leon actually had talent and star quality? If he could be convinced to go in a different direction, maybe the whole thing could be salvaged? He could do R&B songs—really croon out the ballads. But he obviously didn't like that kind of music.

I looked back at Gordon. He seemed judgmental. He was playing ska in punk clubs after the Sex Pistols. Then he switched to jazz. If he could do that, why couldn't Leon rap? Because My Gordon was still from the working class, not the prep school suburbs. His authenticity came from his economic background, not his race. And that was going to be Leon's issue.

Then I got pissed off at the way those of us from the suburbs seem to be judged. Just because you didn't live in a gang neighborhood or in extreme poverty didn't mean you didn't get bullied or have sadness or problems. Maybe we were better off in terms of schooling and food, but if you get a cut, it hurts whether you live in a Bedford-Stuyvesant apartment or in an Essex County colonial. No matter what your circumstances were, you could still have insight and creativity and deep feelings!

My worldview was not going to help sell Leon as a gangsta rap artist, though. I was pretty sure that I was in the minority on that thought process.

IT TOOK ME ANOTHER COUPLE OF DAYS TO RECOVER FROM MY Monday. After the run-in with Kenny, I laid low. I walked around in a bit of a daze and went through the motions of answering phones, tracking back catalog production, and sitting in meetings, all the while politely avoiding LaKeisha and outright hiding from Kenny. Through all of this, I realized that I had not seen Michael since Monday night, which was highly unusual, because as a rule, he was in my face at least twice a day.

Thursday lunchtime found me in the cafeteria munching away, rabbit-like, at my chef salad. I sat perusing my complimentary issue of *Soap Opera This Week* (another perk of knowing people at the bottom!), when I was besieged by Tony, Jenny, and Alejandro at my table.

They all settled in, chatting and joking, and generally interrupting my quiet funk with their ruckus. Alejandro sat next to me. I asked Tony where Michael was, and he shrugged me off, claiming he didn't know.

Just as I was about to pursue a more detailed line of questioning, Tony, in an extremely unsubtle move, said, "So Alejandro says you've been avoiding him."

Alejandro practically choked on his ham sandwich.

Jenny backhanded Tony in the bicep. "What is your problem?"

"What?" he said to her. "He wants to go out with her. And she supposedly agreed."

"Maybe he wants to be a gentleman and for things to take a natural course?" Jenny replied.

"Right. He's a regular Colonel Pickering, but that's not gonna get him anywhere."

Alejandro and I watched them banter back and forth like bleacher spectators at Wimbledon, both of our faces turning multiple shades of red.

It was true. I had been avoiding him, and everybody, for the past few days. And they didn't even know half of the reason why.

Tony was right on one level. I needed to get on with my own life. I could not hide behind *Soap Opera This Week* headlines for the rest of the year, until Leon and his issues blew over.

Tony and Jenny went on bickering about us in the third person, as if we were not sitting right here with them. Alejandro and I made eye contact. He signaled with his eyes toward the door of the cafeteria. We both slowly got up, leaving our food, and headed for the hall.

"Did it ever occur to you that she needs to recover a little bit after what happened Monday night?" Jenny was saying.

"What better way to recover than going on a date with a Latin 'gentleman'?" Tony retorted, completely oblivious that we had disappeared from the table.

Out in the hall, I turned to him.

"I'm sorry about dissing you," I said. "Things have been weird this week. Not only the thing with Ronald, but also work stuff. Leon, I mean, 'Doggie T.'"

"The rapper guy?"

"Yeah, the 'rapper guy.' What do you think of him?"

"Seems kind of cocky and full of himself."

"Well, that's what he's supposed to be. That is the MO of star quality."

"Really? OK, then, he's perfect for the job."

I had a feeling Alejandro was simply indulging me to get me to go out with him.

"Listen, Jill, I get it," he told me. "Things happen that are unfair. Not all of us men are like Doggie T or your 'Ronald.' Jill, I just like you. That's all. "

How could a guy be this sweet? This was outside my normal scope of reality. What was wrong with him? Did he fall on his head as a baby?

"Look." He leaned his shoulder against the wall, which made him appear even more attractive. "Are we still going out on Saturday? My dinner offer is still good."

"Dinner out on a Saturday night." I tried to picture it.

"That is the idea."

I finally gave in to the fantasy. Maybe he was for real and I would never know if I didn't give it a chance.

"Yeah," I told him. "I'll go."

TWENTY-ONE

I WAS TAKING WAY TOO LONG TO FIGURE OUT WHAT TO WEAR. HE SAID "dinner." What did that mean? *Fancy* dinner? *Casual* dinner? *Hot dog cart* dinner? He wouldn't take me to a white tablecloth type of place, would he? I put on some tight black pants and a slouchy zebra-print shirt. I took it off. I put on a pair of acid-washed jeans and a silk blouse. I took it off. Finally, I settled on a black linen top and a miniskirt. I couldn't go wrong with this, even though it was kind of boring. It would look all right if I wore my leather jacket and some great earrings.

"All right," I said, finally coming out of my room. "How about this outfit?"

Luann, Joanie, and Alyssa looked up from their cards.

"Where is he taking you?" Luann asked.

"I don't know," I said, putting on my dangling earrings.

Alyssa got up and motioned me into her chair. "Makeup coming up!" She rummaged through her purse and produced a variety of pencils, bottles, and tubes.

"Now it's Saturday night in New York City! Smoky eye! Smoky eye!" she chanted. This was her expertise. She came toward me with an eyeliner pencil. I sat at the kitchen table, occasionally closing my eyes or pursing my lips as she instructed.

"OK." Joanie began to pace between the dining area and the

couch. "Don't order anything with weird sauces. Don't eat more than he does. Keep the conversation light—y'know, favorite foods, that kind of thing."

"Sounds kinda boring," I said, with my face turned up toward the ceiling as Alyssa dabbed my closed eyelids with something creamy.

"No, you can talk about your favorite TV shows." Joanie was taking my wallet out of my huge black bag and putting it into a smaller black evening bag as she said this. Something I had not asked her to do. "Talk music. You already know that he likes music."

"Everyone says they 'like' music," Luann said sarcastically. She was still sitting at the table, picking her fingernails. "Don't listen to her. Talk about something juicy and see how he reacts. Religion. Politics. Abortion. That's what I do."

"Yeah, when was the last time you had a second date?" Joanie retorted.

"I see this guy almost every day at work. We've already done all the introductions talk," I said.

"I suspect there are subjects in between," Alyssa chimed in. "Just don't talk about babies or weddings or married friends. That scares them, for sure, if you get into that on a first date."

There was a buzz of agreement on this point.

The doorbell rang and everybody jumped in surprise.

"What? He's early!" I blurted. The three girls all ran into my bedroom, still arguing with each other about what should happen on a first date. They opened the window and leaned out to look down at the sidewalk for him. None of them had met him yet.

"Stop it! Don't do that? What are you trying to do? Scare him?" I ran after them.

We didn't have a buzzer to let people in. If we wanted them to come up, we would put a front door key into a sock and throw it out the window to them. There was no way I was doing that with these girls here. I shoved my way through them and waved to Alejandro, whose face was turned up, searching the building for the commotion we were creating at the fifth-floor window.

"I'll be right down!" I called out to him and anyone else on the street who might be interested.

The girls offered their opinions of Alejandro. "He's cute." "Tall, dark, and handsome." "Ooh la la."

"Wait, one more thing . . ." Alyssa came at me with a lipstick.

Then the clichéd teasing began in earnest. "Don't stay out too late." "Our little girl is all grown-up." "Don't do anything I wouldn't do!"

I waved them all off as I bolted out the door. I prayed that they had not gone back to the window during the four minutes it took me to get down the stairs.

Out on the street, I greeted Alejandro with a short hug, looking over his shoulder up to my window. They were all there.

"I hope they didn't give you a hard time," I said, as I moved to put distance between them and us.

"No, but they said you forgot this." He held up a knotted striped sock.

I unraveled it enough to see there was a condom scrunched into the toe. I shoved the whole thing into my purse, turning red in the face. Very funny. I'd have to figure out how to get back at them.

"So where to?" I asked him.

"Dinner? There was this place in Alphabet City I wanted to try—Two Boots?"

It was a relief to hear that we were going downtown to some-place casual.

He continued, "Then Tony gave me these." He held up passes

to CBGBs. "And LaKeisha gave me these." He held up more passes for the Blue Note.

"Well, the whole office has your back, huh?" I pondered.

We walked toward midtown to get on the N or the R train and chatted as we headed downtown. We would be doing a lot of walking, since that was the way of New York. We came out of the subway at NYU and walked east. That was one of the great things about Manhattan—you could always figure out the compass directions based on the street grid.

"Do you come down here a lot?" I asked Alejandro.

"Almost never," he said. "I'm more of a homebody, really. But I like good food."

I took that in. I loved to be out almost every night, but lately, it had been getting old.

At the restaurant, the menu was full of Cajun and Italian entreés. "Oh! I get it! Two boots! Italy. Louisiana. That's cute," I mused.

I ordered an entreé with a lot of spicy sauces. So did he. He ordered wine for both of us and seemed to actually know what he was talking about.

We talked easily with each other. I learned that he was into folk art, mostly Mexican. His uncle had turned him on to every Latino art outlet in the city, which was a lot. He took photographs and liked to go to museums, but he didn't consider himself an "artist."

We talked about Mexican food and the differences between life in New York versus life almost anywhere else in the country. We both pined for a slightly slower pace that didn't turn into total boredom.

This was going really well. I was smiling a lot. So was he. His smile made me smile even more. It was a smile-fest.

We walked down the street toward CBGBs. All kinds of people were hanging out in front of the club, smoking and talking. Every time the door opened to let out or in another boisterous group, the loud music jabbed into the night street. The passes got us in and the band was heavy. We pushed toward the stage. The usual crowd makeup was there: friends, lovers, and roommates of the band members; tattooed guys there to find girls; the occasional group of suburbanites who had decided to go slumming. We tried to communicate over the noise and were pushed into each other by the crowd at the bar. The band was not that great, so we spilled back out onto the sidewalk.

Shops were still open. We strolled and talked.

"So," I asked him, "how's your Spanish?"

"Muy bien. I spoke Spanish before I learned English."

"I love the way Spanish sounds. I took some Spanish in high school, but I don't think I retained anything. Say something in Spanish."

"Eres una mujer hermosa!" he said wistfully.

"Ohhh, that's good. What does it mean?"

"It's poetry. Very complicated."

He grabbed my hand and held it as we walked. It felt so sweet and innocent, like we were in the sixth grade. I looked at him sideways. I might have blushed.

"Do you remember any of your Spanish from high school?" he asked me.

"Not a lot. Some verbs. I really need to learn, though. Everywhere I go around here, there are people speaking Spanish. I feel like they are talking about me sometimes."

"Try something."

"Well, umm," I racked my brain for a Spanish word. "I can't. I don't know . . . Yo? Estoy . . . ummm . . . embarasada?"

He started laughing uproariously.

"What?" I demanded in mock fluster. "What did I say?"

"You just said that you were pregnant! You're not, are you?"

"No!" I tried to laugh with him, but I could feel my face burning with shame.

He paused for second, thinking. "Do you . . . will you want to be a mom, I mean, someday?"

Now I paused. "The girls warned me not to talk about babies and that kind of thing on a first date."

He looked a little abashed.

I didn't want him to feel weird about bringing it up. The girls meant that I, the woman, was not supposed to start the subject of the future and having families, so I quickly continued. "But, yeah, I definitely want to have kids. I can't imagine *not* wanting to have kids and a family and all that. In the future."

He seemed to squeeze my hand a little as we walked and looked into shop windows. We stopped at a street vendor selling knockoff purses and scarves. The vendor was a small Chinese man.

"Very good leather. Real leather," he said to us, pointing to the purses. "You like color or natural?"

"I like the blues," I said.

"Oh, yes. Here. Here. Good quality." The man smiled the smile of a true salesman, indicating a section of his table with colorful bags.

Alejandro watched me as I pulled out a bluish leather bag with an interesting curlicue design etched into the leather. Finally, he said, "Y'know, Tony gave me the third degree after he found out we were going on a real date."

"Oh yeah?" I wasn't sure what to make of that. I supposed I should be happy, but I didn't know how he got to be appointed my romance guardian, as if he was an authority on relationships.

He hadn't had a steady girlfriend since I'd met him. "Sorry about that," I offered.

"It's OK. It means something when people are looking out for you that way. You've got real friends. That's a good thing."

"Yeah, but that can backfire sometimes. Look at what happened when my cousin's family tried to 'look out' for me?"

I glanced at him while I fiddled with the zipper on the handbag. "Did you pass?" I asked, trying to sound nonchalant.

"Well, neither of my kneecaps are broken and we *are* on a date right now, so I guess so."

I put the purse down and faced him. He suddenly encircled my waist with his arm and pulled me toward him. It was like a one-armed hug that brought our bodies together. He looked into my eyes for just a moment, then kissed me, for real, on the lips.

The vendor began to make noises like "ohhh" and "ahhh" and moved around to the back of the table again, as if to give us a moment of privacy. He picked up the purse that I had been looking at. As we pulled apart and looked at each other, the man interrupted our mushiness by pushing the blue purse practically between our faces. Smiling broadly, he said, "Nice gift for the lady?"

I JAMMED JOANIE'S MINISCULE EVENING BAG INTO MY NEW BLUE leather purse and flung it over my shoulder like it had always been mine. We kept walking and holding hands and now, I was more than smiley: I was giddy.

We wound up in front of a bar that was packed with people. Clear windows flanked the whole side of the two-story building. There was not even a sign on the building. There was no music playing, which was weird for a New York spot on a Saturday night.

I was glad to see that Alejandro wanted to check it out, not knowing what the place was. We went in and got a couple of drinks from the bar and stood next to a spiral staircase that led to the second floor. The people around us began talking to us and joking around.

"What is this place?" Alejandro asked them.

"I don't know," a cute blond girl answered, "but it's open every weekend and filled with people. I live around the corner. They don't even open the doors until ten."

"There is no name? No bands? No food?" I asked.

"Nope, just people talking and drinking. I don't even know if it's legal. During the day, it's closed up with corrugated garage doors."

Everything in the room was either black or clear glass, from the tables and chairs to the clothing of almost every person there —including me. I fit right in.

As I glanced toward the doorway, lo and behold, who did I see walking in at that moment? His aura was so intense that everyone standing around the door stopped talking and looked at him for a moment before resuming their conversations.

"Look." I nudged Alejandro. "It's Leon 'MC Doggie T' over there."

He was with Shandra and Jackson, the two friends from the fight night at Clinton's. I tried to remember if I'd seen any paperwork with his address on it. Did he live around here?

Alejandro craned his neck in an obvious way. "Oh yeah, this doesn't seem like the kind of place a rapper type would hang out," he said.

"Yeah, I know."

Kenny's and Michael's faces swam to the front of my mind. This desperation to keep Leon's background a secret was just so wrong. I knew it. They knew it. I thought that even Leon knew it. If it took Michael one trip through a yearbook to find out the truth, how long would it take some music journalist at *Rolling Stone* to figure it out?

Not long, that was how long.

Then it would be over.

At best, Leon would be a one-hit wonder and footnote as another fake in the entertainment industry. Maybe Kenny, Michael, and I would keep our jobs if we all acted surprised at the truth, but we'd still be laughingstocks of the music scene for supposedly being duped.

I was not a good liar. And here I was having to lie to keep my job.

Looking at Leon, now, here in this club, I knew he had so much more talent than that. When he closed his mouth and covered the weird, probably faux, gold tooth, he was really handsome. If he had been signed as an R&B singer, he might not reach the top of the charts, but he might have a long career. For all we knew, he'd still fail if he went with the rap stuff on his own.

My Texas conscience tugged at me. I knew I was probably about to make the biggest mistake of my life and possibly end my career in music before it even got off the ground.

I had to talk to him. "C'mon," I said to Alejandro, "I need to talk to Leon about something. Can you follow along and maybe distract his friends?"

Alejandro's eyes lit up, like there was going to be some kind of adventure here.

They had gotten their drinks and sat down at the corner of a long table. I headed over there with Alejandro in tow and sat right next to Leon.

"Hey!" I chirped at him as Alejandro sat opposite me, next to one of his companions.

Leon did a double take, then looked around, as if I was

talking to someone behind him. Then he said, "Aw, hey, Jill."

"Hi, Shandra, how are you doing?" I reached across the table and shook her hand. She got all excited.

"Hey, Jill," she said. "Jackson, you remember Jill from that night at the studio." Jackson did his cool nod in my general direction. "Jackson scratches at Drop Zone, too! We was just down at that jazz club on Avenue A. Doggie says it's the old sound." She was genuinely enthused. That was nice to see.

I introduced Alejandro, who nicely maneuvered Shandra and Jackson into going to look for a made-up game room on the second floor.

As they got up, I gently placed my hand on Leon's forearm. He remained seated and turned to me once they stepped away.

"You hangin' with that computer type?" he asked.

"Funny you use that phrase. He called you a 'rapper type,'" I said, then looked directly into his face. "So?"

"So? What?"

"What are you doing? Really?" I knew I didn't have a ton of time to get my point across to him, so I spilled it all at once. "If you present yourself as a ghetto kid, even if you get away with it at first, you'll get shot down after the first hit—figuratively and maybe literally. If you're not dead, you'll be a joke for a while, then you'll just fade away quick. Do you want that?"

He regarded me with an ambivalent expression.

I continued, "If you take this chance to be authentic, be who you really are, you might have a shot at a real career."

I paused, picturing Kenny with that vein popping in his forehead, and doing a summation of my packing plan to move back to Conroe.

"I got myself signed with Mega Big Records as a gangsta. How am I supposed to change it now?"

I relaxed a little bit. At least he would talk to me about it.

"We liked you that first night because of your stage presence," I told him. "You commanded the room. The rap we heard wasn't that great and you know it! The senior VP was enthralled by your attitude and cockiness in person. He had only heard one song on a tape—and he probably only listened to half of it."

"I don't know, Jill." He was nervously looking around for his friends. "I got myself in deep, here. If I change it up now, they'll drop me for sure."

"Not if you can come up with something better."

Skepticism was written all over his face.

"Seriously, Leon," I continued. "Kenny is just in to keep his job at this point and he doesn't think past next week. That's why he's such a bad A&R rep in the first place. I know you can actually sing! I mean croon. I heard you that night in the studio. And I saw your high school yearbook —the lead in *Music Man*?"

He turned and stared down at his drink. I could see his mind working.

"And here you are taking Shandra to jazz clubs! Who do you think you're going to fool in the long run? Shandra might not put two and two together, but you think the music critics at Spin and MTV don't know the history of pop music?"

There was a pause.

"I do have an idea," he said into his drink.

"Yeah?"

"I've been playing with some of Cookie's tapes and doing a kind of mix of rap and hard rock. He really knows how to rap."

"Does he still want to kill you?"

"Nah." He seemed sure. "We're cool. Jackson smoothed it with him. He was just real mad that night at the studio."

"I could see why."

"Yeah, I'm an idiot. Cookie? He's quiet most of the time—shy, even. But his rap? It's all real."

"And that's what you want."

"He wouldn't do it unless it's his way."

"So we've got to get Cookie on board."

"Yeah."

There was a pause while we both let that settle in our minds.

"I'll probably lose my job over this either way," I said.

"Why you wanna do that kind of thing for me?" he asked, perplexed by my absurd willingness to throw my career away.

I thought again for a second. Why, indeed? Why did I love the bands I loved? Because the music was their own self-expression spilled over into my world. Sure the hype around it might be all showbiz, but the music that stuck was written from deep down and performed from the heart. If a singer didn't "get it," no matter how great the song, you could always tell. If the song was hack, it was usually because it wasn't written from the soul.

I came here in the first place because my soul was driven to be involved in music. Mom and Dad had supported it this far because they knew you had to follow your heart. It was the only way to know for sure that you tried.

Now it was my turn to talk into my drink. "I could not live with myself if your real voice didn't even get a chance."

He shifted his weight toward me slightly. He gently touched the bicep of my arm, just for a moment, then pulled away again. His face softened with a realization of some kind, but immediately came back to attention as Shandra, Jackson, and Alejandro walked back to the table.

"They ain't got no pinball here," Shandra informed us.

"This place don't even have fries!" Jackson added.

Leon and I both smiled up at them.

TWENTY-TWO

By Monday, I was walking around the office like the cat who swallowed the canary. I had a great date with a guy I was really falling for and I might have saved the day with Leon and helped to create a whole new sound.

I was sauntering back from the copy room when I saw Michael turn the corner and head toward me. I turned on my heel, trying to scoot away before he realized it was me.

"Jill Dodge!" he called out to me. "I see you. Stop right there, young lady!" He caught up with me.

"Hey, Michael, thanks for feeding me to the jackals last week. It was so fun to have to wrestle with a horny middle-aged divorced guy," I said sarcastically as I turned to face him.

He pulled me into the empty Admin Pit and leaned in close. "Don't give me that. That's not why you were runnin' just now. I just got off the phone with Leon. What are you doing?"

"I'm trying to save Leon's ass!" I said emphatically. "More than you are doing."

"Why do you think I should give a rat's ass about Leon's ass anyway? You think I should be his best friend because we're both black and . . . what? Went to the same school? Are you best friends with every short girl from your high school?"

"Look, are you going to get mad at me because I came up with a plan, an actual good idea to try to make this work?" Now it was my turn to give him that bug-eyed expression. "What did Leon tell you?"

Michael sighed. "He said that you all went to see a drug dealer in the worst part of Queens in the middle of the night! Are you tryin' to get yourself killed?"

"Nothing happened! And Cookie's not a drug dealer. He just happens to live in the same building with a drug dealer . . . or two, but it's not his fault. It's just a mistake of birth location. Apparently, that's what happens sometimes when you grow up in certain parts of Queens."

"Who are you? The Florence Nightingale of the projects?"

"Hey, I sacrificed the first official date of my adult life for this," I explained, poking his lapel with my finger, "and you don't even seem to care what came out of it, do you? The date was actually going quite well at the time, too!"

He grabbed my fist, engulfing it in his big hand, leaving only the bitten-down nail of my index finger exposed. "OK, then, what came out of it?"

"Shandra and Jackson took us over there to talk to Cookie. That is all. Cookie and Jackson are cousins. What you don't understand is that Cookie is the one with the poetic talent! But Leon? Leon's rap is so-so and he knows it. He has the musical arrangements and the voice."

Michael bugged his eyes at me, in his personal sign of disbelief, releasing my balled-up fist.

"He can really sing!" I informed him.

"What are you talking about?"

"Leon has charisma, good looks, ego, personality AND I heard him singing a crooning ballad that night when they had that fight at the studio. It was beautiful. You are the one who showed me that he's an actor with your high school yearbook."

Michael glanced down at his hands.

"Meanwhile, Cookie is the writer. He has the rhymes. And he was open to the idea, but he's also suspicious, which frankly I don't blame him."

"All right, let's start from the beginning, shall we?" he said in a show of exaggerated ultra-patience. "What, exactly, happened?"

"We went over there with Jackson and Shandra."

"Went where?"

"To Cookie's apartment. He lives with his mom and ten-year-old sister. His mom is really nice. Mrs. Davis. They bake these amazing cookies."

"Are you joking?"

"No, she and Cookie bake cookies at home and sell them through local food trucks and delis. That's how he got that nickname. His real name is Mark."

"Jill . . ."

"Some of them are Cookie's recipes. They have this oatmeal kind, but instead of raisins, it has dried cranberries and these big pieces of chocolate bar. They're amazing."

Michael could hardly contain his exasperation. He wiped the length of his face with his open palm. I was kind of enjoying it.

"Calm down," I told him. "All we did was talk to him about teaming up with Leon. Cookie writes the rap, and Leon sings most of it. Onstage, he would basically be the sideman. He doesn't like all the attention of being in the spotlight anyway. And Whiskey stays in as the DJ. And," I added, "his mom liked the idea, too."

"What about Kenny?"

"What *about* Kenny?"

"Did you let him in on this little experiment?"

I paused. I had totally avoided the concept of Kenny in my thought process. Both Kenny and Michael were willing to throw

Leon to the dogs, just to get their short-term gain. I was not sure I wanted to let Kenny in on this just yet. Besides, I was pretty sure that Kenny would try to make it look like his idea if it worked.

"Don't you think we should see if the music is good first?"

Michael seemed to chew on the inside of his cheek, silent.

"This is not gonna be 'gangsta,'" he finally said.

"Well . . . it might be . . ."

"Leon is a prep school math whiz and you just told me this Cookie kid bakes cookies with his mama! Does that sound low-down to you?"

I bit my lip. "LaKeisha can spin it?"

"No matter how she spins it, if they try to come up with raps about gunnin' and crack, it's going to sound like shit."

"Wait a minute." I suddenly realized something. "Why was Leon calling you?"

A guilty look passed over Michael's face.

"We been talking," he mumbled.

"What? Sorry, I didn't hear that?"

"We've been talking. All right? I was gone last week after . . . your problem . . . because I went out to Jersey to see his people."

"His people?"

"Yeah, his mom and dad."

I pursed my lips and folded my arms, staring at him hard.

Michael suddenly sighed. "The kid's got too big of an ego. He needs a hand, that's all."

So my words had gotten through to him in the limo that day. He was looking out for little Leon.

"So maybe the sound doesn't wind up alongside N.W.A.?" I said. "Maybe it'll be better, something completely new? I still think that putting them together is better than what Leon and Whiskey did on their own. They were falling apart in the studio because they both knew Leon was a poser. Living a lie doesn't work."

"Well, it looks like they want to try it your way," Michael finally gave in, but added, "But we'll have to let Kenny in on it."

"Let them get a track down before we spring this on Kenny. He's the one that wanted to keep up the charade. We can convince him and the higher-ups if there is something good to show. Their imagination doesn't extend that far."

"All right," Michael agreed.

I felt relieved and scared at the same time.

"And if it doesn't work, remember, it was *your* idea." He did his bug-eyed look at me.

I sighed. My stomach bunched up again at the thought of the gamble that I was making. "Yup, and my big career in the music biz will have ended before it started," I agreed. "And if it *does* work, do I have your word that was *my* idea, too?"

He cocked his head to the side with a toothy smile.

"Yes, ma'am," he assured me.

"We are on the same page then?" I put my hand out, Texas home-style, for him to shake.

"Same page." He shook my hand quickly as we heard a couple of administrative assistants talking in the hall on their way into the Admin Pit.

Then he suddenly shot down the hallway in the opposite direction. I scanned the desk I was standing in front of and asked, "Were there any messages for me?"

I HAD TO MAKE IT UP TO ALEJANDRO FOR DRAGGING HIM AROUND AS my personal schemer and bodyguard during a first date. Now we were officially "a couple" to our friends in the office, although we still did not want to flaunt it. Alejandro and I agreed no PDA in the building, especially after we were caught in an embrace in the copy room by none other than LaKeisha. What an embarrassing moment. Her scorn could be heard all the way down the hall.

So we agreed—no hand-holding, smooching, hugging, or anything like that. No. We were going to behave in a professional manner. Like grown-ups.

Meanwhile, I invited him over to the apartment on Wednesday night to make up for our date being cut short. My brand-new VCR machine and several videos from the publicity department's promotional closet acted as the excuse.

On the way to my apartment, we stopped at a deli to get some dinner. The minute we were inside the door of my building, Alejandro dropped the plastic bag with our lo mein in it and grabbed me. We necked against the mailboxes in the narrow entranceway.

I kept looking toward the door and hoping in the back of my mind that Luann was not home.

"Hold it! Wait a minute!" I giggled, grabbing up our dinner bag. "Necking makes me hungry!"

"After you." He motioned toward the stairs, and I started the long climb up.

"So that is a perk for a 'gentleman,' huh?" I joked over my shoulder.

"Hmmm?"

"You seem to have the perfect view of my posterior, sir, when the lady goes first!"

"Chivalry has its advantages, yes," he mused. "It helps that you are wearing those jeans!"

Luann sat on the couch opening mail when we came in. Earlier in the day, I called her at work to let her know that I was bringing him home. I begged her from my desk to hers for her to get home early, clean up the front room, and make my bed. It looked like she did it.

"Hey," she said, jumping up.

"Hi! Luann, this is Alejandro. Alejandro, Luann."

They shook hands.

"I've heard a lot about you," she said to him.

"And I about you." He was so formal, but then added, "It's nice to meet you close-up, instead of from the sidewalk."

Luann actually blushed a little bit, probably recalling the condom in the sock, which still sat, unused, inside Joanie's purse inside my date-bought blue purse, which was on my nightstand.

I saved us both from her flashback by offering dinner. "We brought some Chinese food. You want some?" We headed into the kitchen for plates and serving utensils.

"Yeah, sure." She followed us into the kitchen, giving Alejandro the once-over.

These moments were always so awkward. Old buddies meeting new boyfriends. New boyfriends coming over for the first time. We were all still in the getting-to-know-you phase. Just because you liked someone didn't mean your friends would like them. I'd learned that the hard way. It was good to go one friend at a time. If Alejandro won Luann over first, then the others would be more open.

After we ate, Luann suddenly announced that she was leaving.

"I'm meeting some friends for drinks," she pointedly said. I knew what that meant. I could already see Joanie and Alyssa sitting at Hancock's waiting with bated breath to hear that she had left me alone with a man in our apartment.

Oh, the scandal!

After she left, I started to go through the videos that I had hauled out of the office in my bag.

"You want to watch the 'British Invasion Collection' or the 'Southern Rock Collection'?" I asked him.

"They both sound fine. Is there anything in there that is not music videos? Any movies?"

I brought them all out and began to lay them on the coffee table.

"Well, I picked through a box of catalog and traded videos at work, so maybe not."

I stopped and looked at him.

"I never thanked you for being such a good sport about cutting our date short on Saturday. I mean, you helped me out a lot with Shandra and Jackson. And coming with me all the way to Queens."

"It was interesting. Besides, I wasn't going to let you go off with them all alone."

"Why, don't you think I could handle myself?"

"Yeah, but . . . that was a bad neighborhood, you have to admit. You sure are committed to your job."

I studied him for sarcasm, but did not see it anywhere.

I held up a videocassette. "Here is the box set of all the episodes of *Hill Street Blues*!"

"Not my favorite."

I put the box on the coffee table and kept rummaging in the bag.

"So, San Diego? You grew up there?" I asked him.

"Yup. I'm going back for vacation in a couple of weeks. Seeing my parents and my brother."

He picked up the box set of the TV series, studying the back of it and shaking his head.

"Why don't you like that show? I always thought it was all right."

"The same story over and over. The bald guy is always right. The black man always has a gun. Then there's the Mexican with a knife." He pantomimed a classic stance of a gang fight à la *West Side Story*.

I laughed at the exaggerated mean-face he made.

Alejandro put the box back down. "I mean, at least the black thug gets some firepower." He laughed it off, but I could see some of the bitterness coming through.

"Aha," I said. "Here is one. *Tommy*. The Who. Music video and movie in one. Ever seen it?"

"Yes, but I'd see it again."

I handed him the brochure from inside the video sleeve. There were photos from the movie, the band, Tina Turner.

I put the video in the player and sat on the couch. He plopped down next to me as the sound started up and the FBI copyright warning appeared on the TV.

Again, the new boyfriend awkwardness came back. His leg paralleled mine as we sat there, side by side on the puffy couch. He inched closer. I leaned my shoulder into his. I didn't pay any attention to Roger Daltrey's blond curls because I could not focus enough on the TV screen. Within five minutes, we were kissing again.

Alejandro pushed me down into the cushion and his hands reached up to caress my hair. I pulled him toward me with my hands along his muscular back. We wrestled to keep from falling off of the couch.

"Ow!" I suddenly yelped. A lock of my hair had lodged in his wristwatch, yanking it from my scalp.

"Oh, sorry." He tried to pull his hand back, but the strands of red and brown entangled in the tiny knobs on the James Bond–style gadget.

I cried out again as he pulled my hair. My head followed the movement of his wrist, and I wound up bumping his nose with my forehead. Now it was his turn to say "ouch!"

"Wait. Stop. Don't move at all!" I cried. We both froze. He examined how my hair wrapped around his watch.

He unbuckled the band of the watch and it fell from his wrist. That part of my hair was too short for me to see the watch, so he did his best to detangle it from my hair without making me bald.

We both talked at the same time. "If you just gently pull it out . . ." "No, I've got it. I just need to unwrap here . . ."

He finally gave up, checking my face for levels of pain or exasperation. I slumped down in the cushion with the watch dangling off my head next to my cheek.

This was not a good start to a romantic evening. There was a beat as he looked at me with a puppy-dog expression.

"This could become the next big teen fashion," I finally said, trying to make light of the situation. "You can tell the time by just rolling your eyes!"

We both laughed. At least that was a good sign. Then he got serious again.

"We might need scissors," he announced solemnly.

I went to the bathroom and took a pair of hairdresser scissors out of a drawer. Alejandro followed me right in. We stood in front of the mirror, and he gently tried again to remove my hair from the watch dials. His coordinated fingers moved delicately along the strands of hair like he was a surgeon fixing a broken heart. He concentrated on the task, just as I had seen him do with his computers, his face in clear focus on the small items in front of him.

My hair was just like all the wires and chips he worked with every day. He stood so close to me that I could feel the rise and fall of his chest all along the side of my body and shoulder. I wondered if I would finally see that chest tonight or not.

Most of the hair finally shook loose. Our eyes met in the reflection.

"You're being a good sport about this," he said.

"It's not over yet, is it? I'll be less of a good sport depending on how it looks after the shearing."

I reached up and quickly cut the final strands of hair, and the watch dropped into his hand.

He shoved it in his pocket and reached his arm around me, pulling me to him just like he did when we were on the street in front of the purse vendor. Maybe I could not see his chest, but at the moment, I could definitely feel it and I felt some other things too. The embrace lasted for a long time and we began moving as we kissed, out of the bathroom, through the living room, and into my bedroom. We fell in a heap on the bed as I reached for my blue purse.

TWENTY-THREE

WHILE I HAD SPENT THE WEEKEND WHISPERING IN THE EAR OF MY new boyfriend, Michael had spent it whispering in the ears of Whiskey Fizz and Robert Washington. Apparently, Whiskey was all for bringing Cookie in and even came up with a catchy name for them: Professor T and the Cookie Monster.

Things were finally coming together in both my personal life and my career. I could hardly believe it. I floated around the Berber-carpeted halls of our building for the early part of the week.

When I hurriedly entered my office for the fifth time on Thursday, there was someone sitting at my desk. The chair was swiveled with its back to me, and whoever was sitting in it was inspecting my CD collection on the back wall shelf.

"Excuse me?" I asked the trespasser.

The head of long, dark hair popped up. Jonathan's chiseled cheekbones and Irish blue eyes turned toward me. My heart leapt into my throat.

"This CD collection sucks," he said with a sardonic grin. "Where is the Led Zeppelin?"

Seeing him sitting there, looking all cocky and cute, made my stomach lurch. It felt like I'd just been punched.

He leaned back in my chair and appraised me with a delighted expression. "Nice," he said. "Your own setup. That's pretty cool." He swung his feet onto the desk.

"You've got some nerve!" I barked, finally able to speak.

"Oh, Jill, c'mon. I didn't know Jacklyn called you like that. She's bonkers. Total."

"That didn't keep you from sleeping with her!"

"Aw, we were on the road. Nobody is attached on the road."

"Surely you could have come up with a better excuse than that."

The six feet of space in between us was like a running river. I could not wait to see the leaky raft he would try building to cross it. He put his feet back down and lifted his hands in the "be still" stance used to calm wild animals.

"All right. Okay. You're right, of course," he said, getting up slowly and moving around the desk. "I admit, I should have called you back. But man, we had a time in Austin. There were no phones around. I barely got home at all."

"How did you get back here?"

"The Reivers, a band from Austin." He started crossing the imaginary troubled waters between us. "They're touring the East Coast and gave me a ride in exchange for sound work until their guy wrapped up at South by Southwest. They're playing in Hoboken tomorrow night. Wanna go? You'll like them. They've got chicks in the band!"

He was looking me in the eye, the smile never leaving his lips.

"I don't think so," I sneered.

"Jill, really, it was a hard road trip." He paused. "You look good as usual."

My arms dangled at my sides as he moved closer. I didn't know what I was going to do. I wanted to hate him, but his wiry, disheveled cuteness brought on some kind of hormonal response that made me hesitate to throw him out of the office.

Which I definitely planned to do.

Any second now.

He stopped short suddenly, looking over my head. I felt another presence behind me. I turned to see Tony filling the doorway. His arms were crossed and his feet hunkered into the thin carpet. The two of them locked eyes and coldly acknowledged each other.

"Tony," Jonathan said with a nod.

"Jon," Tony said, then added, without moving his eyes from Jonathan, "Jill, we have a computer meeting in the conference room."

Then he walked off.

"Whoa!" Jonathan reacted by lunging at the doorframe and slapping the wall as he leaned out. "Nice talkin' to ya!" he called down the hall. Tony responded by silently flipping him the bird as he turned the corner.

"So is Tony into you now?" he asked obnoxiously.

"No," I answered, "but he knows a mistake when he sees one." I moved toward the desk, away from my spot by the doorway.

"Oh, ouch!" He mockingly grabbed at his chest. "That hurts."

"Well, 'ouch' to you, too."

"I'm sorry. I'm sorry."

Was he being sarcastic? The attitude was getting absurd.

I studied his face, thinking that there must have been a reason that I called him my boyfriend for so long. When he wanted to be charming, he was. He was a salesman. That was it. I had been the willing customer, sold a bill of goods that turned out to be worthless.

"Why, exactly, are you here?" I asked.

"I live here."

"Ugh! Quit playing. I mean, 'here'—in my office?"

His shoulders relaxed into a tired slump.

"Looky, I want to make up!"

I regarded him skeptically.

"You and me," he continued, "between the two of us, we're in the back room all over the city. It's 'rock 'n' roll!'"

I crossed my arms and leaned back on my desk. "Yeah, that's really convenient and all, but I don't like getting dicked around."

"Hey," his voice softened. "We're good together, when we *are* together. Isn't that enough?"

"Not really."

He was close enough now that I could smell his aftershave, which meant he had actually shaved before coming to see me. His white T-shirt was clean. He had primped for this.

"Did it ever occur to you that I might be seeing someone else by this time?" I asked.

He stepped up to me and leaned his chest onto my still-crossed forearms, completely ignoring what I just said.

"Jilligan, Jilligan," he cooed. "We do a lot of great things together."

I was not exactly resisting as much as I should. His arms snaked my waist and he gently leaned his hips against mine.

"I don't know, Jonathan." I had already let my guard down too much.

He leaned in, trying to kiss me on the lips. I abruptly turned my head so that his smooch ended up somewhere near my ear. He used the opportunity and kissed down my neck. My folded forearms still blocked his chest from touching mine. I closed my eyes, trying to decide how long to let this go on.

"C'mon," he said between pecks. "You're a rockin' chick. Isn't that all about the sex?"

I stiffened and my eyes flew wide open.

"What did you just say?"

He leaned back with his arms around my waist. "Rock 'n' roll? Sex?" he offered. "I didn't say drugs. I could throw in gin though, just for you." He had felt me tense up though and asked, suddenly confused, "What?"

I stared at him, taking in the concept of the label—"rockin' chick." Here he was, using the exact same words as Ronald to get me into bed, based on . . . what? A label that came from my taste in music and my outfit. It was extrapolated into an entire persona that I was not—some hard-drinking slut with no scruples whatsoever.

As I processed this, I put both of my hands on his chest and began to push him away. I looked around the room, trying to make sense of what I was allowing to happen here.

Suddenly, Alejandro's face appeared in the doorway.

He saw Jonathan and me seemingly in an embrace, even though I was in the action of pushing him away. Alejandro's face clouded, his eyebrows knitted, and his cheeks flushed. Then he was gone.

I shoved Jonathan hard. He stumbled backward, losing his balance. I flew out into the hallway in time to see Alejandro turn the corner. I ran after him, almost crashing into Jenny as she stepped out of her office.

"What's going on?"

I pointed back toward my office and gasped, "Jonathan," then pointed in the direction where I was going and said, "Alejandro . . ." and then kept going.

She got the gist of the situation and headed toward my office. By the time I got to reception, I didn't know which way Alejandro had gone. Sheila saw the expression on my face. She pointed out into the hall toward the elevator banks.

I bolted to the elevator in time to stick my hand into the closing doors. It reopened.

Alejandro stood in the corner of the elevator like a statue. His hands were in fists down by his hips. I jumped into the elevator as the doors closed. The two of us were trapped there together.

"It's not what you think," I said. My heart pounded in my ears.

"You don't know what I think." His jaw barely moved with the statement.

I stayed three feet away from him, realizing that I did not have any idea how he was when angry. Geez, it was a dumb idea to run after him.

His chest heaved. His eyes hardened on me.

"I don't appreciate getting played, Jill," he said too evenly. His eyes flitted over the floor buttons looking for an out. There was a little electronic readout of the floors we were passing. Twenty-two, twenty-one . . .

"He's my ex." I rushed as the numbers descended. "He's a jerk. He was trying to convince me to take him back."

Twelve, eleven, ten . . .

"I'm not . . . I am totally done with him," I fumbled.

"I know who he was. It didn't look like anything was 'ex' to me." He knew who he was? How? Ugh! Tony!

"I'm not a player, Alejandro, honestly."

Four, three . . .

"I should have known better than to fall for some . . . rocker," he said, almost to himself.

One.

He brushed gruffly past me out of the opened elevator doors into the lobby.

I started to follow him. There it was again. He was not even giving me a chance to explain! If he would just look at me! But he was walking away.

It wasn't fair. I didn't do anything wrong. My cool was officially lost.

"Fine," I yelled. He wouldn't hear what I was saying anyhow. "You go ahead and think that! It's not real. I live in fucking 3-D!" People who had been minding their own business on their way through the lobby turned to look at me. I continued, "You're a jerk, too! You think you own me because of one weekend? What kind of Mexican macho shit is that?"

He stopped and turned to face me. His expression had changed from anger to some other kind of upset that was all too familiar.

"Don't. Follow. Me. Jill." He turned and stalked off, out of the revolving doors.

I stood rooted to the shiny floor as he disappeared into the sidewalk crowd.

TWENTY-FOUR

FIVE HOURS LATER, I PACED THE FLOOR IN MY SMALL LIVING ROOM.

"This sucks. This is so stupid. I cannot believe how stupid this is," I said.

"Just call him," Jessica ordered from inside the speakerphone on the coffee table.

"I did call him. He hasn't answered his phone. I don't even know if he went home."

Jenny and Luann were sitting at the kitchen table, quietly watching me wear a hole in the frayed carpet.

"I have no idea where to even look for him."

"I cannot believe you used the words 'macho Mexican,'" Luann scolded me for the tenth time. "Seriously, you know better than that."

"I know. I know. I know." I threw my butt down onto my fancy couch and put my head in my hands.

"Look, you just have to wait until you get to the office to-morrow," Jessica's canned voice advised. "I've got to go. Ara's got homework, and I've got to get dinner started. Are you going to be all right?"

"We've got her," Jenny announced.

"OK, well, call me tomorrow." Jessica hung up the phone.

I leaned back on the couch and began to jiggle my knee.

START WITH THE BACKBEAT

Luann and Jenny looked at each other.

We sat there for a minute with the air growing thick. Jenny got up and went into the kitchen and came back with three juice glasses and a bottle of tequila. In the silence, we watched her pour a shot into each glass and hand one to each of us.

"Salut," she said and drank. We all did.

Suddenly the phone rang. Luann visibly jumped as I dove for it.

"Hello?" I eagerly answered.

"Get in a cab and get over here to Clinton's." It took me a second to figure out that the voice belonged to Michael. "Your little experiment is about to hit the fan."

JENNY CAME WITH ME. WE HEADED OUT THE DOOR AND ACROSS TOWN. As we got out of the taxi at the recording studios, I saw Cookie, Shandra, and Jackson standing against the brick facade.

"They won't let Cookie in on account of what happened last time," Shandra informed me the second she saw my face.

"I don't know why the fuck I'm here," Cookie said, insecure about his role.

Jackson put his hand on the larger man's forearm. "C'mon, man, this is your chance." Jackson was gentle with the hulk of a guy that was leaning against the wall. "Seriously, cut the shade, cuz."

"Don't worry." I assured them that Michael and Leon were on their way over. Then we could all go in together.

Cookie let out a frustrated sigh. I wasn't sure what to say, so instead, I introduced Jenny to them.

There was a pause as we all looked at each other.

"So." Jenny tried to break the ice. "You grew up in Queens?"

Cookie leaned back against the wall. "Yeah."

"I'm from Jersey."

227

"Hmm," he said, looking her up and down.

Then nothing. We stood there for another moment in silence.

"Here," Cookie said abruptly, holding out a paper gift bag that was closed with a pink ribbon and had a tissue paper spilling out the top. "Mom sent you these."

"Oh, thanks! That's so sweet."

"They's the chocolate chunk and some kind of nuts. You ain't allergic or nuthin'?"

"No, wow. I love that," I said, showing the bag off to Jenny. She nodded in amusement, glancing over at Cookie.

He stared down at the concrete sidewalk, obviously embarrassed. Baked goods were not very "street."

I opened the bag and pulled out a huge cookie, then tilted the bag toward Shandra, who delightedly reached in and took one.

A cab pulled up at that moment and Michael, Whiskey, and Leon got out of it. I was beginning to feel whiter and shorter with each passing second.

We approached the reception area like an army, with Leon and Michael in the lead. They checked in with the receptionist. The security guys, with their slicked-back hair and dark jackets, stood around, conspicuous on purpose, eyeing us.

"Hi, how ya doin'? Hey there," Michael greeted them each individually, smiling all the way, as he led us all through the glass doors into the hallway. It was a little bizarre.

In the studio, the producer, who I'd never seen until now, was already in the control room with an engineering assistant.

"What are we doing here?" he asked.

Michael and Leon went into the control room and closed the door. Whiskey picked up an electric guitar and started playing riffs. He fiddled with the knobs on the amplifier and created odd sounds and reverb. The rest of us milled around in the studio, stealing furtive looks through the soundproof glass into the control room.

Michael and Leon were animated as they explained themselves to the producer. He was nodding, looking out at us, eyeing Cookie, then nodding again.

Eventually, Michael sat down on the couch behind the soundboard and Leon came out into the studio.

"OK," he said. "He's on board."

Cookie and Leon appraised each other.

"So?" Cookie said, finally. "Are we gonna do this thing or what?"

MY OFFICE WALL APPEARED TO PULSE. THE TOP OF MY DESK WAS A garbage dump of spent fast-food bags and dirty paper coffee cups. The past few days blurred in my head.

Cookie, Whiskey, Leon, and the producer were eating and sleeping at the studio. Michael and I took turns taking in food and taking away snippets of the sound. There was a song track in there somewhere. More than one, actually. But they wouldn't let me hear the whole thing until it was done. There was nothing I could do but provide cover and wait.

Jenny and Tony ran interference for us with Kenny and everyone else at the office on Friday and most of this morning. They told them we were at the copy machine or in the bathroom, that they had just seen one of us down the hall, while we snuck in and out of the building all day and evening. I spent most of the weekend at Clinton's, lurking around the periphery like a scullery maid, catching only a few hours of sleep each night, worrying about what else was happening in that dim studio. This was what it must be like for the father-to-be during baby gestations and deliveries—feeling useless yet needed.

I shuffled the crumpled burger wrappers on my desktop aside to see My Gordon.

"Is this normal?" I asked him.

He squinted at me with empathy. Surely, the creative spark was not always this hard? Finding a true voice crying out in the city was tough enough. What would happen if you roughed it up too much or coddled it too much? Either way, you might kill it. Like with all living things, the most dangerous time was when it was young.

As if the weekend had not been stressful enough, Sunday afternoon, while Michael and I sat in the lobby of Clinton's, trying to figure out how to tell Kenny about what we were doing, Jonathan popped up out of thin air and sat down on the pleather couch right next to us.

"How the hell did you get in here?" Michael demanded, jumping up from the couch like a spider just crawled onto the cushion.

"My friend Joe is an engineering intern here," he answered with confidence.

Like I said, Jonathan had a handle on the entire bottom of New York City, affording him entrance into every club, restaurant, and apparently, recording studio. I wondered where else he could suddenly appear.

Michael took on the air of a Secret Service agent. He stood two feet away, arms crossed, feet apart, just watching, as I explained to Jonathan that we were no longer a couple.

Jonathan was genuinely miffed.

"I don't get it," he said. "You would rather go out with this geek from nowhere than with me?"

I had to expound on the idea that there was a little more to it than that, like, y'know, him sleeping around? He was confused, but not exactly heartbroken.

Just like him.

In the end, he went out to get all of us Chinese takeout and even brought me an extra fortune cookie. The fortune inside read, "Seek allies among the enemies you know well." That said just about everything I needed to know.

Now, at one o'clock on Monday afternoon, the whole thing was catching up with me.

I stared blankly at the vibrating blue screen of the computer monitor. The computers were on in individual offices, but I had yet to send or receive an electronic mail file.

Just touching the keyboard made me think of Alejandro. The vision of his angry face from days ago came back to me like a bad LSD flashback—or at least what I thought might be like a bad LSD trip, seeing as I had never taken LSD. Had it already been three whole days since that moment?

He was unreachable over the weekend and I had not seen him today in the office. *One thing at time*, I told myself. But really, I simply didn't have the guts to face him, explain myself, and beg forgiveness. I needed to do something nice for him if I wanted to make up. I looked to My Gordon. He observed me with concern. It suddenly occurred to me that there was an old box of promo cassette tapes in the closet behind my former desk. I vaguely recalled there being some Pink Floyd in there. I jumped up from my seat, checking back to My Gordon's photo for confirmation of action.

He seemed to approve.

I could start with a music bribe for Alejandro, then move on to groveling.

I headed over to the Admin Pit where the interns and admins had cleared out for lunch. Making my way to the back corner, I squeezed behind the chair of my old desk to the cabinet. I had to reach up on tippy-toes to hook my index finger around the edge of the box, which was positioned on the very top shelf. At that moment, the printer beeped and began printing, startling me and making my hand jerk. The box tipped and cassette tapes rained down on my head, bouncing off my shoulders and scattering all over the floor. I dropped down to my knees between the chair and the desk to retrieve them. As my head ducked under the desktop to reach the scattered tapes, I heard Tony's voice enter the Admin Pit.

"It's printing out here," he called back down the hall, his voice full of frustration. I was about to pop up and say "boo!" to him, when I heard a second voice.

Alejandro.

"That's not right," he was saying as he caught up with Tony a mere five feet away from where I crouched. "It should be connected to the printer by Sheila's desk."

I froze like an ice sculpture.

I could hear Alejandro scraping the printer around on the table as Tony berated him.

"Well, Paco? You got it all mixed up! Just like your love life."

Alejandro sighed loudly.

I turned and parked my butt on the floor under the desk, so I was hidden. I silently folded my body and legs into a "C" shape in the opening of the desk well. A hard plastic cassette tape case jammed against my jeans, denting the flesh underneath, but I held my breath and didn't move.

"Yeah, well," Alejandro said. "It turns out that both ended up more complicated than I predicted. The wiring in this old building goes every which way, just like the whims of a woman."

"Very poetic," Tony responded in a skeptical tone. "But Jill doesn't have 'whims.' She's the most straightforward chick I know. With her, you get what she has. And in your case, she's handing out a lot. She really digs you, man."

Aww, Tony was sticking up for me. How sweet.

I heard the sound of the printer door clicking. Alejandro must be opening the machine.

"'Digs me,'" Alejandro repeated without inflection. "So that is why she is calling me racist names?"

"What, do you think she's prejudiced?" Tony snorted. "Yeah, that's right. That's why one of her best friends is a black guy. That and the fact that she even looked at your skinny ass in the first place. You think she'd be putting herself on the line for the likes of Leon and Cookie if she had an ounce of racism in her? Hotheaded? Yeah. Racist? No."

There was a beat and I could hear there was more fiddling with the printer.

"You're probably right," Alejandro mumbled.

Tony continued, "She's looking for the real thing. And she deserves it. You got the balls for the real thing, Don Juan? Or are you messing with her?"

"Huh? Me messing with *her*? What about her messing with me?" Alejandro retorted.

"How so?" Tony shot back.

Alejandro asked, "What is all that going on with her old boyfriend?"

"She's finally got his number and it's in the negative. That dude is poison and you, amigo, are the antidote."

"If you think Jill is so wonderful, why aren't you going out with her?"

There was a pregnant pause. I could imagine the grimace on Tony's face as he answered, "It'd be like dating my little sister. Yeah, she acts all hard on the outside, but inside, she's a big marshmallow."

Another pause, then the short slam of the printer door clicking shut.

They must be facing each other. I tilted my toes toward my face to keep my calf from cramping. I needed to move my leg, but could not risk making noise.

"And speaking of Leon and Cookie, this whole thing with them?" Alejandro went on. "Does she have to be so involved? Why her?"

"Because it's her job and she does it with passion. That's what you liked about her in the first place! Why do you have your mitts on those stupid satellite phones and all these goddamn machines?"

I heard his calloused knuckles rap the plastic of the printer as he spoke. "It's the same crap. You afraid of a woman with some passion in her?"

Silence.

Alejandro sighed again.

Was that a good sigh or a bad sigh? Was he shaking his head? Or giving in? I couldn't tell. There was no way to know since I could not see him. I wedged down a little to look through a crack in the wood of the desk back, but could only catch a glimpse of Tony's Converse sneaker.

Alejandro's voice came in a little softer this time. "Yeah, she's passionate. About her career—but where does that leave me?"

He sighed again, then said somewhat slower, "And I do 'dig' her too. I think I am falling hard."

I almost gasped.

Tony chewed on this revelation for a moment, then went in for the kill.

"You're a fucking idiot if you think you could find another girl like her willing to be with a geek like you. Have you taken a gander in the mirror, buddy? The supernerd act here ain't getting you nowhere. And on top of it, you are a shrimp." As he went on, his voice cracked a little. "You gonna be home making love to your circuit boards, all alone. Like my grandma always says, you'd better get while the gettin's good and that is now!"

Wow, Tony was getting all emotional.

There was another pause and I heard Tony start to move away.

Alejandro seemed to follow, saying under his breath, "Who was the marshmallow again?"

I realized how far up I had scrunched my shoulders in an effort to remain still. Since Tony and Alejandro were now gone, I relaxed and allowed my cramped limbs to spill out from under the desktop. I pulled the cassette out from where it was wedged into my hip. Pink Floyd's *The Wall* demos—a famous bootleg tape hidden among all the B-side bands in the back of the closet. See? Sometimes, it helps to be one of those at the bottom.

TWENTY-FIVE

WRAPPED IN BLACK PAPER AND A BLOOD-RED RIBBON, THE LITTLE package was burning a hole in my jacket pocket. It was obviously a cassette tape. I didn't write a note or anything. What was I going to write that didn't sound cheesy? I'd have to say it when the time was right.

I actually did have to do something that resembled work. The computers were on in the individual offices, but they still were not connected to each other for sending e-mail or files. I sat, trying to catch my breath, when I realized that I still had to take a finished schedule for another act to Jenny. So I fumbled around in the top drawer of my desk, pulling out one of the floppy disks that looked like a square black envelope of thick paper. I figured I would just save the file and walk it over to her. I turned on the computer.

It whizzed and buzzed, but I could not be sure of life until I saw the little green blinking cursor on the monitor screen. I worked the floppy disk into the computer's flat slot and followed my scratched out instructions from a pink memo sheet where I had written down how to save a file.

The computer made a "dink" noise, indicating the file was saved. If only I could be "saved" so easily. I pushed the button to eject the disk. I gingerly held it in my slightly shaky hand and made my way down the hall into Jenny's office.

As I walked in, I heard her saying, "No! I tried that! I swear, I did exactly that, but then the screen went blank."

She sat there staring at her computer screen, seemingly talking to it. I could not register what I was seeing until I heard Alejandro's voice coming from the floor on the other side of her desk.

"Try it now," he commanded.

I froze. I was not mentally prepared for this yet. His face popped up from behind the corner of the computer monitor. He saw me before I could back out of the room undetected.

"Ah!" Jenny exclaimed. "It worked!"

Then she noticed me stiffly standing there.

Her look quickly moved back to Alejandro, who also seemed locked in stiffness.

"Oh, for God's sake!" she said loudly. "Just make up already and get it over with. I can't stand this."

She got up and stalked past me out the door, closing it behind her. I reached for the knob and tried to pull, but the door didn't budge. She must have been standing on the other side of the door holding it shut.

I sighed.

Loudly.

Meanwhile, Alejandro stood up from his place on the floor, a place where he seemed to spend an awful lot of time.

I turned back to him, noting that he had not moved from the far end of the desk. I stepped forward to my end of the desk and gently tossed the floppy disk onto it.

"I brought that for Jenny," I offered, searching his face.

He just nodded. I gathered up my breath.

"I'm so sorry!" I gushed. "You walked in at the exact moment that he tried to kiss me. I was pushing him away. Really! He was the one that cheated on me and we weren't even that tight to begin with and then I got mad again because he assumed that I would take him back, that I'd jump at the chance to sleep with him, just because I'm . . . I'm a 'rock chick' and then you said the same, exact thing, which is the same thing that my personal creep from New Jersey said, and I lashed out at you about it and I'm sorry. So, so sorry I insulted you in the exact same way."

There. I drew in my breath.

Alejandro just stood there, coolly still. I couldn't tell if he had even heard anything I had just said. He stared at me. It was like he was in a trance.

Finally he said, "Are you done?"

"Um, yes." I folded my hands in front of me. I felt a hot blush rush up to my cheeks.

"I know exactly who that guy was," he started. "I also know that I am not like him in any way, shape, or form. If you want a guy like that, then you don't want me."

"I know that," I answered sheepishly.

"I'm not a 'player,' Jill. I'm not trying to crash into fame. I'm quiet and uncomplicated."

"And smart," I added for him.

"I know who I am and it's not a caricature from a Frito commercial. You'll have to settle for honest and steady."

"Yes, of course. That's what I like about you."

Our eyes met and his shoulders relaxed a little. I didn't know exactly what else I could say, so I tilted my head, did a little shrug, and tried to smile.

"Oh." I remembered my gift. "And I found you this!"

I held out the wrapped tape.

He was tentative. He reached out to take the small package, but did not move toward me, so I had to take a small step forward for him to reach it. We remained three feet apart.

He was just staring at the object in his hand and thinking.

He said simply, "I need a little time."

I slumped. Then I recalled what he had said to Tony earlier. This was going to work. I knew he liked me, and now, he was measuring his words, protecting himself.

"I'll make time," I assured him. And this time, I was the one to cross the waters.

The kiss was not full of passion. It was a vulnerable peck on the lips. Both of us feeling and wanting the warmth, but, again, this was a new thing, easy to snuff out with one wrong move.

But then, he put his arms around me and we just stood there in a long embrace, leaning into each other.

He finally pulled away. "I really don't want to be mad," he said. "Let's just rest on it for a day or so, OK?"

This was new. Thoughtful. I would even call it mature! But I had to get in one last thing, however corny it might come out.

"I really like you, Alejandro."

"I really like you, Jill."

There was a silent moment.

"OK, then, we'll make up all the way tomorrow?"

"Tuesdays are good for that," he answered, with a hint of a smile.

He moved passed me and yanked at the doorknob. This time it offered no resistance. People scattered away on the other side like cockroaches. It was like turning on the light in a dirty Texas kitchen at midnight. Jenny stood in the hallway, feigning impatience to get back into her office, but Michael headed away in one direction and Tony in the other. And I even saw LaKeisha's ponytail bobbing away at the end of the hall.

Alejandro's cheeks flushed and he put his head down as he scurried past Jenny.

"Show is over!" I said to her. "I left the schedule on your desk." I walked away, hopeful.

LATER, I DID A TOUR AROUND THE FLOOR OF THE BUILDING TO SEE IF Alejandro was still around. It was technically "after business hours." In regular businesses, the workday actually ended. People were on their way home for the evening. In my current world, especially this week, time was a matter of opinion.

Of course, he was not here. He had left for the day, like a normal, working person.

I wound up in Tony's office, where, as I expected, he sat at his desk with the phone still to his ear. He seemed to be listening more than he was talking, which was extremely unusual for him.

He motioned me into the room. I didn't spend much time in his office. It felt like entering the cave of a bear. He never had the overhead light on. There were a couple of dimly lit lamps on various surfaces. Heavy metal band posters, whose names all seemed to include the word "death" in them and whose members were all pictured in near-Renaissance clothing, haunted the walls. The vibe was dark and earthy with the feeling of impending doom.

Merely a few hours ago, he was waxing poetic about love, but you would think from the décor of his office that "love" was something he might be a bit cynical about.

He put his hand over the receiver, nodded toward the chair in front of his desk, and whispered to me, "Sit down."

I sat.

He turned back to his phone with an expression of consternation.

"Where are you, anyway?" he said into the phone. A pause. He looked at me. "OK, we'll be over there in a minute."

He hung up the phone and I smiled at him, like a stupid kid sister.

"You," he informed me, "are in deep shit."

TEN MINUTES LATER, WE WERE IN FRONT OF THE PARTY VENUE FROM Crystal's release reception. I was literally shaking in my boots. The fading light of the evening cast orange and purple reflections onto the brick building. The sidewalks were bare of humanity except for us. Again this area of Manhattan felt like a deserted warehouse district from the street, even while the rooms on the other side of the wall teemed with activity. Apparently, Kenny and Michael were here because of another industry cocktail hour and that was Kenny calling Tony from his brick phone a few minutes ago.

Before we could even enter the building, Michael came bounding out of the door, right up to me.

"Brace yourself!" he quickly warned me.

My wide eyes lost focus on him as Kenny rushed toward me right behind him, leaning down to my eye level and putting his nose an inch from mine.

"You are the one!" he hissed, his hot breath on my face.

That little red vein was popping out of his forehead, and I was sure he was about to lunge for me with both hands. Both Tony and Michael had stepped up on either side of him, ready to protect me.

I opened my mouth, but before I could get out a syllable, he was already raising his voice above my intention.

"What do you think you are doing? You little peon. You'll never work again in this industry. Who the hell do you think you are? You came here from a cow paddy in the sticks and think you can walk all over ME? ME?"

His whole body was a mass of tension. Any minute, he might spontaneously combust right in front of us. I stepped backward, feeling the cold sweat that had broken out under my hair take over my whole body. What was I supposed to say?

"Look, man," Michael jumped in, "take it easy. It's already done."

With that Kenny turned on him like a jackal defending his scraps. "NOTHING is done!" he shouted. "Nothing is done until I say it is done." Now he scooted toward Michael, sticking his finger out to wag it. He had to rise up to his full height and then up a little higher to get face-to-face with Michael.

"This is the end of my career, and yours, and yours." He pointed back at me. "Do you hear what I am saying here? We are all fired. Especially you, little Miss Punk! You're supposed to be tough, with your goddamn spiked bracelets and skinny legs! You're a fucking pushover for Leon and his charisma, like some kind of white trash!"

My cold sweat turned hot. That was enough! Kenny and his selfish, cheating attitude could kiss my ass. I finally found my voice. "Are you insane?" I asked, my voice higher in pitch than even I had heard it before. "It would have been worse if people found out after he was a hit! You can't just lie like that and get away with it." Now, I was yelling. "If you keep lying, you are going to get fired anyway! Just later! You're like a spoiled baby because you can't have your bottle right this instant!"

Kenny put his head in his hands and turned back toward the facade of the building.

Tony, Michael, and I all exchanged worried glances.

I followed Kenny toward the building. "Kenny, it's going to

work." I tried to sound assuring, which probably wasn't working since at that moment I pretty much hated him. That and also the fact that I was not exactly sure it would work, either. I gambled myself into this corner based solely on my personal morality. That was not a valued commodity in this business. I matched his step, back and forth between the curb and the building as he paced the sidewalk like a caged animal. "Everyone in the studio loves it," I said to him. "The producer loves it."

"It's not going to work! He's from New Jersey! He's rich! His father is a fucking dentist! That is not 'cool,' Jill." He made exaggerated finger quotes, his voice taking on a sardonic, patronizing tone. "That is not 'down.' That is not 'fly.' And on top of it, you don't even bring in a real street kid. No, you bring some baking Neanderthal. Mike Tyson in a fucking bread apron!"

I stopped in mid-pace and searched out Tony and Michael, who were just standing there watching as if Kenny and I were a TV show.

"Who told him? How did he find out?" I asked them.

There was a beat.

Michael finally said, "People in the studio are talking. Some session musician heard what they were doing and told his friends, who work for these guys." He motioned toward the door, indicating whatever band or label was in there having their party. "All of the musicians in there are talking about it . . . in a positive way."

"See!" I grabbed onto the straw. "Positive—that is a good thing."

"If they know, then their managers know. If their managers know, then their publicists know. And then everybody knows!" Kenny said, filling in the blanks that did not need to be filled in, still on his own train of thought.

I looked back at Tony, who seemed to be awfully quiet during this whole exchange.

Michael followed my gaze and turned to Tony now. "Well, what is your take on this thing?" he asked him.

We all stopped to wait for his answer, as if it might part the thunderclouds that were figuratively bearing down on us.

He shrugged and asked, "Is the music any good?"

TWENTY-SIX

THE HUGE POSTER OF CRYSTAL RENEAUX STARED AT ME FROM BEHIND Jenny's desk. A flowery autograph cascaded down the side of the ethereal photo: "To my breeze on top of the mountain, lovingly, Crystal."

"So are you, in particular, the 'breeze,' or does she write that on all of her autographs?"

Jenny looked up from the paper she held in her hands and rolled her eyes. "Apparently, I'm the only breeze. Leah is the 'dusky light.'"

"Hmmm," I mused, from my seat in front of her desk. "I wonder what she wrote on the senior VP's poster." I still had not told Jenny about the pornographic scene Alejandro and I had almost witnessed. I had kind of blocked it out of my memory until this moment. Trauma had a way of doing that, I'd heard.

We sat there, waiting.

Leon and Cookie were scheduled to come in this morning to present one of their tracks. I looked sort of businesslike today in the same royal blue silk blouse and black pants that I wore for the in-laws' Easter party. I knew I would have to talk in front of the senior vice president this morning. Well, that, and Michael had ordered me to appear like I could be taken seriously. Our task was to convince everyone that Cookie should be brought on the contract as cowriter.

Obviously Kenny's reaction last night had cut our excitement to the quick. After an hour or so, he had finally stopped yelling, at least. Then it took the rest of the evening to convince him that Leon, Cookie, and Whiskey could show us all how great they were. He put in a call from his ridiculous phone to the senior vice president, which led to the final ultimatum.

"Show me. Tomorrow morning. 9:00 a.m." was basically all the senior vice president had said. Then we scrambled over to the studio and made sure they could deliver. This was the exact reason we didn't tell Kenny in the first place. He would have squashed it.

Now, my career hung in the balance over the opinion of an old white guy and how much he thought the music would sell.

I sat facing Jenny's desk and jiggled my knee up and down. I noticed the cuticle of my thumb and brought it up to my front teeth, stopping myself in mid-motion. Oh God! I was turning into Kenny!

In addition to the nerves, the half-gallon of acidic coffee from the deli this morning knotted up my stomach.

I broke the silence in Jenny's office. "This whole thing has been really weird. What if they came up with a bomb? What if pairing them up was a mistake? What if the contract gets canned and I have the Incredible Hulk of the Ghetto and a prep school egomaniac as enemies? Then I get fired for messing with an artist and screwing up the contracts—my very first assignment!"

"Chance you took."

"That helps. NOT!"

"It's already done, so you have to own it, or you'll come off like a wimp."

"Right." I took a deep breath and got up to pace the floor in front of her desk. "If I get fired, I get fired. That's all. You'll still vouch for me, won't you?"

"Of course!"

I truly did not know if I could believe her. This was a fickle business. If I got blacklisted, I knew I would probably wind up behind the appointment computer at my father's vet office.

"Don't worry. It'll turn out all right," Jenny offered.

I paused. My heart was racing.

"I'm getting fired, for sure."

"No, you're not."

Uncertainty filled my head along with the sound of my pounding heart.

Jenny's phone buzzed. My knees went a little weak and I sat back down. Jenny picked it up.

"Yeah, she's in here . . . OK, I'll tell her." She put down the phone. "They are here. Everyone is heading to the conference room."

I took a deep breath.

She came around the desk, telling me, "OK, head up! Shoulders back. Be a man!" She handed me one of the chocolates from her candy bowl. I shoved it in my mouth.

"OK! Got it!" I left the office and immediately met up with LaKeisha. Here was the first line of defense to break through.

She stopped when she saw me and gave me her inspection position—hand on one hip, head tilted slightly back, squinting at me.

"Well, well, well, this should be interesting," she said.

I braced myself.

Then she relaxed a little and grabbed my arm, smiling the warmest smile she had ever offered me or anyone that I knew of.

"You go, girl," she almost whispered, then stalked off down the hall toward the conference room.

I stared after her for a moment with amazement. Then I followed her.

As I turned into the conference room, I expected some of what I saw: the senior vice president, sitting at the far end of the table, back to the wall; Kenny doing a nervous walk back and forth behind his chair; Robert, Cookie, Leon, Whiskey, and Michael, all seated to the right, bunched up together; and LaKeisha, calmly leaning back in her chair, slightly separate from them all. She waited for the show.

What was there that I was *not* expecting was Alejandro.

The network of computer parts was still on the table as it had been for weeks. This had been his spot for the past month and for some crazy reason, that had completely slipped my mind. Why they had not made him leave for this meeting was beyond me and his presence just added pressure.

He looked up as I came in. I had no idea what my face betrayed, but I had to keep my cool here. I nodded at him.

He looked back down and concentrated hard at his wires, twisting them together and moving them around. All I was thinking was, *Oh my God. Oh my God. Oh my God.*

I turned toward the others.

"Jill, sit down," the senior vice president ordered. "Can you explain exactly what is going on here?"

I searched the faces at the table. They all seemed a little frazzled. I guess there had already been some explaining that didn't go over too well.

After a slight pause, he continued, "We thought we would sign the next big scandal, put out the bad boys, and make music history. Kenny went all around the boroughs, seeking out . . . Kenny, what was your phrase?"

"Gangbangers," Kenny hissed.

All of the black people sitting at the table grimaced ever so slightly.

"Yes, looking for 'gangbangers,' and instead we have here a recent graduate from an honors math program and a baker of gourmet sweets?"

He looked directly into my face for probably the first time since I'd started working at this company. Obviously, Kenny's spin on things was not exactly flattering.

I took a deep breath. Everyone watched me, waiting.

"Right, yes, well," I began in utter disarray. "Sir, what you have here are some extremely talented people," I said, waving my arm in the general direction of Leon, Whiskey, and Cookie.

"Extremely," Michael echoed.

"Yes, indeed," Robert said.

I glanced at Alejandro. He was still twisting the same wire as a few minutes ago. His face was bent toward his hands, but his pupils were decidedly looking in my direction.

"Leon is not just a math whiz," I continued, walking around the table toward Leon, "but a charismatic performer who can command a room, a whole nightclub, a stadium! Whiskey is a musical giant, able to create hooks and grooves with nothing but some old LPs and his nimble fingers." I had practiced this part. "And Cookie," I said, slapping my hand on Cookie's shoulder, like I'd seen Tony do to people of importance, "has the poetic writing ability of . . ." This was as far as I had gotten in my rehearsals over the past twelve hours. Now, I searched my brain for a name that an older white guy would relate to and love. *C'mon, Jill—think great '60s and '70s writing—NOT one of the Beatles.* "An inner-city Bob Dylan—a troubadour of real-world problems."

"Yeah!" Leon jumped in, genuinely surprised at my words. "That's exactly what he is!"

Cookie stared down at the tabletop.

"He's not part of this deal," Kenny's crazed voice stabbed into the room. "We contracted a thug rapper. That's what we paid for."

I eyed him venomously. I was not going to become a "Kenny." I was not going to be looking for the quick buck and willing to sell my soul to do it. Even though I knew that was what everyone in this room, this building, even this city might be about. His comment catapulted me into preaching mode.

"This is going to be better than the gangsta rapper that you asked for," I said adamantly. "This is the start of something bigger than a one-hit wonder that will get played for a year and then fade away. This is authentic art with sustainability. A dance rhythm all its own. But don't take my word for it. Where is the tape? Music can't be explained! It has to be heard!"

Leon jumped up and jetted toward the tape player on the back wall. He put the cassette in and pushed the play button. This was a state-of-the-art sound system with speakers in every corner.

First, there was a bass drum beat. Then a guitar swelled in the background with an almost Hendrix-style guitar sound, but choppy. The backbeat was deafening, with a weird metallic sound as an upbeat. The voices were obviously from two very different people. One voice was a smooth tenor, talking the rhyme like a fairy tale poem. The other voice boomed in heavy response. Of course, I figured the smooth voice was Leon and the lower voice was Cookie.

I'm in the street, baby, waitin' for the drive by
when can we meet, baby? nothin' else to do t'night

My mama said,
"boy, don't be a deadbeat,
out there in the street,
just like all them creeps"

I know she right,
you, out there sellin' crack
now you got some cash
get shot in the back

It sound like Funk (-riff ----beats) in the background
It sound like Soul (-riff -----beats) in the living room
It sound like Rock (-riff ------beats) doggin' it like a hound
yeah, yeah, here we go (-riff ----beats) that's what you gonna do!
me and my crew, we got nothin' but some cousins and a hobby
what I gotta do? shed my culture, wear a sweater like a Cosby?

When you walkin' down the river, you're the man with a plan
are you following the moon or do the moon follow you?

Do the moon follow you?
Do the moon follow you?
Do the moon follow you?

So here we be, on the curb, doing what we can to keep it legal
and with the beat, what's the word, got to fly up like an eagle

I told you boys,
"I ain't got no sax,
I ain't got no ax,
so why you askin'?"

All I got
is my crate of vinyl
and this here turntable
put me out a label

It sound like Funk (-riff----beats) in the background
It sound like Soul (-riff-----beats) in the living room
It sound like Rock (-riff------beats) doggin' it like a hound
yeah, yeah, here we go (-riff----beats) that's what you gonna do!

me and my crew, we got nothin' but some cousins and a hobby
what I gotta do? shed my culture, wear a sweater like a Cosby?

When you walkin' down the river, you're the man with a plan
are you following the moon or do the moon follow you?

Do the moon follow you?
Do the moon follow you?
Do the moon follow you?

The song was a mix of funk, hard rock, and rap. I didn't know how they did it, but there was a rapped verse that led into a funky chorus then to a poetic third part, then back again.

Just the fact that the tape played the whole length of the song without interruption was some kind of feat. Sitting here was the jaded music industry. Very little impressed people like us. But now, we all simply listened. The shiny surface of the table reflected the patchwork of our faces.

At first, the senior vice president's eyebrows knitted, like he didn't understand what he was hearing. Kenny stopped pacing, but was still doing his cuticle chewing. LaKeisha leaned forward on her elbows, delightedly looking back and forth between me and the rap crew. Robert and Michael were both patting the table in time to the music, Cheshire cat smiles across their faces.

Whiskey, Cookie, and Leon sat next to each other, all looking straight ahead. None appeared to be breathing.

As the song went on, the senior vice president's face changed from confusion to recognition. Then he began to nod his head to the beat. By the end of the song, he was actually smiling, too.

Even Kenny, with his pained expression, was moving with the rhythm.

But the full song blew me away. I had only heard bits of it in the studio.

The music stopped and for a second, the sound of kinetic air filled the room.

Leon audibly let his breath escape.

Cookie finally made eye contact with the senior vice president and said the first thing I'd heard him say in days: "Ain't that the bad truth?"

We all stared at him.

Suddenly the senior vice president jumped up from his seat.

"This is fantastic!" he cried. "This is going to work out great!"

Everyone stood up and started talking at once.

Robert was shaking Michael's hand. LaKeisha was hugging Leon.

Relief washed over me and my knees gave out. I sat down where the senior vice president had just been sitting.

He took command of the room.

He turned to Kenny. "Kenny, get down to legal and have them change the contract. Bring it back to my office." He sent LaKeisha and Robert out to discuss press ideas and Michael out to tell the radio department to scratch the gangsta talking point in their pitches.

Then he went over to Leon, Whiskey, and Cookie, who stood at the tape player, doing his glad-handing and loud talking. It began to blur together. I looked over at Alejandro. He was just kind of staring at me. I couldn't read the expression at all.

Suddenly, there was a commotion at the door. We all looked up to see an odd apparition.

There was a light flowing dress, but it was soiled. Copper-tinted hair, but it was stringy. Smooth skin, but it was white as a ghost. It was Crystal Reneaux. She had obviously been crying.

Sheila came up behind her, but before she could get to the door, Crystal had shoved herself up against the conference table.

"You," she croaked in a witch-like bark, pointing at the senior vice president. "You betrayed me!"

"Crystal?" he answered.

"'Don't worry,' you said, 'I'll make you a star. You'll be famous.' They haven't played my video on MTV once!"

"Honey, let's go to my office and talk." He put his hands up, arms out over his end of the conference table where he stood next to me.

"Miss Reneaux, I told you they were in a closed meeting." Sheila had reached Crystal and lightly touched her arm. Crystal turned and shoved Sheila hard, throwing her against the doorframe with a thud. Sheila scrambled back out of the room and down the hall.

Crystal began to walk around the table in Alejandro's direction. We were sort of backed up against the wall.

"You lied!" she screamed loudly. We all flinched in disbelief.

I began to stand up. The men in the room were all frozen.

"And now, I'm a laughingstock. I gave you all I had!"

"You have more . . . There is time . . ." The senior vice president obviously didn't know what to say.

"No, I don't," she wailed. Her eyes were turning more and more wild. "You are the devil!"

She had reached the part of the table that was full of computer parts. She was about seven feet from us and maybe three feet from Alejandro.

She suddenly grabbed one of the hard plastic boxes and hurled it in our direction. She was obviously aiming for the senior vice president, who stood right next to me. The rap contingent sped away from him on the other side.

Before I could tell what was happening, she had catapulted some kind of circuit board, a ninja-like object when thrown at high speed. It embedded into the drywall directly in front of Cookie's nose, like a circus thrower's knife.

"Damn!" Cookie said. "Girl got an arm!"

Another electrical item went flying, this time with better aim, toward the senior vice president. He grabbed both of my upper arms from behind and dragged me in front of his body. I became a human shield. The hard metal object ricocheted off my shoulder, and a stabbing pain shot all the way down my arm.

I cried out. I tried to shake his hands off of me.

Alejandro rushed toward me, and deflected the next incoming item, sending it back in an arc. He wrenched me from the senior vice president's grasp, pulling me toward him and Crystal. But we were around the curve of the table, so now her direct aim would miss us and make a chord between her and her target.

Crystal ranted and yelled about how she had given herself to him, how he was a user, how he had "taken all of her breath." All the while she was reaching for more things to throw at him.

He was now trying to dodge all the incoming debris and talk her down with a barrage of condescension, calling her "Honey" and "Baby."

By this time, Cookie had made it around the huge table from the other direction. Crystal was so focused on the senior vice president that she was not prepared as Cookie put his arms around her from behind, locking one of her arms by her side, and lifting her up off the ground.

She totally lost it at that point. She flailed with the rest of her limbs, screaming like a wild animal. Leon and Whiskey tried to catch her kicking feet, telling her, "You've got to calm down," and "It's gonna be OK."

Alejandro went toward her from our direction. "Stop kicking, now." His voice was trying for soothing, but not quite making it.

Suddenly, Jenny appeared behind Leon as Sheila, Michael, and a bunch of others blocked up the doorway.

Jenny yelled, "Crystal!" Her booming voice cut through all of the commotion.

Cookie instinctively turned toward the source of the yell, and Crystal saw Jenny standing there with a perplexed and scared look on her face.

Crystal went limp and began to sob. Cookie didn't let go of her, though. He simply sat down on the nearest chair with Crystal sitting on his lap. Jenny came up and kneeled in front of her, speaking in calming tones and reassuring her that everything was going to be all right.

I glared back at the senior vice president. He was still backed up against the wall at the far side of the conference table. He returned my look with a contrite expression. I reached up to hold the pain in my shoulder and felt wetness there. Looking down, I could see a spreading stain of blood discoloring the nice blue silk. I suddenly felt dizzy and everything went black.

TWENTY-SEVEN

"OUCH!"

"Just lay still," Jessica ordered me. "For God's sake, you are the worst patient, ever."

"You're the worst nurse, ever!" I protested. "You are pressing too hard and it's cold!"

"Ice packs are supposed to be cold."

She finally let go of the ice pack that was pressed against my bandaged shoulder and started to fluff up the pillow behind me as I lay on my fancy couch. My silk shirt had been torn at the sleeve up through the neckline, so now it looked like a tattered blue toga.

I touched Jessica's hand and said, "Thank you. That's enough. If you take any more 'care' of me, I think I might pass out again."

"OK, OK." She sat back at my side and looked at me.

Apparently, after I fainted, they called an ambulance. I had come to in time to see Crystal being led away by the proverbial "men in white coats," along with a policeman. A paramedic helped me to get up from the floor. Alejandro had caught me on the way down, so I was told, but I didn't see him after that.

Jenny called Jessica at her office downtown and she met me at the hospital. She called my mother, then waited with me all afternoon for my discharge so she could bring me home and nurse the life out of me, per my mother's strict instructions.

Now, it was 6:00 p.m. and I was exhausted.

"I still cannot believe that snake vice president actually used you like that! What a worm!"

"More than you know," I answered dryly.

Just then, Luann burst through the front door, directly into the living room.

"Oh my God!" she exclaimed. "Are you all right? They didn't tell me where they took you! Everyone at work was talking about Crystal Reneaux going nuts."

Jess and I stared at her questioningly.

"Leah sent out a press release," she said.

I just sighed.

"What? That's just wrong!" Jessica said.

"My friend at Condé Nast said that her friend at the Post said it was going on Page Six tomorrow," Luann informed us.

"The gross part is that *now* they will probably play Crystal's video on MTV," I said.

"What a great precedent to set," Jessica added. "You'll have to build a padded room at the office for all the new musicians on the label."

"Did your magazine get the release?" I asked Luann.

"Yeah, I brought you a copy. Your name is in it."

She dug in her bag and produced a crumpled paper. She handed me the photocopy of the faxed press release.

Yup, there was my name, along with a whole paragraph about how Cookie was the street-poet hero who saved us all.

How was I supposed to feel here?

It was crappy to be publicly declared "the victim," but at the same time, this meant we were also getting national attention for the music. Thanks to Crystal's meltdown, all of our careers were going to go nowhere but up.

The door buzzer rang. Luann ran to the front window to see who it was.

She came back with a weird look on her face.

"Is someone coming up?" I asked.

"Yeah," she answered. "Tony and Alejandro!"

"Oh no! I've got to look terrible!" I said.

Jessica sprang into action. She ran into my room and came back with a hairbrush, lipstick, and a sweet pinkish sweater.

She handed me a Kleenex. "Wipe the black smudges from under your eyes."

I moistened the tissue by licking it and dabbed my face as Luann grabbed the brush and stroked it a few times through my tangled hair.

Jessica disappeared again and returned with a hand mirror from somewhere.

"Here." She shoved it at me along with the lipstick.

We could hear them clomping up the last flight of stairs and talking. They paused at the landing, right on the other side of the door, probably to catch their breath before they actually knocked.

Luann stood at the door when they finally knocked, checking for my signal that I was ready. I nodded and she let them in.

Tony barreled through the doorway and came straight for me.

"Jill, man oh man!" He actually had a bouquet of flowers in his hand, which appeared odd and out of place. He peered into my face, then at my shoulder. "You don't look too bad."

"Thanks," I answered. "I think?"

Alejandro was hanging back. Tony sat down on the coffee table, facing me.

"Alejandro, here, told me the whole thing. Everyone is talking about it. I can't believe . . . what a nut case!" Tony rambled. "Your office is already filling up with gifts and 'get well' flowers." He finally paused and noticed there were others in the room.

"Hey, Jess. Luann. So what's here? How many stitches?" He used his sausage-sized thumb and forefinger to try to gingerly lift the bandage and look under it.

"Twenty-five," I said.

"It'll be a hell of a scar! You'll have to start wearing more tank tops."

"Seriously?" Luann asked.

"Oh yeah!" Tony cried. "Scars on a woman? Well, not the face, but certain places—very sexy."

"To the biker crowd, maybe," Jess added.

He reached past my shoulder to the prescription bottle on the side table.

"What'd they give you? Vicodin?"

"Sorry, just Tylenol 3." I took it back from him. "Although I thought of asking for something stronger, just to have bribe material for you."

"Hmm" was his response.

"Tony," Jessica said. "Here, let me take those." She took the flowers and somewhat poignantly looked at Alejandro as she walked to the kitchen to put them in water. Alejandro awkwardly stood in the middle of the living room rug.

"So you were the hero!" Luann said to him.

"Not really," he replied. Again, his head was down but his eyes were looking at me.

"What? Of course you were!" Tony jumped up and put his arm around Alejandro's shoulders, robustly shaking him. "Our Clark Kent! The mild-mannered computer guy! Who knew the geek had it in him?"

"You want something to drink?" Luann said to Tony. She

motioned for him to come into the kitchen, doing an eyeball communication of "shut up and let's let these two be alone for a minute."

Tony looked at her, then me, then Alejandro.

"Oh, yeah, yeah. What've you got? Any tequila?"

They walked behind the kitchen wall where I could hear Jessica filling up a vase with water.

Alejandro stood there for a second, then came a little closer, but didn't sit down.

"So I'm glad that you're OK."

"Yeah, better than OK." I tried to be flip and held up the copy of the press release that was still sitting on my lap, and said in an exaggerated southern accent, "Ahhh'm famous!" I switched back to a normal tone. "And so are you, even though they spelled your name with an *h* in it."

His smile seemed too small.

"Really," I said sincerely. "You were fast on your feet. Thank you so much. I would have been torn up if you hadn't helped."

"It was a normal reaction," he said modestly.

"Normal for *you*. That's what's so great about it."

I smiled at him. Again, he didn't really smile.

Something was up. As my knight in shining armor, shouldn't he be a little more cavalier?

There was a beat of silence and I glanced over at the wall that divided the kitchen area and the living room. They were being too quiet in there.

"Jill." Alejandro took in a deep breath. "I was thinking. You and me? I don't think it's going to work out."

I was stunned. That was the absolute last thing I expected him to say at this moment.

"What?" I whined. "We were supposed to be making up,

weren't we? It's Tuesday! Like you said! I thought we were going to be good. Great, even!"

"You are a very passionate person. You have your career. It's very exciting. But . . . it's too much."

"Look, this kind of thing is not a normal part of my job. Well," I stumbled. "Generally, it's really much more dull than this. I mean . . . I thought you thought it was fun? What do you mean 'too much'?"

I could see he was struggling for the words to explain himself.

"I don't know what to say." He looked down at his hands. "You have a great group of people around you. You are one of those people that has everything under control. You don't need me."

"You call this control?" I cried, indicating my bandages.

"I'm not like you."

I couldn't believe this.

"Of course you're not like me!" I exclaimed. "You're like YOU! That's the point! Maybe you have this idea of what I'm like that's not actually like me at all!"

"You're beautiful and funny. A lot of exciting and rich men will want to be with you."

"What does that have to do with anything?" I said. "The whole reason I liked you in the first place is because we seemed to be able to get over the veneer and the arm candy idea. We talk to each other about real things—goals in life, not just to the end of the week or how it all appears to other people!"

His expression seemed confused.

"I don't know," he said. He stood there silently for a few seconds, staring at the carpet.

I was bewildered too. It sounded like he was breaking up with me because he thought I was "too cool." That would be a first!

"My flight for California is tomorrow," he sighed. "Maybe the time away will make it easier."

He stepped slightly closer and handed me something from inside his jacket pocket. It was the hard metal thing that had torn open my shoulder. There was a tuft of blue silk stuck in one of the corners.

"I'm sorry. I hope you feel better."

With that, he walked to the door and then through it.

"What the hell?" I asked the back of the closed door.

TWENTY-EIGHT

WITHIN TWO WEEKS, LAKEISHA HAD A PRESS PARTY PLANNED WITH A short performance by "Professor T and the Cookie Monster" and their DJ, Whiskey Fizz. It would happen at The Bottom End, a small club on Fourth Street. It was the usual place to have acts premiere to the press and the others in the music industry.

She made Leon ditch the golden tooth.

They went back into the studio to put down three more tracks. They were on a roll.

I was healing fast and was back in the office after a few days. I didn't get to go back to the studio to hear some of the other tracks that Leon, Cookie, and Whiskey were creating, though. And I didn't hear from Alejandro.

Jenny reported that Crystal was currently an inpatient at the emergency psych ward at Bellevue Hospital. How was that for a cliché? She was doing fine and would be out, with meds, by our press party. The good news was that her video was being played all over the TV and she was even mentioned on some news shows and was invited to model for a spread in *Vogue* magazine. Apparently, the "psycho" look was all the fashion.

By the time the night of the party rolled around, I was able to lift my arm without wincing and put on a regular shirt all by myself. Luann was coming along for the big reveal. She said there was no way she was missing this one.

They called from the office to tell me that a car would come to pick us up.

"Finally, some appreciation!" I told Luann. "And all it took was blood!"

"You may not want to get used to that," she cracked.

The buzzer rang and we both bolted to the window to look for a big stretch limo.

"I don't see any classy car," Luann exclaimed.

Looking down at the street, there were all kinds of taxi cabs and town cars driving by, but parked directly in front of our building was a huge Caribbean blue boat of a vehicle with LaKeisha waving up from the open passenger window. I smiled. "I do."

THE CLUB WAS BUZZING WHEN WE ARRIVED. LAKEISHA BREEZED PAST the intern at the door and was immediately in selling mode. Tony, Luann, and I trailed behind her like members of her court. Tony drifted off.

LaKeisha held my elbow delicately while she introduced me to people, one after another. She'd mention to each one of them that I was the person responsible for what we were about to see. Then she'd casually add an offhanded remark about my shoulder or blood or fainting. They'd all heard the story. Just as the curious recognition began to show in their eyes, she'd drag me to the next person.

"Smile and act mysterious," she instructed. "We are trying to pique interest here. If you talk too much, it won't work."

I nodded, wide-eyed at her take on it.

"By the way," she said after a while, "your boy, Sting, might be here tonight."

My wide eyes widened.

"Yes ma'am," she continued, speaking out of the side of her mouth at me while stalking her next prey. "He is in town rehearsing for some highbrow, depressing play. Something about money and opera. 'A Nickel for an Opera'? Something like that."

"*Three Penny Opera*?" Luann chimed in.

"Yeah! That's it," LaKeisha replied absently as she looked around for important people. "I invited all the I.R.S. people."

I.R.S. was a record label owned by the big blond Miles Copeland, brother of the medium blond Ian Copeland, who ran a booking/management agency, and also brother of the small blond Stewart Copeland, drummer of the all-blond rock band, the Police. Of which, "my boy Sting" had been the lead singer. If they showed up, they showed up as a towheaded pack.

I turned to the room with my heart in my throat and did a quick search, but came up with nothing in the blond category.

Before LaKeisha could parade me in front of another journalist, I loosened myself from her grip. "I want to see the guys before they go on," I told her. Still doing radar scans of the club, I picked my way around the side of the stage, trying to figure out which hallway to go down to find the greenroom. Along the way, I ran into Tony again.

"You gotta see this," he said and led me down some stairs that I didn't even know existed.

When we entered the greenroom, they were all there. Leon, Whiskey, and Cookie—our stars, plus Michael, Robert, Shandra, and Jackson.

Leon rushed me as I walked in.

"Jill, this is great. My parents are even here, sitting in the VIP section." He was so excited and looked more handsome than ever with all his teeth showing. His cocky act had fallen away and I liked this new guy, or rather, I liked the person he really was.

Whiskey and some others converged on the snack table and Cookie sat on the black pleather couch, kind of staring at the floor, then looking around the room. I greeted everyone.

Cookie only nodded at me and quietly said, "Hey."

"Is Cookie feeling all right about everything?" I asked Leon in a lowered voice.

"He's fine. A little nervous."

Kenny entered the fray.

"All right everybody. You are going on soon. You need anything else?" He marched around the room, inspecting each of them, as if he had a clue about what he was inspecting them for. "You know all the words?" he asked, without exactly waiting for an answer. Leon laughed out loud. Shandra and Michael both hooted.

Tony pulled a Ritz cracker from his lips and sent an exasperated call from his spot in the midst of the snack table party, "Kenny, c'mon." Leon began to rap some of the song, "My mama said, boy, don't be a deadbeat . . ." Whiskey joined in with a simple beatbox, pursing his lips and hitting his own chest.

I thought to myself that if all went well, they would be so sick of that song in a year, they would never do it voluntarily. I was pretty happy.

Kenny then stopped at the couch. He sized up the Cookie situation. He still had an underlying animosity about Cookie's involvement and the fact that Michael and I were the ones who brought him in.

"This night has to go perfect. You have to impress these people. We've got everyone from *Ebony* to *Rolling Stone* out there! MTV! CBS Radio!"

"You're not helping, Kenny." It was my turn to call from across the room.

Jackson even spoke up. "Why you illin', man? Who let him in here?"

Finally, Cookie stood up and walked calmly up to Kenny. He towered over him and would only have to nudge him with one finger to send him flying. Kenny visibly shrank as Cookie placed his hand on Kenny's scrawny shoulder. "Man, you gotta be cool," his baritone offered. "We got this. This is what we do."

I came up to them and laced my arm through Kenny's. This time, I would be the rescuer. "Kenny, can I have a word?"

I led him out the door and back toward the staircase. We began walking up to the main club. "Why don't we find the senior vice president so he can do the introductions?"

Halfway up the stairs, Kenny stopped and turned to me. He searched my face for a second in the dim fluorescent lighting.

"This will work," he said. It was more of a sudden realization than an assured statement.

"Yup, I think so," I replied.

He patted my shoulder and we continued up into the club's main room.

When we got there, I again scanned the room. LaKeisha was working the room like the pro that she was. There was a sea of industry people milling around, drinking. Luann stood at the bar with Jenny. And standing with them was Alejandro.

My heart did a flip.

Kenny said, "All right, there he is. I'll go get him." Obviously not referring to the person I was looking at. I nodded mutely. Kenny left me standing there. I suddenly felt like the biblical pillar of salt.

Jenny noticed me and held up her glass in my direction. Alejandro's gaze followed the arc of her arm, but he made no move. He seemed to look right through me, then looked away. My vision suddenly blurred with tears. I didn't want to be a whiny dumped girl who trailed behind ex-boyfriends. So I spun around and made a beeline toward the bathrooms.

I stumbled in there and leaned over the sink breathlessly, the tears dripping off of my chin. I heaved a few sobs, oblivious to the surroundings. Who brought him here? And there Jenny and Luann were, just chatting away with him. They were supposed to snub him for dumping me, weren't they? *Wow*, I thought, *I really am in love*. What was I going to do?

"Are you quite all right?" a British accent asked me.

I turned to look into the face of a thin blond woman.

"I'm fine. I'm OK. I just . . . y'know, boy trouble."

She mouthed the word "Oh" but no sound came out. She put her hand on my back in a sign of comfort. Once I accepted her touch, she said, "We've all been there, haven't we?"

"It doesn't make sense," I confessed to this complete stranger. "He goes on about how great I am, then dumps me. I thought I could get over it or something, then I see him here and fall apart!"

She quietly handed me a tissue and rubbed my back in a circular motion. "Maybe he's simply scared?" she offered.

"Of what?" My voice sounded angry.

"Most men are afraid of strong women, you know," she observed.

"How do you know if I'm strong?"

"It shows on your face, my dear," she answered without a trace of irony.

After a moment, she said, "I need to meet someone. Are you better now?"

"Yes, of course. Thank you so much." She left me to my own recovery.

When I came out of the bathroom a minute later, she was still in the dimly lit hallway. She smiled empathetically and nodded toward the men's bathroom. I guess she was waiting for her date to come out of there.

As I turned to walk away from her, I stopped short in the narrow entrance of the hallway. Alejandro stood there, blocking the exit.

I glanced back at the woman who would be witness to this. She wasn't going anywhere. She saw my face, then looked off to study the "Men's" sign on the door in front of her.

"Hi," Alejandro said simply.

"Hi," I replied, trying to sound just as simple.

There was an awkward moment of silence as Alejandro seemed to be gathering himself up.

We both spoke simultaneously.

I said, "How was San Diego?" He said, "I've been looking for you."

The men's bathroom door opened and shut. The momentary shaft of light illuminated Alejandro's chocolate eyes. I tried to blink away my emotion, but it didn't keep the blur from returning.

I heard the woman whispering behind me.

Now, all I saw was Alejandro's silhouette in front of me—his broad shoulders and the crumpled outline of his shirtsleeves, which were rolled up to that perfect place on his forearms.

"I've been looking for you," he repeated with slightly more confidence.

"Yeah?" I tried to sound like this was one of those everyday conversations that you have with a coworker. I could tell it was not working.

"Jill, I wanted to try to explain."

"You don't have to explain anything. Whatever." My voice

quivered slightly. It would be the absolute worst thing for me to actually cry at this moment. I took in a deep breath.

The whispering behind me was answered with a low murmur. A man had joined the woman and she was probably filling him in on my little drama. I felt a current of warm air from them, somehow. Alejandro didn't seem to notice them. He was caught up in whatever he was about to say.

"I was in California with my family," Alejandro began to explain. "I was there, a stone's throw from what I thought was my holy land. But just walking on the beach wasn't the same anymore."

"What do you mean?" I was able to get out.

"I walked a lonely mile in the moonlight, Jill. And even though there were millions of stars shining, my heart was lost. I stared up at the April moon, just sad."

My eyes had adjusted to the darkness in the hallway and I could see his imploring face.

"I walked along that beach for hours," he went on. "Every step I thought of you. Every footstep—only you. Every star became a grain of sand, like some dried-up ocean in the sky. I kept asking myself what I was doing."

He remained about two feet away from me. My voice seemed to have left me. I raised my shoulders in hopes that my body language would lead him to keep talking.

"Jill, I don't want to be alone," he concluded. "I want to be with you. I'm mad about you."

I realized that I had been holding my breath during his heartfelt soliloquy. I let the air out in a sigh.

Alejandro's face changed a little in the shadowy light. "But I understand if you don't feel the same way." Then he abruptly turned and walked away.

My shoulders slumped and I turned back toward the woman. There was a blond man standing next to her now. He stepped up to me as if he knew me, stooping to look directly into my face.

It was Sting.

Gordon Sumner, front man of my favorite rock band, actor, intellectual, saver of the rain forest, my muse, *My* Gordon.

Face-to-face with my teenage idol, here I was—mute, tear-streaked, and stitched up like Frankenstein.

My shock was complete.

"So are you mad about him, too?" he asked me in a serious voice. His accent rolled around in my ears.

My lips seemed to be glued together, so I just nodded at him with big, glassy eyes.

"Listen, my dear," he said intently, "if someone I loved ever said something like that to me, I certainly would not let them walk away."

Again, I nodded mutely. He didn't seem satisfied with that response. He shifted his chin downward, moving his eyes even closer to mine. He was so close that I could smell the scent of whatever shampoo he used.

He said pointedly, "There are no victories without love."

Our eyes met and something finally clicked. It was like a dam broke in my brain, flooding my whole body with sudden understanding. My voice rode this wave over my lips. "Yes," I said. "Yes, of course, you are so right."

I threw myself at him and hugged him, pressing my face into the middle of his chest. He hugged me back in a fatherly gesture, then let go as I pulled away from him and ran back out of the hallway into the main room of the club.

The lights had gone down. I searched the tables for Alejandro. I scoured the back of the room. Then I saw him on the other side of the small stage, standing next to Tony. His head was down and Tony was talking in his ear. As I picked my way through the tables to get to him, the lights on the stage went up and everyone went quiet. The senior vice president came out onto the stage and made a little speech. He thanked everyone for coming. His voice droned about this and that. I had almost made it across the room when I heard my name from the stage and suddenly a bright spotlight was shining in my face.

"We have to thank Jill Dodge for bringing this all together and sacrificing herself for music!"

I grimaced into the light. People applauded. I waved weakly.

Then the spotlight was off me and back on the stage, where a ghostly figure had appeared. It was Crystal Reneaux.

"I'd like to say how sorry I am to Jill. And now, let me introduce to you, the future of rap music in America, Professor T and the Cookie Monster!"

The rest of the stage lit up and the pulsing backbeat began.

I finally made it to the far side of the room. I calmly walked up and stood beside Alejandro. He shifted his weight toward me, waiting. I could see Sting and his wife still standing at the entranceway to the bathrooms. They were both watching me with curious faces.

Leon and Cookie burst onto the stage from opposite sides of the turntables.

I smiled as I grabbed a hold of Alejandro's hand.

ACKNOWLEDGMENTS

The first person I want to thank is YOU – for reading this book. I hope you enjoyed it.

I'd also like to thank the following people:

- My kids Sofia, Adrian, and Zabel for the hugs, smiles, and cheerleading.

- My husband Javier, for setting up a home office and for occasionally handing me my laptop when I was cranky with a suggestion that I go write for a while.

- Beth Dandy Atkins, Norman Green, and Caroline Leavitt for being the very first readers of the full manuscript. Without your initial encouragement and suggestions, this book would be lounging at the bottom of my desk drawer on a thumb drive.

- Zabel Isassi for the very '80's cover illustration.

- Caitlyn Levin, for being a great project manager, Pamela Long for editing, Julie Metz for the cover design.

- The Gaithersburg Book Festival staff, committee, authors, and volunteers for the opportunity to work with so many talented and smart people. You all inspired and encouraged me to write this novel.

- Every musician, singer, songwriter, music teacher, music industry person, music store clerk or owner, nightclub owner, and band fan, that I've ever seen, met, worked for, jammed with, hated, yelled at, cried with, been facebook friends with, been a fan of, or loved – Thank you for making music happen. Keep doing it.

And a special thanks to Brooke Warner, Crystal Patriarche, and the staff at She Writes Press for daring to buck the system and succeeding. It's very rock'n'roll of you.

ABOUT THE AUTHOR

Garinè B. Isassi is a former singer/songwriter who grew up with one foot in Texas and the other in New Jersey. A graduate of the University of Texas at Austin, she is a lover of music, chocolate, and altruistic sarcasm; a writer of post-punk humor; and the illustrious founder of Helicopter Moms Anonymous. She is proud of her Armenian-American heritage, but tired of explaining it. She currently lives in Maryland, where she works full time in marketing communications, sings in a gospel choir, is the Workshops Chair for the Gaithersburg Book Festival, over-volunteers for a variety of community organizations, writes when everyone else is asleep, and lives with her husband, three kids, a cat, a dog, and a gecko. It's the gecko that sent her over the edge. You can read her blog, "Hi!" from the 'burbs, at her website, garineTHEwriter.com.